Other Books by Kathleen Williams Renk

FICTION
The Rossetti Diaries

Vindicated: A Novel of Mary Shelley

Orphan Annie's Sister

CRITICISM
Caribbean Shadows and Victorian Ghosts:
Women's Writing and Decolonization

Magic, Science, and Empire in Postcolonial Literature:
The Alchemical Imagination

Women Writing the Neo-Victorian Novel: Erotic "Victorians"

No Coward Soul Have I

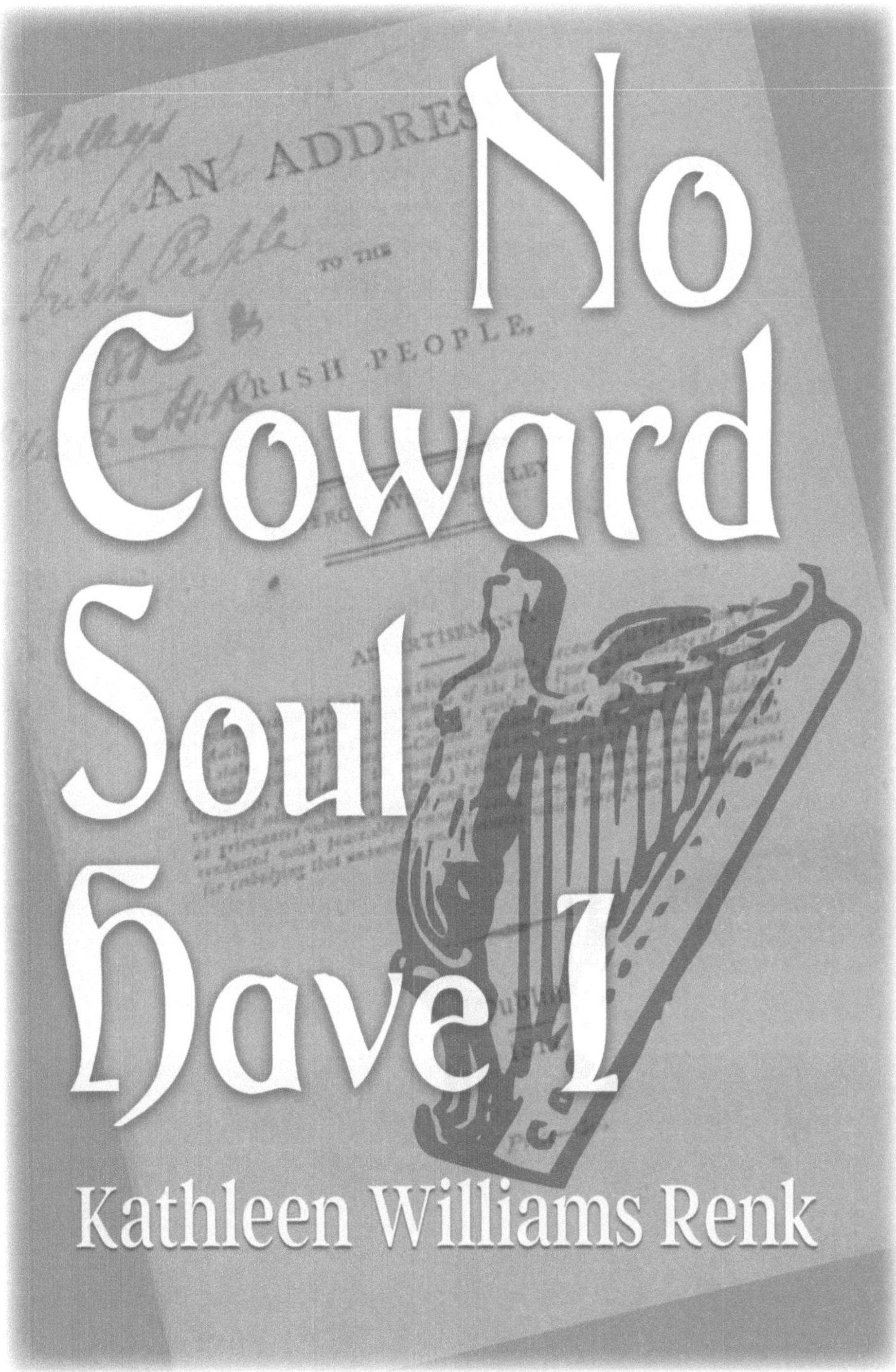

No Coward Soul Have I

Kathleen Williams Renk

Bink Books

Bedazzled Ink Publishing Company • Fairfield, California

978-1-960373-59-5 paperback

Cover Design
by

Sapling
Studio

"Outside History" reprinted with permission from Eavan Boland's *Outside History:
Selected Poems 1980-1990*, published by W. W. Norton and CO., 1991 and by Carcanet
Press Limited, 2009.

Bink Books
a division of
Bedazzled Ink Publishing Company
Fairfield, California
http://www.bedazzledink.com

*Dedicated to Stephen Carl, who always supported
my desire to learn and to teach*

No Coward Soul Have I

There are outsiders, always. These stars—
these iron inklings of an Irish January,
whose light happened

thousands of years before
our pain did: they are, they have always been
outside history.

They keep their distance. Under them remains
a place where you found
you were human, and

a landscape in which you know you are mortal.
and a time to choose between them.
I have chosen:

Out of myth into history into history I move to be
part of that ordeal—
whose darkness is

only now reaching me from those fields,
those rivers, those roads clotted as
firmaments with the dead.

How slowly they die
as we kneel beside them, whisper in their ear.
And we are too late. We are always too late.

From Eavan Boland's, "Outside History"

Prologue

1803 Kilmainham Gaol, Dublin

Anne Devlin

Everything became a shadow, a shade. I had descended into Dante's hell with no guide. Like being buried alive, but on my feet. I was still standing. Stretching my hand out and feeling the sodden, slimy wall, I wondered whose hands had touched these walls before me. I kept reaching until I had walked the pit's circumference.

Mr. Emmet told me about the French *oubliette*, far worse than a mere dungeon. The *oubliette* is a hole in the ground that the French tyrants push people into, and then they cover the hole with a grate. As the ultimate punishment, this is the place where you are forgotten and then starved to death. You may cry, scream, beg for mercy but to no avail. Is this Kilmainham Gaol's version of the *oubliette*, I wondered? Will I be ignored, forgotten? Will they feed me? Will I ever see the sun and stars again? What did I do to deserve this? I'm a simple country girl who loved Mother Ireland. My only crime. Oh, that and devoting myself to Mr. Emmet, whom the British called a traitor. I would have to atone, but I would leave that between me and God. Until then I needed to keep my wits, my faculties. I would have to trust that God would not fail me, even after Robert Emmet had.

One

Becoming Irish

12 February 1812
Dublin

Steel-gray clouds shrouded the sky, blocking the light of the morning star. The passengers in the coach, Percy and Harriet Shelley and Harriet's sister Eliza, were shaken and spent, for while crossing the Irish Sea, their craft nearly capsized when a tempest arose and tossed the ship like a toy boat. Then the vessel ran off-course near Wicklow, far from their Dublin destination. The travelers wondered whether the distant stars ultimately foretold doom regarding their Irish sojourn.

After hiring a coach to take them to Dublin, the trio tried to settle their nerves and rest. Their spirits brightened and then soared as they looked west into the twilight.

They felt charmed as they perceived, within the verdant fields dotted with pink cyclamens and purple and yellow pansies, stone circles, ringforts, and cairns. They asked each other about the history of these mystical, mythic places. Who had inhabited or was buried in such sites? Kings, like Brian Boru, who handily defeated the Viking invaders? Druids who resisted the interloper Patrick? Mythical creatures, like the leader of the Fianna warriors, the giant Finn McCool who ate the salmon of wisdom and strode across the sea to battle the Scottish giant Benandonner? Magical folk, the fairies, whom the Irish called *aos si*, who smuggled humans into their mysterious realms and fed them sumptuous feasts? They spoke of the differences between history, legend, and myth and Percy wove a tale of the hero Cúchulainn and his faithful hound Bran, while Harriet claimed that fairy folk were the ancient Irish who burrowed and hid underground after the English had invaded the island.

As the coach approached the city, the travelers viewed the Georgian red-brick buildings and dirty narrow cobbled streets that reminded them of London. They had left behind the emerald fields of the Irish countryside, where they imagined fairies twinkling in the gloaming. As if they had been sprinkled with pixie dust, they peacefully drifted to sleep to the repetitive tattoo of the horses' galloping hooves.

The splattering of raindrops on the coach's roof woke Harriet from a serene dream of visiting a fairy fort where she and Percy devoured ambrosia. The fairies fed them as if they were divine, not mortal, beings.

She opened her eyes, lifted her head from Percy's shoulder, and stretched her stiff neck. Shivering from the cold, she pulled her lap robe closer and tucked it under her cloak and gown. She peered out the window as the coach trundled across the bridge spanning the murky River Liffey and saw waves splashing against the stone walls. A gust of wind blew the dusky water high into the air, reminding her of their perilous journey. She shook again but this time in fear. She didn't relish recalling that memory so instead, she shut her eyes and imagined she was feeding Percy pieces of pomegranate dipped in nectar as they lounged on a sun-lit cloud.

The bells of St. Patrick's Cathedral chimed, rousing Harriet from her reverie as the carriage halted. She looked lovingly at Percy who was fast asleep. He was as handsome as Adonis. His dark curls bobbed as the carriage rattled over the cobblestones, his long eyelashes fluttered as if he were dreaming, and his pink lips were pursed as he breathed softly. His black waistcoat was bunched up as he leaned against the carriage wall.

She pulled at his waistcoat to straighten it. "Darling, wake up. We've finally arrived. How thrilling. Now you can begin your political work." She pecked his cheek and caressed his shoulder.

They pulled in front of a three-story brick building—the lodgings Percy had rented on Sackville Street, the bustling main artery through Dublin City. Excited to begin their Irish life, Harriet slipped her lap robe onto the coach's floor, tied her silk bonnet, and grinned at her husband. Percy yawned and then rubbed his eyes. He glanced out the window and noticed a large crowd encircling the coach. He smiled.

"Perhaps Dubliners have somehow learned that I'm here to rescue them, like Brian Boru did. But this time from illegitimate British rule. I'll complete Robert Emmet's rebellion," he said. "Sir Charles was right about the Irish. Look at the warm welcome we're receiving."

But as the footman held out his hand to help Harriet descend from the carriage, no one welcomed her. Instead, the drenched, quivering crowd pressed closer as each extended their hands, not in prayer or thanksgiving, but silently to beseech her to physically save them from starvation. Resembling the living dead, the women and men were dressed in rags and their faces and hands were filthy. As Harriet struggled to enter the crowd, she covered her nose with her lace handkerchief, for some petitioners smelled as if they had never once bathed. And many of the mendicants were wee wailing children with rotund bellies that indicated they were in the last stages of starvation. One woman, whose face was so etched with lines that she resembled the legendary *Shan Van Vocht*, the Old Woman of Irish lore, pointed a bony finger at Harriet and begged, "Miss, do you have a coin or bread to spare? My children are hungry." Then another woman came forward, and another, and another, all pleading for mercy.

Harriet couldn't hold back her tears. Even though she and Percy had recently learned, from their friend and benefactor, Sir Charles the Duke of Norfolk, that their Irish cousins had suffered from centuries of English and then British occupation and rule, she did not expect to be greeted by the ravenous.

She felt helpless and turned to Percy who was still sitting in the carriage and said, "These people are our kin, darling. Look at the children. We must help them. What can we spare?"

Harriet knew they had little to spare. Percy had borrowed funds from Sir Charles to travel to Ireland, for Percy's father, Sir Timothy, a Member of Parliament, had recently withheld Percy's allowance because Percy had tarnished the family name by being expelled from Oxford University. The Masters and Fellows labeled Percy Bysshe Shelley a heretic and blasphemer because he had audaciously penned a pamphlet, with his friend Thomas Jefferson Hogg, entitled "The Necessity of Atheism." His father, like the university dons, pronounced Percy a heretic, and told him that he had ruined every opportunity he had possessed to be a great man and a MP.

"Percy, I pampered your ridiculous flights of fancy for too long and now you've disgraced us," Sir Timothy said. "We raised you to be a good Christian but now you exhibit no charity or compassion for your family."

Harriet didn't agree and believed that Percy was inspired and noble and as charitable as Christ himself, but now he remained hidden in the carriage and seemed reluctant to distribute coins to the distraught people who were seeking physical salvation.

"What would you have me do, my love?" Percy asked from the shadows. "Of course, I wish to aid my Irish cousins, but we need to conserve our funds until my poems are published. I need to take care of my family before I care for others."

Harriet was stunned. Percy had never been frugal in the past; in fact, he was often a wastrel who never abided by Polonius's advice to be neither a borrower nor a lender. He was often generous. Once he gave his cloak to an old man who had none. And Percy had always preferred the company of those whose birth did not equal his. Why was he now withholding charity?

"You would rather have these children perish? I implore you, Percy, open your purse," she said as she wept. The hungry continued to surround her.

Percy reached into his purse, took a deep breath, and pulled out a handful of coins. He donned his hat, climbed out of the coach, and dispensed a couple of them into the hands of those who appeared to be the weakest and the most desperate.

Harriet wiped the tears from her cheeks and beamed as she stole coins from Percy's purse and distributed them to all within her reach, especially to the children and women.

"God bless and keep you, lass," the beggars each said as they received the coins. A few women touched Harriet's silk dress and bonnet.

Eliza leapt from the carriage and pushed through the crowd. She grabbed Harriet's arm. "Come, sister. Our lengthy sea voyage has wearied you. You must rest before you collapse. Percy, close your purse, tell these ruffians to go away and then quickly seek our landlord. Harriet must go to bed."

13 February 1812

Percy Shelley did not enjoy being lorded over by his overbearing sister-in-law, who often acted like their mother, but he had to admit she rescued them from the rabble, who immediately dispersed after she ordered him to shut his purse. He was here to save the masses, and like Harriet, he now identified with the Irish, but he did not relish being confronted by them as soon as he and Harriet alighted from the coach, and he later agreed with Eliza that some of the hungry women seemed to threaten his bride. Eliza's intervention had saved Harriet and helped him secure sufficient coin so he didn't need to seek another loan from one of his countless benefactors; at least not yet.

Still, once they had settled into their modest lodgings and had slept for a few hours, he argued with Harriet because she had become angry after he fastened his purse. She reiterated her unhappiness with his seeming lack of compassion for their Irish kin.

"Percy, didn't we agree that we are ashamed of John Bull and what he has done and continues to do to our Irish cousins? Do you no longer identify with the noble Irish?"

"Of course, I do, Harriet. That's why we're here. We will help them get the foot of the British off their necks, and return their country to their own rule, but in the meantime, I need to ensure that we have sufficient funds to pay for our lodgings and to feed ourselves. I can't feed the entire world. I can only help the oppressed achieve freedom through my art and pen."

"Freedom isn't free if you're starving, Percy," she said.

"I'd rather not contribute to our own deprivation and hunger," he replied as he took a bite of a scone that Eliza had procured early that morning at a nearby bakery.

Harriet scoffed. "You appear to have lost your ideals."

Percy gave Harriet the side-eye. He was used to her being docile and deferential. What was she up to? She looked the same, as lovely as ever with her alluring figure, her long, flowing nut-brown locks, and her sea-green eyes. But somehow, she had been internally transformed. Had his devoted tutelage changed her personality and made her bold?

"You assume wrongly, my love, and I'd rather not continue this conversation. You're rather peevish. Perhaps your sister is correct—you need more rest. I must get back to my writing, for writing will feed us and help us rescue the poor Irish that you and I desperately wish to save."

Harriet was livid with the way Percy now presumed that he could tell her what to do and supervise her activities. He had always advocated for equal rights for women but now he was treating her as if she were a child and not his equal. They were both admirers of Mary Wollstonecraft's *A Vindication of the Rights of Woman*; he and Harriet had read it aloud to one another. Harriet felt that being told that she was tired and testy resembled the way her father treated her; it was patronizing and unbecoming of the husband who, until now, had seemed as heroic as Perseus.

Just the day before, during their sea voyage, which lasted days rather than the promised hours, Percy, a seasoned sailor, soothed Harriet and her sister when a squall arose at night while they were gazing at the canopy of stars. "The heavens are illuminated," Percy announced as lightning pierced the sky. He told them about how ancient the stars were in relation to human struggles. "The stars stand outside of human history. And yet many people trust that the stars govern our lives."

As they gazed at Andromeda chained to the sky, threatening clouds appeared, torrential rain fell, and seawater swamped the deck. Captain Holbrook ordered the travelers below and told them to remain there until dawn. Percy grabbed Harriet's and Eliza's hands and raced them through the knee-deep water and then down the slippery steps.

The three of them rode out the storm in utter darkness in their cabin. Percy withstood the tortuous waves, but the ladies were terrified, for the table, beds, and trunks slid back and forth across the floor. At times, it seemed as though the ship might overturn but then it righted itself. Percy wrapped his arms around Harriet and tried to placate her fears. Even so, Harriet repeatedly cried, "God save us! I don't wish to die." Percy didn't remind her that they didn't believe in God, for he knew that her sensibilities were stoked by her fear of perishing at a tender age.

Before they set to sea, Harriet had dreaded the voyage because ever since she was a child, she had dreamt that she would drown. After she eloped with Percy, she frequently had nightmares where she saw herself flailing in the water and then sinking. When she awakened in terror, Percy would stroke her hair, console her, and say, "My love, you are safe. You're on land. The sea is far away. I'm here to protect you and always will be." She snuggled next to him, and her heart settled when she felt his strength and then she returned to sleep. On other occasions, she dreamt that Percy perished at sea, but she never warned him of these terrifying visions.

In addition to heroically saving her during the storm, Percy had also rescued her from her domineering father who insisted that she continue her education at the frivolous Miss Fenning's School for Girls, where girls were taught nothing other than how to become submissive, mindless dolls for male amusement, the performance of which Harriet detested. She couldn't bear the idea that a female education consisted of learning to dance properly, drink tea correctly, speak a modicum of French, and make odious small talk. She did not want to learn how to be man's perfect, subservient helpmate, which was the goal of female education.

Like her idol Mary Wollstonecraft, Harriet thought that girls should be educated just as boys were. They too should learn Latin and Greek and read the classics and history. And now that she and Percy were wife and husband, he served as her mentor, remedying her lack of an equal education.

As her tutor, Percy even rectified Harriet's orthodox, rigid, and fearful thinking. He awakened her sensibilities and conscience and shaped her thinking, so she no longer believed that atheists, like himself and Hogg, had horns and cloven feet and she no longer dreamt that the devil spirited her soul away to hell. As a child, she worried that devils would snatch her from her bed and cast her into their dark, sweltering lair where they would brandish her with pitchforks or hang her from hooks while their pet ravens pecked out her eyes.

"Harriet," Percy said, "you've listened to too many horrifying sermons that clergy use to scare people into believing in God and hell. There is no hell, except for the one we create here on earth."

This revelation eased her mind. She could accept that there was no physical hell ruled by a defiant fallen angel and his followers. Even so, she was not at ease with Percy's atheism. She had been saddened when, while she was at school, he professed his lack of belief in God in a letter to her that was confiscated by a teacher. The entire school learned of Percy's atheism and thought that Harriet also denied God's existence. She was brought before the head mistress who questioned her. Harriet denied she was an atheist and firmly attested her belief in a good God. Even so, a rumor spread throughout the school that she didn't believe in the Almighty, and all the girls, except for Percy's sister, Hellen, shunned her. Harriet sequestered herself and silently professed that God was equated with all that was good in the world. When humans acted charitably, as Percy ordinarily did, they performed God's work.

But now, she needed to consider whether Percy was as noble or as much of a savior as she believed. Rather than acting benevolently when confronted with genuine suffering, he seemed fearful of the famished; he acted as though the Irish were devils.

Ignoring his admonishment to rest as if she were a child, she donned her cloak and bonnet and opened the door.

Eliza looked up from her darning. "Where are you going?"

"Out."

"Wait, I'll go with you," Eliza said as she placed her sewing on the end table and started to rise from the chair.

Harriet stood in the doorway, allowing the frigid air in. "No, sister, don't bother. I wish to walk alone. I need some air. It's oppressively hot in here."

Percy finished his breakfast of tea and soda bread, and then warmed his hands near the glowing hearth. He thought about his *Address to the Irish People*, which he had written during a recent visit to Robert Southey in the Lake District. Originally, Percy wished to visit Wordsworth and Coleridge, whose poetry he deeply admired, but they were unavailable, so he settled for Southey, whose work, in Percy's view, was not as inspiring as that of the other Lake District poets. He did enjoy some of Southey's early poetry though, especially Southey's thoughts on human potential. He recalled and agreed with the lines:

> Oh what a glorious animal were Man
> Knew he but his own powers, and knowing, gave them
> Room for their growth and spread.

And he knew that Southey, Coleridge, and Lovell had once planned to establish a utopian community in America that would transform society. Percy had similar plans whereby he would create an Academy like Plato's where he and his fellow philosophers would walk, think, and talk as *they* reformed the entire world.

Based on these sentiments and a similar worldview, Percy believed he might learn something from Southey. So, after he and Harriet eloped in the fall of 1811, they traveled to Keswick in the Lake District, and he introduced himself to Southey.

One evening as they sat in Southey's parlor discussing the poetry and politics of Thomas Moore, the Irish poet, Percy brought up his interest in Irish culture and politics that he had gleaned from his friendship with Sir Charles. Southey told Percy that he had lived in Ireland while serving the Crown as the Secretary to the Irish Exchequer and initially enjoyed Irish wit and wisdom; now he despised the Irish and viewed them on par with what he called African "savages."

"The Irish are ignorant and foolish, given to superstition and whimsey. They talk of fairies and changelings. They keep beasts in their hovels and are nothing like the ancient Irish bards and druids of whom I read," Southey said as he sipped his Irish whiskey and petted his Irish wolfhound that lay at his feet.

Percy was appalled by Southey's change of heart and mind. "Perhaps it's the penal laws that forbid Irish Catholics an education or owning land, or of having any power, which diminishes their brilliance, that and the abhorrent Act of Union of England and Ireland that deprive the Irish of their own parliament."

"You lack historical perspective, Mr. Shelley. Those laws and the Act of Union were instituted following deadly revolts against the Crown. The Crown seeks to protect the Irish."

Percy rose from his chair and paced the room as if he were arguing a point in parliament. "I understand history perfectly, Mr. Southey. The Crown patronizes the Irish, acting as if the Irish are children who must be supervised, and the Crown will not tolerate dissent. However, the Crown has established an illegal government in Ireland, for history teaches us that English men and Irish Protestants confiscated Catholic land while the Crown and the British parliament and their lackies, penalize, torture, and even kill those who defy them."

"And you refer to whom in particular that is being penalized, tortured, and killed?"

Percy stopped pacing and stood in front of Southey. "Peter Finnerty the journalist was pilloried and jailed; Lord Castlereagh, the Crown's henchmen, sent him there after accusing him of libel when he merely reported the truth. And of course, the 1798 rebels and Robert Emmet and other United Irishmen were tortured and killed."

"They were traitors. Traitors get hanged. Your man Moore was friends with Emmet. Luckily, he did not swear an oath to the United Irishmen like Wolf and Emmet did." Southey crossed his legs and bent down to feed his whimpering dog a bit of biscuit.

"Mr. Southey, Emmet, and Tone were heroes and statemen. They sought Irish independence and bravely led their revolutions. Tone defied the British by courageously slitting his own throat before they executed him. Emmet spoke eloquently at the dock before he was hanged."

Southey raised his eyebrows and then stared at Percy as if he were studying his face and physiognomy. "Mr. Shelley, unfortunately, you remind me of Emmet, whom I met during my tenure. Like him, you are young and foolish but if you manage to live long enough to mature and attain wisdom, you will agree with my point of view. You are a naïve idealist; long ago I was like you."

"I know myself well enough to know that whatever my age I will always side with the oppressed, even those you condemn, the Irish."

Percy remembered that upperclassmen at Eton had treated him as a rural idiot. Southey was treating him similarly. The upperclassmen had belittled him and mocked his Latin pronunciation as well as his idealism. Even so, he excelled and shamed all of them when examination time rolled around. Because of this, he always sided with the underdog, for he knew that greatness often resides in those who first appear simple or powerless. Whenever he saw someone mistreated, he felt great empathy and from this experience, and from pondering Plato, he had developed his notions of ideal justice.

"You're partially correct—I am an idealist, but I am not a naïve one. And wisdom is not necessarily an attribute of the mature. My foolishly wise idealism will help me create a world built on equality and justice. I intend to complete Emmet's revolution but through peaceful means. I've written my *Address to the Irish People* that speaks to the common man. Would you care to hear me read it?"

Southey smirked. "No, I have no interest. Perhaps, we had best refrain from talking politics, for we will never agree. Let's stick to poetry. Have you read the latest from Wordsworth, who now writes against the French Revolution and its barbarism?" He stood and walked to the heavily ladened bookshelves that lined the room and pulled off his copy of Wordsworth's new work. He leafed through it.

"I haven't; of course, I agree with Wordsworth regarding the French Revolution, for I am a pacifist. If you wish to discuss poetry, I'll share some stanzas from my poem 'The Mask of Anarchy,' written about Lord Castlereagh's treatment of his fellow Irish."

Before Southey could reply, Percy pulled a piece of paper from his waistcoat pocket and unfolded it. "I wrote this after the detestable Castlereagh tortured five hundred United Irishmen and executed fifty of them in Ulster."

Percy solemnly recited:
I met murder on the way
He had a mask like Castlereagh—
very smooth he looked, yet grim;
seven bloodhounds followed him:

All were fat; and well they might
be in admirable plight,
For one by one, and two by two,
he tossed them human hearts to chew,
which from his wide cloak he drew.

"Now Castlereagh's hounds chew and grow fat on Finnerty's heart," he said smugly as he slipped the poem into his pocket.

"Perhaps poetry is off limits too, Mr. Shelley," Southey replied. "Care for a game of whist?"

The turf fire roared, sending sparks up the flue. Percy felt energized. He opened his desk drawer, grabbed a quill and ink, and set out to revise his *Address*. In the first paragraph, he pointed out that he was an Englishman but that did not prevent him from relating to his Irish cousins or preclude him from administering advice. One's birth in whatever nation was merely an accident, one turn on Fortune's whimsical Wheel, and being born in one country or another did not prevent a man from feeling for the plight of other men. And hearing the views of an empathetic Englishman, a would-be, honorary Irishman, might help an Irishman better know his own interest. All of this was sound reasoning, but Percy thought it best to seek the opinions of Irishmen before he altered anything in the *Address*, so he decided to visit a public house where men often gathered to discuss politics. Naturally, he would have preferred a teahouse. He did not imbibe spirits because he thought they impeded rational thought, but he knew that the Irish were fond of their porters, stouts, and whiskies. So, he walked the short distance to The Brazen Head, a pub he had spotted from the carriage window the previous day. At the time, he had noted a sign that designated the pub had been founded in 1198, so he surmised that politics had been discussed and debated there ever since Henry II had sent the Lord of Leinster, Richard de Clere, otherwise known as Strongbow, to invade the island.

Percy indulged in a favorite pastime of observing people and studied the other patrons in the public house. History and the voices of patriots seemed to ooze from the very stone and vibrated in the air. But not quite enough to drown out the three men standing at the bar, having a heated discussion about the Prince of Wales.

The tallest man, who resembled the prince with his wild locks, picked up his whiskey and swirled it around in the glass. "We cannot trust the Prince of Wales. He says one thing and does another. And how long will it be before the crown is his? His father, King George, continues to talk to angels and oak trees, but there are other folk who do likewise. Fitzgerald here does the same on occasion and no one calls him a crazy loon."

His friends laughed.

"Lawless, you've been known to converse with the Little People yourself, ain't that right?" Fitzgerald replied.

Lawless shrugged. "Sure, many of them are my kin. And Murphy, you ain't right in the head yourself so I don't know if we can expect better from old George." He turned to and motioned to the bartender. "Another round for me friends."

Amused and eager to join their discussion, Percy walked across the sticky beer-soaked floor.

He leaned on the bar. "I couldn't help but overhear your discussion and I agree, the prince can't be trusted." He held out his hand. "Percy Shelley."

Lawless shook Percy's hand. "John Lawless. This here's Seamus Fitzgerald and that's Liam Murphy." He nodded in their direction.

"A pleasure to meet you," Percy said. "May I join your discussion?"

"You're most welcome to join us, young man," Lawless said as he waved the bartender his way. "You appear thirsty. The first drink is on me. What'll you have? A pint?"

Percy smiled and shook his head. "Thank you, no; I don't imbibe spirits. But if there's tea available, I'll gladly drink a cup of Earl Grey."

Lawless looked at Percy as if he were mad. "This ain't a tearoom, young man. Go down the road if you want a cuppa." He raised his pinky finger.

"No, I'd prefer to stay here and speak further about the Prince of Wales and those who advise him."

"Based on your speech, you ain't no Irishman." Murphy pointed a finger at Percy. "You sound like an Englishman, sir. Don't he, Fitzgerald? He sounds like some of your English cousins."

"I'm loathed to admit it, but I am English. Still, I feel great kinship with you. I've learned your history. I align my politics with yours and would happily become Irish," Percy replied, relaxing his stance against the bar.

Fitzgerald raised his eyebrows. "How does one become Irish? If that's possible, I'd like to see how you unbecome Irish." He laughed. "Politics aside, are you a Protestant like most of your countrymen?"

"I'm neither a Protestant nor a Catholic."

"What are you then? An infidel?" Murphy asked.

"I've been called a heretic," Percy said with a hint of pride.

"You don't believe in God?" Fitzgerald asked.

"Not in the way God is imagined. I believe in Truth and Justice. Perhaps those ideals are God. And no man should be called a heretic just because he believes differently than you."

"You have radical ideas, lad," Fitzgerald replied.

"I've been accused of that before."

Lawless lifted his glass. "Hold on, boy. You say you feel kinship with Irishmen. Few Englishmen have a liking for we Irish. They think us animals, closer to apes than fellow human beings."

"I understand the plight of the Catholics and sympathize with them," Percy said. "My Irish friend the Duke of Norfolk was compelled to convert to the Church of England in order to sit in the British parliament."

"So, your friend was obliged to embrace heresy to be welcome in Westminster; of course, that's what your fellow Brits do to legitimize the Irish. They force us to become heretics, condemning us to eternal damnation," Lawless said, staring at Percy.

"Never mind that," Murphy said as he turned to Percy. "What I want to know is why are you talking to us underlings? We know no dukes."

"I believe that no man is better than another. In God's eyes, the king and the peasant are the same. Likewise, the duke who sits idly, and those who labor are equal."

"You hold some revolutionary views, youngster," Lawless said. "We're happy to speak with you. Are you sure you'll have no pint, perhaps you'd prefer a half pint like the ladies drink?"

Percy laughed and shook his head, while the others indulged in another round of drinks.

Lawless brought up how the Prince of Wales had pledged that when he was crowned king, he'd emancipate the Catholics. "I've heard that Georgie Boy ain't long for this world. I'm hoping that the prince follows through and frees us so that we can once again educate our children properly in schoolhouses instead of barns. They forbid us a formal education, you know."

"And we need to be able to hold office," Murphy said. "And restore our parliament."

"I don't think that any of this will happen without organized action," Percy said.

Lawless nodded in agreement.

Percy rested his elbows on the bar. "He says one thing now while prince but there are those in government who seek to dissuade him."

"You know this how?" Lawless crossed his arms.

"My friend the Duke is privy to such knowledge."

"Then how can the prince be persuaded to honor his promise?" Lawless asked. "Charles Fox, who advocates for Catholic Emancipation, no longer advises him."

"He can't be persuaded. Instead, I think that the Irish should work toward freeing themselves," Percy replied.

"You've heard of Daniel O'Connell?" Fitzgerald finished his pint and put the glass on the bar. "He's doing just that. He promotes peaceful ways to liberate us, but I don't believe that our liberation will come about through peaceful means."

"But it must," Percy retorted. "Look at what happened in France. The original liberation was based on rational principles that recognized the rights of man, but then violence ensued, and innocents were slaughtered."

"The French are unreliable. We know that from their capriciousness in ninety-eight. They pledged to help Wolfe Tone, but they never showed up. It's no wonder they couldn't control the masses and lead a proper revolution," Lawless said. "We can't follow their example. Besides, we have our own ways. Do you care to know about them?" He uncrossed his arms. "We have a group that works toward our liberation."

Fitzgerald looked askance at Lawless.

Percy straightened. "If you're talking about the Society of United Irishmen, I've read their prospectus, and I'm well acquainted with Robert Emmet's speech at the dock. I've memorized it. Would you care to hear it?"

"No, lad, we also know the speech," Lawless said.

"I wish to pursue Emmet's agenda. I believe that if Ireland is free to govern itself other countries will follow suit. All tyrants must be removed; all kings toppled. As my mentor the philosopher William Godwin argues, there must be a worldwide revolution that frees people to govern themselves by their rational faculties."

Lawless placed an arm around Percy's shoulder and leaned close to his ear. "It would be best if you lowered your voice. We should talk further in private. You're aware that the Society is outlawed?"

Percy nodded.

"Then, we'd best retire to a private room where such things are spoken of."

The frigid air cooled Harriet's anger. She pulled her cloak closer and strode down Sackville Street with determination to hide her nervousness at embarking out alone for the first time. In the past, she had always walked with her nanny, sister, or Percy. It was frightening to walk alone but also liberating. And she felt righteous, for she was convinced that she could do good in the world on her own.

She glanced around, trying to make eye contact with the people who stopped and stared at her. Why did they stare? Was it because she was unchaperoned and young or that she was dressed as a fine lady in the latest Parisian fashion?

The dirty children lurking in doorways and holding out tiny hands broke her heart. She had to find a way to alleviate their suffering. After all, children were the future. Thomas Paine's words sang out in her mind. " . . . failure to act condemns our children to tyranny." If she couldn't lead a revolution, she could do something practical. Writing could accomplish much, but compassionate, pragmatic action was necessary to genuinely reform the world.

She remembered an afternoon when she was ten. She and her Irish nanny Irene were strolling in Hyde Park and saw a wee girl wearing a torn, dirty dress and sitting alone next to the Serpentine Pond. She was playing with a stick and floating it on the water.

Irene pushed a pram with Harriet's doll in it as if she were a real baby. Sometimes, Harriet placed her dolly in a toy boat and sailed her in the pond, pretending the doll was a pirate queen, like Grace O'Malley, whom Irene praised as a fierce Irish patriot.

Harriet stopped in front of the little girl. "Have you no toys?"

The child shook her head.

"Would you like to play with mine? I brought my dolly, whose name is Grace, just like the pirate queen."

The little girl's eyes grew wide as she gazed at the doll.

"I've never owned a doll. She's lovely," the girl said.

"You can have her," Harriet said, as she handed her favorite toy to the child.

"I can't take it, miss; I have no place to keep her." The girl threw the stick into the murky water.

Harriet felt confused. She looked at Irene who opened the lunch basket she carried. Harriet understood. "Maybe you'd rather have some of the biscuits that we brought to feed the ducks. And some of our cucumber sandwiches. We have too many anyway."

Irene smiled as Harriet handed the child a half dozen biscuits and several sandwiches.

"Bless you, miss," the child said as she ran away. "I'll share these with my sister."

As they watched her run toward an older girl, Irene said, "You have a kind heart, love. How is that so?"

"She looked like how I think you looked when you were a little girl in Ireland. You told me that your papa didn't have a job, and you were often hungry. And you taught me to treat others the way I want to be treated. Besides, we have more than we need. Why not share what we have?"

The clouds parted revealing the sun's face. Irene pulled Harriet close, and they walked hand in hand toward the rose garden. Harriet felt safe with Irene, who acted as her mother. But as they skirted the pond, Harriet felt a little shiver as she imagined herself sinking to the bottom.

Now, walking across the River Liffey Bridge, she thought of that girl as she spotted two girls huddled on the ground. The smaller one's white dress was grubby, and her face and neck were riddled with grime. The older one wore a far too large brown brocade dress. Harriet assumed it was a hand-me-down. Neither of them wore a shawl or cloak. Both children had unbrushed and unwashed hair. The older one had her arm wrapped around the younger seemingly to shield her from the cold. The younger one appeared to be crippled. They had a tin can on the ground in front of them and a sign that said, "Please help."

Harriet wished she could pick up the children and take them home to feed and bathe them. She dropped a few coins in their tin. "Are you sisters? If so, where are your mother and father?"

"Yes, miss, we are. Our da is dead. Our mam is working," the older girl said, as a matter of fact, as if she were quite used to the question and had prepared an answer.

"And where does your mother work?"

The girl paused. "Are you with the Foundling Hospital?"

Harriet smiled to reassure the children. "Certainly not. I'm just wondering how I might help."

"Our mam works at a house on Merrion Square. You've helped enough, miss," the girl said as held up the can and then moved her sister onto her lap.

"If your mother works, who takes care of you during the day?"

"We take care of each other."

Harriet's heart ached as the girls huddled closer together. "Have you eaten today?"

"No, we haven't; thank you, miss."

"Would you like to come home with me? I live nearby."

"No, miss. Our mam told us to stay here; this is *our* work. If we left, she wouldn't know where to find us."

As Harriet was about to add more coins to their can, she saw a fat, red-faced policeman walking toward them swinging his nightstick. What could he possibly want?

He stood in front of the children. "There's no begging on this bridge. Move along, you scamps. Go to Ha'penny where the other beggars rob passersby."

"The one child appears to be crippled, sir," Harriet said, her voice shaking a little, for she had never spoken to a police officer. "And the other said that their mother will meet them here when she's done working."

The officer looked at Harriet as if she were a naïve child.

"Working, huh? She's likely earning her bread by spreading her legs." He turned to the children. "Move along, now, or I'll cart you two to the Foundling Hospital."

"Is there no help for these desperate children?" Harriet asked.

"The Foundling Hospital is their help. Do you know how many of these urchins are on the street? Their parents are scoundrels for leaving them alone."

"Their father is dead," Harriet said.

"That's what they all say. I'd advise you to move along too. If you don't move along, I may have to arrest you and take *you* to Kilmainham Gaol for interfering in police business."

As if she were a grownup, the older child hoisted her sister onto her hip. "Thank you, miss. We'll be all right. God Bless," she said, sounding as grateful as the child Harriet met years ago in Hyde Park.

Harriet stepped into the flat a few hours later. Her legs ached from having walked for hours.

Eliza looked up from the little desk she was writing at. "You really should have waited for me. I went out to look for you, but it was as if you had vanished. I fretted so. You know that ladies don't walk alone."

"Perhaps I'm not a lady or I'm more than a lady."

Eliza frowned. "Whatever do you mean? How can one be more than a lady? You're acting like a petulant child. These streets are dangerous. And obviously, you've forgotten that strangers accosted you."

"I was not accosted. The poor women were merely admiring my clothes. I am not acting like a child and the streets aren't dangerous, sister," Harriet said as she wrapped her indigo shawl around her shoulders.

"You're naïve. This is not home. This is not Mayfair. I traveled to Ireland with you and your foolish husband to protect you." Eliza's tone was condescending.

"I don't need your protection, thank you. I can take care of myself. Now I wish to be left alone," Harriet said, as she closed the bedroom door.

Harriet leaned her head against the cold windowpane. She looked down onto the street and saw pools of water. The oak trees behind the flat bent with the wind. She thought about the children she had met. Had they sought shelter from the rain? Were they safe? Did they find their mother? Did the policeman further harass them?

Percy burst into the room and said excitedly, "My *Address* is done. I talked with some locals about its contents; I didn't get a chance to read it to them, but they are on board. I feel no need to revise; it's perfect. Tomorrow, we go to the publisher and begin my real work. Aren't you pleased?"

"Of course," Harriet said without smiling.

"Then why do you look sad?" he asked as he stroked her arm.

"Ireland, our new home, makes me sad."

"Would you tell me why?"

"I don't wish to talk about it."

"We'll improve it. Don't fret, my love," Percy said as he grabbed her hand and kissed it. He removed her shawl and began to unbutton her dress. "Come closer, my sweet Irish lass; let me comfort you."

Harriet tried to think about how much she adored Percy as they caressed, but all she could think about were the little girls who were likely fending for themselves in the cold. She promised herself that she would look for the wee sisters on the morrow and then closed her eyes and slept a dreamless sleep.

14 February 1812

Percy asked Harriet to go with him to find the publishing house of John Stockdale and Sons. "A man I met gave me Stockdale's address. He publishes radical writing, even though such writing could lead to his arrest. Stockdale bravely published Emmet's address that Emmet aimed to deliver after taking over Dublin Castle."

"Would you be in danger if you published your address, Percy?" Harriet asked as she poured Percy more tea.

"Of course not, love. I say nothing that threatens the government. I'm perfectly safe," he said. "Please, no more tea. I'm ready to meet Stockdale and truly begin my work."

Harriet took one last sip, and then Percy helped her with her cloak. They opened the door. The air was brisk and the sky was cloudy and heavy with moisture. The wind blew off Percy's hat, which he quickly picked up and donned. Harriet grabbed her parasol from the umbrella rack near the doorway and once outside, opened it, shielding Percy and herself from the wind.

Weaving in and out of the poor people who blocked the sidewalk, they traveled south on Sackville Street. More children dressed in tattered clothing beseeched them for alms. Crowds of beggars grew larger as they approached Trinity College and the former Irish Parliament. "Parliament has been shuttered since after the Act of the Union." Percy removed his handkerchief from his pocket and wiped a grimy window. He tried to look inside but could see nothing. "Someday this parliament will be restored. And we'll be instrumental in making that happen."

Then they walked farther south. All along the way, destitute people approached them, imploring a pence or two. Harriet studied the faces of the children, hoping to see the girls, but many of the children looked identical—desperate, sad, hungry, motherless.

As they approached St. Stephen's Green, they saw many derelict Georgian mansions and the nearby Merrion Square filled with weeds and littered with rubbish. Harriet wondered which house the girls' mother worked in.

"It looks as though the gentry have abandoned their homes and returned to London," Percy said. "It's shameful that these houses are empty. They could house many needy people."

"I wonder if some of the poor squat in these places," Harriet remarked. "It's possible, isn't it?"

"Doubtful. I'm sure these estates, though neglected, are protected in some fashion. Wealthy people, like my father, would never allow the indigent to occupy their property."

The address that Lawless had given them was one of those abandoned properties, and three Irish wolfhounds bounded toward the gate and barked madly as they approached.

"Quiet boys, we mean no harm." Percy turned to Harriet. "This can't be right but I'm sure it's the correct address."

"I doubt that a publisher of radical writing lives in such a palatial home," Harriet said. "We should enquire elsewhere."

So, they doubled back toward Sackville Street, where they asked a clerk at the General Post Office where Stockdale's Press was located.

The clerk looked at them blankly. "I dunno. Gillespie, do you know a publisher named Stockdale?"

"Yeah, I think he's on Abbey Street near the apothecary," Gillespie said as he stamped envelopes. "You need to go down the alley behind it and look for the sign."

Following the clerk's instruction, they peeked down an alley littered with broken beer bottles and saw the publisher's clapboard hanging vertically by one chain and swinging back and forth in the wind. The establishment's door creaked as they opened it, and they saw a large printing press and an old, bald man in the back. He wore thick glasses and held a magnifying glass in one hand as he scrutinized what appeared to be metal letters in his other hand.

"Mr. Stockdale?" Percy asked.

The man was intent on his task and didn't look up. "I'll be with you momentarily. I must set this type. Have a seat."

Percy and Harriet sat on a wobbly threadbare settee. A long-haired black cat jumped onto Percy's lap and meowed loudly, and Percy told it to shoo. Harriet petted the cat who curled up in her lap and purred.

"Percy, may I read a few pages of your pamphlet while we wait?" she asked as she stroked the cat.

"Of course, darling. Or I could read it to you."

"No, I'd rather read it myself."

"If you insist," he said as he pulled a stack of papers from his satchel and handed them to her.

"Percy, are you sure it's wise to begin by chastising Catholics in this way?" she asked after a few minutes. "They might be offended. Also, why don't you mention the needy children and future generations, like Paine did?"

"No, it's fine, love, readers will understand the rationale. I intend no offense. And children have nothing to do with my argument."

As they continued to discuss the pamphlet, Mr. Stockdale walked to them as he removed his leather apron.

"Now, young people, how may I be of help?" he asked. "Do you wish for me to print wedding announcements?"

"No." Percy laughed. "We're already married. I have an important pamphlet that I want you to publish. I heard that you published Robert Emmet's 'Provisional Government Address.'"

Stockdale pursed his lips and paused a beat. "Who told you that?"

"John Lawless."

"Lawless is a bit of a rogue; he epitomizes his surname. Are you as radical as Emmet? Do you advocate overthrowing the government, as Emmet did?"

"Certainly not. Well, not in the same way at least."

Stockdale pushed his glasses up to the bridge of his nose. "I will have to peruse your writing first to ensure it's not seditious. Come back tomorrow."

"If you would, please read it now. We'll wait. I'm eager to get it into the hands of Irish citizens." Percy excitedly rubbed his hands together.

"If you insist, but I will read it carefully before I decide."

Harriet handed the stack of papers to Mr. Stockdale who retreated to his office.

An hour passed and Percy paced the room. "I wonder what's taking so long. Surely, he has found nothing treasonous in my writing."

"Percy, try to be patient," Harriet said as she continued to caress the cat that slept on her lap. While waiting, she read *The Mysteries of Udolpho* by the Irish writer Ann Radcliffe, which Sir Charles had given her. The novel focused on a woman held against her will in a sinister castle.

Percy continued to pace impatiently.

Finally, after another half hour, Stockdale opened the door. "I will publish this, but on one condition. I will not place my name on the document. Some might infer much from what you write and cast you as another Emmet and me as a co-conspirator." Then Stockdale said that he fervently feared the British government ensconced at Dublin Castle and didn't wish to become their prisoner either there or in Kilmainham Gaol. He said that the conditions of these places of punishment were the most horrific in the world.

"The dungeons in Dublin Castle and Kilmainham are earthly hells, young man," he said. "They are worse than the Black Hole of Calcutta if you know what I mean. It's even said that some folks are buried alive in these prisons. You'd best avoid these places if you wish to remain free and effect your revolution."

Harriet recalled her demon-filled dreams and shuddered at the thought of being carted away to an earthly hell.

"I appreciate your concern, but I have no intention of spending time in either place," Percy said. "Surely, I'm in no current danger, for what I've written, although passionate, is not irrational. Besides, my father is a Member of Parliament. Which Irishman, no matter how high ranking, would dare arrest the son of a British MP? Thank you for your time and help, Mr. Stockdale. When might I collect the pamphlets?"

16 February 1812

Percy fetched four hundred copies of his pamphlet, and Stockdale promised an additional eleven hundred after Percy paid for the four hundred.

"I'll pay you as soon as I receive royalties from my poems." Percy didn't admit to Stockdale that he had not yet received a contract for the poems. He figured that Stockdale did not need to know that. Percy only had sufficient funds to advertise the pamphlet and mail it to those who would put it to practical use.

With pamphlets in hand, he visited *The Dublin Evening Post* and paid for an advertisement announcing the *Address* and then he visited the General Post Office and mailed pamphlets to Lawless, Fitzgerald, and Murphy, and then to other rebels, whose names and addresses Percy learned from Lawless during their closed-door meeting. They included those remaining patriots who participated in the 1798 and 1803 rebellions and their apologist, John Philpot Curran. Percy also mailed his pamphlet to William Godwin, who, no doubt, would approve of it, for he had inspired its political philosophy.

Feeling elated, Percy proceeded toward the former Irish Parliament and pasted the pamphlet on the door.

Afterward, Percy enthusiastically placed pamphlets in ladies' hoods as women passed him, and when he returned to the flat, he grabbed Harriet's hand and pulled her onto their balcony.

"Harriet," he said, as he handed her pamphlets. "Help me throw some of these from the balcony."

"Why would we do that?"

"We'll surprise people with the gift of my address."

Harriet frowned. "I know you're excited but is this the best way to distribute your pamphlet? This seems absurd—a bit mad."

"Of course I'll hire someone to distribute them in pubs, but for now, please help me get my *Address* out to Dubliners. We must not waste time."

Harriet reluctantly took some of the pamphlets and threw a handful over the balcony. Then she watched as Percy threw dozens. He seemed to be in a fever.

The pamphlets sailed down onto people's heads and some men and women grasped them, glanced at the title, and then tucked them away to be read in private. Others glimpsed at the title and tossed the pamphlets on the ground where they were trampled. But then Percy saw one woman look up after she caught a pamphlet in mid-air. She read the title and then shyly smiled as Percy leaned over the balcony and waved a greeting. Unfortunately, some pamphlets flew far away with a gust of wind and landed in the river.

"Perhaps passersby will pick up the ones on the street and a fisherman will retrieve the wayward pamphlets and join our peaceful revolution," Percy remarked.

Harriet hoped that Percy's pamphlet would work toward the common good. She prayed that her adopted home would no longer be broken and forlorn. She prayed that its four green fields would be returned to the Irish, that they would no longer be squatted on by the merciless and greedy John Bull.

17 February 1812

A woman knocked on their door as they were about to take tea and asked to see Percy Shelley. Eliza invited her in and, as she stood in the doorway, Percy was surprised to see that she was the woman who had smiled at him from the street when he tossed her a pamphlet. A cleanly dressed, middle-aged, plain-looking woman, she introduced herself as Mrs. Catherine Nugent, a seamstress, but then added that she was a member of the Society of United Irishwomen. Percy was astounded and grateful to know that such a women's organization existed and aimed to learn more.

But before he could inquire, she asked, "Are you Mr. Percy Shelley?"

"Indeed, I am, ma'am. Please come in. What can I do for you? Do you wish to join our cause?"

She glared at Percy. "No, I wish to advise you that your pamphlet is troubling and condescending. It belittles the people with whom you wish to engage. It needs to be amended."

Even though he felt rather insulted, for his pamphlet proposed unlimited tolerance, he replied, "Please have a seat and inform me of your thoughts."

She settled herself on the comfortable brocade settee and Eliza asked if she would care for a cup of tea.

"Don't trouble yourself. I won't be long." She drew a deep breath. "I'm quite certain, Mr. Shelley, that you have every good intention, but in your criticism of Irish Catholics, you refer to us as barbarous in our beliefs and actions."

"I find that Protestants too act in barbaric ways, and I said so," he replied.

"That may be, but you begin with your critique of Roman Catholics. Those of us who were raised as faithful members of the Church don't wish to be forced to convert to the Church of Ireland and become heretical Protestants. We most likely fail to read on once you've chastised us for our beliefs."

"I was only trying to show that both forms of Christianity are at fault," he said. "And both need to reform their ways and tolerate one another."

Mrs. Nugent pulled the pamphlet from her cloak and waved it in Percy's face. "You say here that you are kindred to us and that you are a friend to Ireland. That may be your hope. Your error, in part, is the structure and tone of your argument. In addition, you act as though we Irish have never given any thought to bettering ourselves and do not realize that the English treat us as chattel. Mr. Shelley, we have been victims of the English since the twelfth century. Ever since your Richard de Clere landed and aided one Irish king in his quest to attack another Irish king who had kidnapped his wife." She paused and took a breath and then continued with what was becoming a diatribe. "We know our history; our Bards taught us through song and verse. We know how Henry VIII and Elizabeth I stole our land and installed their fellow Protestants on it. We don't need a young Englishman, an aristocrat from the looks of your attire and speech, to remind us of our state. And we don't need to be told to read, think, and discuss. That we do frequently and without British assistance. Even though the penal laws forbid us an education, many of us are properly educated through the outdoor hedge schools. Some of us read and speak Latin and Greek just like British gentlemen, like yourself. Even the illiterate discuss our never-ending plight, the way we are tyrannized by British rule." Flushed, she pulled from her gown's bosom a small green scarf emblazoned with an Irish harp and wiped her brow.

He felt chastened for making this sincere, knowledgeable woman so agitated and unhappy, and he wished to make amends. Initially, he wanted to correct her assumption about his privileged background, for his grandfather was not born to wealth; he came from humble roots. When he acquired his fortune, he bought his baronetcy, but Percy held his tongue and asked, "What would you have me do?"

"Amend your writing; recognize your faulty logic. Change your tone if you truly wish to be a friend to Ireland."

He agreed to consider her proposal and then Mrs. Nugent agreed to take tea with them, and she and Harriet talked about the many street children, and how they might be helped.

As soon as Mrs. Nugent departed, Percy re-read his address and realized that her critique was correct. He felt ashamed but also thankful, that, through some sort of Providence, they had made the acquaintance of an Irish woman who would help him become a faithful friend of Ireland and perhaps a genuine Irishman.

Two

The Unmarked Grave

18 February 1812

Dear Sir Timothy:

I received your correspondence today and feel compelled to immediately reply to your command to renounce my atheism, seek Oxford University's forgiveness, and return to England, commands, which I must, in all good conscience, ignore. Father, I do not believe in your God, and I will not lie and claim to be a believer, just to save your and our family's reputation. You claim that because of my non-belief I will come to a bad end like the brilliant Christopher Marlowe did when he wrote atheistic tracks. I will remind you that this is the nineteenth not the sixteenth century. I do not fear the Crown's ultimate punishment.

Regarding your view of my work, you have never supported my political nor spiritual work, nor my thirst for action. You do not favor Catholic Emancipation. You look upon Catholics as heretics, in the same way that you label me a heretic. I proudly wear that label for I am a heretic who fights for justice and for the rights of others to believe as they prefer and not be barred from education and power as Irish Catholics currently are. I will not be dissuaded from my goals and beliefs.

You say that Ireland is full of fools and drunkards, brutish, ignoble people who live like barn-yard animals. Sir, since you have never visited this isle, this Hibernia, you know not of what you speak. There are people who imbibe spirits too often, and sometimes drink their dinner because they have no food, but have you ever contemplated why they might do so? Perhaps if the British would lift its foot from the neck of the Irish, the Irish would choose temperance over indulgence.

You, sir, misunderstand who the Irish are. This isle is inhabited by many virtuous Protestants and steadfast Catholics who continuously work for freedom for all Irish. And, as it's well known, the Irish saved civilization from the barbarians.

As a member of Parliament, you might consider how you would feel if an occupying force shuttered Westminster and dissolved your seat in parliament, and then ordered Mr. Perceval home, telling him that his services as prime minister were no longer necessary.

Although you have never read my writing, I have enclosed a copy of my Address to the Irish People. *It is time you educated yourself, and that you realize I am not your vassal but your grown son.*

In the spirit of Irish hospitality, I invite you to visit us. As the Irish say, "Tá fáilte romhat anseo"—"You are most welcome here." We will gladly help you acquaint yourself with our Irish cousins and with our political work.

Also, I ask that you reinstate my allowance, which is rightfully mine, until my financial independence is achieved. My poems are in the process of being published but until then I have few funds with which to buy food to feed my wife and her sister. I do not wish for them to suffer from hunger just as many of the Irish do because of British tyranny.

Your "Irish" offspring,

Percy

Harriet needed to find the two girls who had moved her heart to pity. She traveled down the main arteries of Sackville and Grafton Streets, peering down narrow, foreboding alleys, fearing she would find the girls' wee bodies crumbled in a doorway. She visited Ha'penny and Liffey Bridges, but only saw gypsies and Irish travelers holding out their hands. It was as if the girls had vanished. She tried to reassure herself that the girls were safe and warm at home nestled next to their mother by a roaring hearth.

Mrs. Nugent visited each evening after work to help Percy revise his writing. Harriet greatly respected Mrs. Nugent's opinions and wished to show her gratitude so one evening, as Mrs. Nugent stood in the doorway readying herself to walk home, Harriet invited her to join them for dinner the next evening and extended the invitation to her husband.

"Oh, my dear girl, I'm not married," Mrs. Nugent said as she tied her woolen bonnet and pulled on her thin woolen cloak.

"Are you a widow?" Percy asked gently.

"No, I never married, although I received several earnest proposals. I call myself Mrs. to be respected, for spinsters earn no respect. I never wished to be married. I'm happy to be a solitary traveler in life. My only love is my country."

Even though Ireland and its desperate children saddened her, Harriet loved her adopted homeland and agreed that love of country was as compelling as love of another human being.

Harriet figured they would serve their usual fare at dinner—vegetables and fruit—for they ate a strict Pythagorean Diet.

Eliza disagreed. "Mrs. Nugent is likely a carnivore and will prefer eating meat."

Harriet shuddered. Percy had taught her that eating animals was unethical and so she adopted a vegetarian diet like him, and Eliza was forced to eat what Percy insisted on eating. Harriet didn't relish serving a dead animal for dinner but agreed that Mrs. Nugent would probably expect a course of animal flesh. So, she said that she would purchase a "murdered" chicken, if Eliza were willing to roast it.

"I have no qualms about roasting a chicken for our guest who likely doesn't fancy surviving on vegetables as we do," Eliza said as she returned to chopping carrots and potatoes for the soup she was making for dinner.

Harriet entered a butcher's shop on Strand Street and the rancid smells and sights overpowered her, for her stomach had become sensitive ever since she stopped eating flesh; the place was strewn with animal carcasses and large sides of beef covered with flies. She felt sick to her stomach and nearly turned around, but the butcher greeted her before she could leave.

"Good day, miss. What'll you have? I have fresh pork and some delicious beefsteaks." He wiped his bloody hands on his filthy apron.

Harriet winced and tried to ignore her mounting nausea. "Would you please wrap a chicken carcass and place it in my satchel?"

"A chicken carcass?"

"That's what I said."

He picked up a chicken carcass and wrapped it in brown paper.

"That'll be 2 shillings and 6 pence," he said.

Harriet counted out the coins and dropped them into his hand, trying not to touch his flesh.

"Thank you, miss."

She turned her head away as he placed the animal carcass in her bag, and then made her way to the door. She needed fresh air.

Once she was outside, she breathed deeply. She wasn't sure that she would be able to stand the smell of a roasting flesh. She might have to sit on the balcony while Eliza prepared the dead animal. Trying to forget about the fact that she was toting animal flesh in her bag, she began to walk across the street.

The police officer who had threatened the girls was standing in the apothecary's doorway. Harriet noticed he was eating what appeared to be a pie and was licking his fingers. Had he been following her? If so, why? She didn't have time to think about that further. She decided to question him about the girls' whereabouts.

"Have you seen the girls you sent to Ha'penny Bridge?"

The officer took a bite from his pie and wiped away the gravy and bits of meat on his lips. "Hello there, young lady. How's yourself?"

Harriet didn't reply.

He shrugged. "If you must know, I seen them not an hour later. The little weasels were back on the bridge where there's no begging allowed. They should've heeded my warning. I did what I said I'd do. I took them to the Foundling Hospital."

"But they were waiting for their mother, who works as a maid nearby."

"Not likely. She probably abandoned them."

"Have you no faith in your own people?"

"Very little. I ain't blind. I see what goes on every day."

"The children are likely suffering because they have been stolen from their mother who promised to meet them." Harriet stared at the officer who looked off into the distance.

"Their mother is a no account and no, they ain't suffering. They are likely learning a trade other than how to beg," he said, then took another bite of his pie. He belched after he swallowed, and then clenched his stomach as if he were in pain. He turned toward Harriet. "They's in excellent hands. If you want to know, their names are Sinead and Michaela O'Byrne. You can check on them and see that they're thriving. Good day, miss." He threw the remainder of the pie on the street and quickly walked away while whistling. A stray dog ran over and gobbled up the meat pie and promptly vomited.

As soon as Mrs. Nugent arrived for dinner, Harriet wished she could speak with her about the girls but thought it prudent to wait until after dinner. She wasn't sure that Percy or Eliza would understand her interest in the children's welfare; they might insist that she stay uninvolved in their lives.

Eliza served Mrs. Nugent the chicken and when Mrs. Nugent noticed that she was the only one eating meat, she asked, "Aren't you having any?"

"Correct," Percy said. "We eat vegetables and fruit. We find the slaughter of animals for food revolting and unethical."

Harriet looked at Percy. Did he not realize he had insulted their guest in suggesting that in eating meat she condoned the murder of animals?

"I apologize for my husband's poor manners," Harriet said.

Percy scowled at Harriet, who ignored him.

"No offense taken," Mrs. Nugent said. "I don't often eat meat. I can't afford it. We Irish mostly survive on potatoes, but this year there was a blight, which is why you see so many hungry people."

They ate their dinner in an uncomfortable silence, finishing with a bit of trifle that Eliza had made.

"Let's take our coffee in the parlor and sit next to the fire," Eliza said, when they were done.

Eliza and Percy picked up their cups and walked out of the dining room.

Mrs. Nugent stood.

"Please wait, Mrs. Nugent," Harriet said. "I have something I wish to privately discuss with you."

Mrs. Nugent sat down. "What is it, child?"

"What can you tell me about the Foundling Hospital?"

"What do you want to know?"

"What are the conditions there? How are the children treated?" Harriet frowned.

"I haven't visited in years, but at one time the institution was scandalous. It's a former workhouse, but many reforms were put in place by a benefactor, Mrs. Denny, several decades ago."

"That's encouraging."

"Indeed. Before the reforms, the children, who were all Catholic, were forced to convert to Protestantism and they lived in despicable conditions. Women were paid to steal children from parishes and bring them to the hospital. While there, rats often bit children. Babies were fed laudanum to keep them from mewling from hunger."

Harriet's stomach turned at the thought of rats harming children, and that children were fed opium. "How horrifying. I do hope that the hospital has been rid of vermin. And laudanum is not suitable for children and should never be administered."

"Oh, Mrs. Denny eliminated the formula while instituting a regular feeding schedule of wholesome meat and grains. She also sent in rat catchers and had the hospital thoroughly cleaned and then employed fastidious and kind caretakers to mind the children. I believe the reforms are still in place. I think that the children are well cared for. You appear quite concerned, Mrs. Shelley. Do you know children who are housed there?"

"I met two little girls who were taken there," Harriet said as she twirled her cup on the saucer. "I'd like to see how they're faring."

Mrs. Nugent took Harriet's hand. "You have a kind heart, a mother's heart. Don't fret; I'll take you there tomorrow; Sunday is my day off."

"Thank you, Mrs. Nugent. I'm most grateful."

"You may call me Catherine. May I call you Harriet?"

"Yes, of course," Harriet said, as Catherine squeezed her hand.

Harriet knew that she had made her first Irish friend.

While they sat in the parlor enjoying their coffee and the sweet scent of the peat fire, Percy asked Mrs. Nugent about the United Irishwomen.

"Of course, many of us wish to keep a low profile, but I will tell you about my own experience. I was so involved in Wolfe Tone's rebellion that the authorities at Dublin Castle repeatedly threatened to hang me, even though, as far as I know, no woman has ever been hanged in Ireland," she said. "After the charges against me were dropped, I continued to aid the cause by ministering to those imprisoned in Dublin Castle and in Kilmainham Gaol, where I exhorted state prisoners, like the patriot Anne Devlin, to have courage and never abandon hope."

Percy's ears perked up. "Who is this Anne Devlin and why she was a state prisoner?"

"She was Emmet's associate," Mrs. Nugent said.

"Were you one of the leaders?" Harriet asked.

"No, our leader was Lady Mont Cashell, the former Margaret King, whose governess was the young Mary Wollstonecraft," Mrs. Nugent said. "She said that Wollstonecraft shaped her revolutionary spirit. Did you know that Wollstonecraft's mother was Irish; she was from Ballyshannon in Donegal."

"No, I didn't," Percy said. "I do know that Mary Wollstonecraft was the first wife of my mentor William Godwin. Tragically, she died after giving birth to her daughter Mary, who is now fourteen years old."

"How unfortunate to have lost such a brilliant and influential mother," Mrs. Nugent replied.

"It must be a great loss for the child but also for the world," Harriet said, who felt strongly for the plight of the motherless child.

"Would it be possible to meet Lady Mont Cashell to learn more about her role in the rebellion?" Percy inquired. "Might you arrange a meeting?"

"No, I'm afraid not, Mr. Shelley. Lady Mont Cashell lives in exile because she left her husband, in order to marry the man she loves."

Ah, Percy thought, the former Margaret King is indeed a kindred spirit; a free love advocate and non-conformist. Perhaps one day I will have the pleasure to encounter her, and we can discuss the audacious courage it takes to break with tradition.

Harriet was disappointed that she could not meet the former Margaret King, but also thought about the child Mary Godwin and wondered if someday she might be able to meet her and help her grow into womanhood, since Mary had never had the privilege of knowing her own mother.

19 February 1812

Dear Godwin,

Thank you for your quick reply to my missive. I know that your remarks intend to safeguard me, my family, and Ireland overall, but I must disagree with your thesis. You said that if I awaken the Irish poor, "they will rise up like Cadmus' seed of dragon's teeth, and their first act will be to destroy each other." You don't know the Irish like I do, so I intend to ignore your ill-founded prediction. Even though Lord Castlereagh betrays his fellow Irish, I trust that other Irish will never turn on one another.

Respectfully,
Percy Bysshe Shelley

The long wall of the Foundling Hospital stretched near St. James Gate, the gate where beggars entered the city. A patch of waste ground ran alongside the wall, and the height of the wall made the Foundling Hospital look more like a fortified prison than a refuge for poor Catholic children.

Harriet and Catherine walked along the ditch and located the hospital's entrance. Catherine lifted the knocker.

A white-haired, portly porter opened the door a few inches. "If you're delivering children, take 'em around back and leave them on the wheel. Someone will fetch them directly." He began to shut the door.

"Wait!" Catherine said. "We're here to retrieve two children who were brought here erroneously. We would like to speak with the supervisor in charge."

"He's in a meeting."

"We'll wait," Catherine said.

"May we see the children that we are looking for, Sinead and Michaela O'Byrne?" Harriet asked.

"I'll ask the matron," he said as he limped away.

Harriet thought the porter was clearly disabled but at least he had a job and needn't beg. Perhaps this hospital was a good place after all.

In a few minutes, the porter returned. "Follow me."

Harriet and Catherine entered the courtyard and then they heard childish cries rising from a nearby building with bars on the windows.

"Are those children being tended to?" Harriet asked.

"Never mind them. They're the loonies or the ones who refuse to obey the matrons," he said gruffly. "They'll spend some time in the Bridewell; that usually cures them of their rebellious behavior."

Harriet's heart sank. She wondered what it took to end up in the Bridewell, a virtual prison. Were children sent there if they attempted to escape? Were they confined if they spoke out of turn and refused to remain silent?

Arm-in-arm, Harriet and Catherine followed the porter into a cathedral-like building.

"Remain here," he said. "The matron will be with you directly."

On the wall hung a painting of a beet-red-faced, corpulent man, the founder, Archbishop Hugh Boulter.

"Looks like he never missed a meal or a Guinness in his life," Catherine said, shaking her head in disdain.

As they waited, they heard children praying in the nearby chapel. Harriet recognized the prayers, one of which was, "I acknowledge my transgressions, and my sin is ever before me . . . Oh Lord, correct me but with judgement, not in thine anger, lest thou bring me to nothing."

"They're reciting Anglican prayers," Harriet remarked. "I thought the children were no longer forced to practice Protestantism."

"I'm surprised. I was certain the reforms included no forced conversion," Catherine replied. "You're right. I hear no prayer to our Holy Mother."

The feeble cries of those in the Bridewell mingled with the strident Protestant prayers as if to say, "Someone, anyone, please have mercy on us."

A stout, middle-aged woman entered the foyer and wiped her hands on her apron. "What can I do for you ladies?"

"We wish to see Sinead and Michaela O'Byrne who are not foundlings. Their mother says they were stolen from her," Harriet said. She thought that this white lie would help the children. Catherine looked askance at Harriet, and Harriet felt her cheeks warm, but she did not acknowledge Catherine's dubious look.

"When were they brought here?" the woman asked.

"Nearly a week ago," Harriet said.

The woman walked to a large ledger, pointed a dirty fingernail at the page, and traced the writing until she stopped at the bottom.

"Here are their names. Sinead is in the infirmary, and Michaela is in number eight."

"May we see them?"

"They are sleeping."

Harriet wondered why they were sleeping during the day.

"We wish to see them sleeping then," Catherine said.

From her apron, the matron fetched a large set of keys and jangled them. "If you insist, follow me." She led them to a staircase, slowly ascended the steps, and unlocked the door at the top.

"Must the door be locked?" Harriet asked.

"Yes, some of the children are old enough to open it, and we don't wish for them to tumble down the steps."

Although it was midday, the room was dark, for the curtains were drawn and a lone candle sat on a table at the far end of the room. After their eyes adjusted to the dim light, Harriet and Catherine saw many beds pushed together, and three or four children in each. The children looked to be in a stupor. Harriet noticed that each child had a number etched with what she thought was Indian ink into their skin on their right forearms.

"Why are these children marked?" Harriet asked.

"That's so's we can keep track of who they are and when they came here," the matron said.

"You don't use their names?" Catherine asked incredulously.

"Rarely. There are too many, you see. Numbers are easier." The matron lifted a child's arm and examined the number etched into her skin. She dropped the flaccid arm. "Here's the one you're looking for, #2201812, Sinead O'Byrne."

Sinead appeared half dead. Her eyes were glassy, and her mouth open. She was cradled in the arms of another child who appeared as stupefied as she was.

"She looks far worse than when I saw her on the Liffey Bridge," Harriet said to Catherine.

Harriet touched the child's arm and began to lift her.

"Leave her be," the matron said, gruffly. "She's had her medicine; she needs to sleep."

"What medicine is that?" Harriet asked.

"The one that helps her sleep."

Harriet looked at other children who sucked on bottles filled with milk and wondered if the children were drinking milk laced with laudanum. Harriet stroked Sinead's face. She didn't respond to her touch.

"We wish to see Michaela now and hope that she's faring better than this child," Catherine said as she glared at the matron.

"This child is faring quite well, madam. And the older child's busy working."

"I thought you said she's asleep," Catherine replied.

"I misspoke. After prayers, the children learn a trade."

"And what is she learning?" Harriet asked.

"Lacemaking or beating hemp. I don't know which trade she was assigned."

"What do we need to do to remove the children from your care? Their mother says they were stolen from her," Catherine said, adopting Harriet's lie.

"That's not possible without the Governors' approval." The matron rattled her keys once more. "I have rounds to make. I trust you ladies can find your way out?" She opened the door and motioned for them to leave.

Harriet looked one more time at Sinead who had not moved. Reluctantly, she turned to leave. "We'll contact the Governors and then we will be back to fetch the girls."

"As you wish," the matron said.

On their way toward the exit, they saw rows of fresh graves behind the main hall.

"Oh, dear Lord, are children buried here?" Harriet asked.

"It appears so." Catherine clasped Harriet's hand.

"We must get Sinead and Michaela released before they end up in one of those unmarked graves," Harriet said as tears rolled down her cheeks.

Catherine reached into the bosom of her dress and fetched a handkerchief. "Dry your eyes, love. We'll do what we can for the girls. It's what Mrs. Denny would want us to do." She wrapped her arm around Harriet.

They returned to Harriet's lodgings and discussed how to convince the Governors that the O'Byrne girls were not foundlings and that their mother could provide them with a proper home. But first, they had to find their mother to ensure that this was true.

20 February 1812

Ever since his conversation with the three men in the pub, Percy wished to learn more about the fabled Robert Emmet, whom he had admired ever since he had read the broadsheet about his execution. As if he were his brother across time and nation, Percy felt great kinship with Emmet and believed that visiting his grave would further inspire him and prepare him to speak to O'Connell's Catholic Committee, which Lawless had arranged. Perhaps he would be able to channel Emmet and his message. Mrs. Nugent had told him that an uninscribed tomb in St. Michan Church's graveyard was thought to be Emmet's resting place.

"After he was hanged and decapitated, his corpse was returned to Kilmainham Gaol and then his body was interred in Bully's Acre, where paupers are buried," Mrs. Nugent had said. "Some of us patriots dug up Emmet and moved his body to St. Michan's, a Dublin church frequented by United Irishmen."

Harriet was surprised. Mrs. Nugent didn't seem like a graverobber, but Harriet supposed that Mrs. Nugent had likely participated in all kinds of terrifying activities as a member of the United Irishwomen.

Percy seemed undisturbed by the graverobbing. "I'd like to pay my respects and visit Emmet's grave."

"I know where the grave is in the churchyard," Mrs. Nugent said. "I'll meet you there at half six tomorrow. Follow the river westward and turn right once you arrive at Church Street. You'll find it easily."

Percy did not fear graveyards or meeting the dead. He believed that the dead sometimes walk among us. Perhaps Emmet patiently paced that graveyard, waiting for someone to champion his goal.

21 February 1812

On his way to the graveyard, Percy made a short pilgrimage while reflecting on Emmet's rebellion. He stood in front of the entrance to Trinity College and thought about how Emmet, like himself, had been expelled from an elite educational institution founded to educate Protestant gentlemen. Unlike Percy though, Emmet did not deny the existence of God, but challenged the authority of God's supposed regal representative, the king, an opinion with which Percy agreed. Percy personally called George III "an old, mad, blind, despised and dying king," for George once addressed an oak tree as the King of Prussia and claimed to converse with angels. Emmet refused to take an oath to George, not because the king was mad and supposedly chatted with angels (and the occasional devil), and often thought he was persecuted like King Lear, but because Emmet would not pledge his allegiance to an unlawful government. Instead, at the age of twenty, he swore an oath to the United Irishmen.

Percy continued west on Dame Street, which took him to Dublin Castle. At the formidable, locked gates overseen by an enormous statue of Britannia, he imagined Emmet's plan to storm the gates at dusk on 23 July 1803, to seize the British Viceroy and Privy Council, and then hoist the green flag emblazoned with a harp over Dublin Castle. The plan utterly failed; the rockets that Emmet designed to alert his troops were useless; some of Emmet's rebels were drunk and many deserted him. The men who were to arrive from Counties Wicklow and Kildare were not summoned. Some of the drunken rebels attacked a carriage entering the castle gates and pulled a gentleman from the carriage and murdered him. When Emmet saw the brutality, he became irate, for the gentleman was a barrister Emmet recognized, Lord Kilwarden, a Privy Councilman who had defended Wolfe Tone. At that point, Emmet and his lieutenants called off the rebellion and hurriedly sought refuge in the Wicklow Mountains.

At Thomas Street, where Emmet was executed at the age of twenty-five on 20 September 1803, Percy could picture him speaking to the people who had gathered around the gallows. Emmet stood valiantly; he did not tremble. He helped the executioner place the noose and then asked to speak to the people but was denied. Even though the executioner tried to silence him, Emmet shouted above the crowd, "My friends, I die in peace and with sentiments of universal love and kindness toward all men. I may have betrayed England, but I never betrayed Ireland." Before giving the executioner his consent, the plank was kicked out from under Emmet's feet and he dropped; because of his light frame, he was suspended for thirty minutes before he ceased breathing. No one was allowed to break his legs to end his suffering. Afterward, the executioner chopped off Emmet's head and hoisted it, saying, "Here's the head of a traitor—Robert Emmet."

Percy's heart was troubled when he finally crossed the bridge at Church Street and entered the graveyard, knowing that, even if he found Emmet's grave, he would never find the man himself or learn much more about him.

Sitting on a bench outside the church, Mrs. Nugent motioned to Percy as he entered the graveyard. They then walked amongst the dead.

Feeling a chill, Percy remarked, "I feel Emmet's spirit. He's still restless, hoping that someone will carry out his work."

"That's fanciful mad talk. You sound rather like an Irishman who believes in sprites and fairies. Are you whimsical and superstitious, Mr. Shelley?" Mrs. Nugent asked, laughing.

"I wouldn't say so, but I often feel the spirits around me, for souls of the departed sometimes linger on earth when their work is thwarted. I've witnessed such lingering. When I was a lad, I spent considerable time in graveyards." He thought about how, as a member of the Resurrectionists, he "chased ghosts" and helped robbers steal corpses for physicians so that they could discover the human body's secrets. And when he experienced melancholia, which he often did, he walked graveyards while carrying pistols in case his melancholy compelled him to take his own life.

They passed graves ornamented with large Celtic Crosses. Mrs. Nugent showed Percy how such crosses told a biblical story, like the Cain and Abel story, or Eve and Adam's banishment from Eden, carved in figures for the illiterate. They walked past ancient tombstones, many toppled and shrouded in moss, thus obscuring the names and dates of the silent departed. After Mrs. Nugent pointed out the fresh grave of a month-old baby, they heard a gate clang.

"We're not alone, Mr. Shelley."

Thinking perhaps his idol had manifested himself, Percy felt his heart tremble. But instead of seeing Emmet's spirit, they beheld a woman in a black dress, her hair covered with a black shawl, bent over a grave. After placing something on the grave, the woman stood upright and looked directly at them.

Mrs. Nugent's face brightened, "Why I know that woman. I visited her in Kilmainham Gaol. Anne," she called. "Anne Devlin, is that you? It's me, Catherine Nugent."

Percy grew excited because he recalled that Mrs. Nugent had mentioned that Anne Devlin was a patriot who had been incarcerated in Kilmainham.

Mrs. Nugent rushed toward her, but before she could reach her, the woman had disappeared, as if she had never been standing in their midst.

"What happened, where did she go?" Mrs. Nugent asked. "I'm sure that she was standing here at Emmet's grave. And look, she left Deora Dé."

Delicate, tear-drop-shaped pink and purple flowers lay on the tombstone. They appeared to be what the English called fuchsia.

"What does Deora Dé mean?" Percy asked.

"Tears of God," Mrs. Nugent replied.

How appropriate that such flora should be left on Emmet's grave, Percy thought. If such a good God exists, which I highly doubt, he or she would naturally weep for the loss of such a brave individual who hoped to free humanity.

"Perhaps we frightened this Anne Devlin or her spirit that had traveled here to see Emmet's grave," he replied. "You mentioned that she was a state prisoner. Why was she imprisoned in Kilmainham?"

"She was Robert Emmet's housekeeper, not in the euphemistic sense, mind you . . . She was his colleague who helped plan and organize the 1803 rebellion. For that, she was arrested, charged with sedition, imprisoned, and tortured by the British and their Irish cronies for three years and during that time she never once revealed anything about Emmet, or any other rebel associated with the cause. Before she became Emmet's housekeeper, she was a member of a rebel family and Lady Mont Cashell swore her in as a member of the United Irishwomen."

Ah, Lady Mont Cashell was a hero, Percy thought. Clearly, Mary Wollstonecraft's instruction benefited her young charge.

Percy felt excited. If he couldn't meet the former Margaret King, perhaps he could acquaint himself with Anne Devlin so he could learn more about Emmet and fulfill his rebellion. He would not fail, as Emmet did. And, in doing so, perhaps he would dry "God's" tears.

22 February 1812

Lawless gave Percy Anne Devlin's address and he offered to accompany him. "No, I wish to meet Anne Devlin on my own. I believe she will see me as a true Irish patriot and will gladly speak with me."

The excursion took him to the Liberties, the poorest part of Dublin. The Liberties were ironically named, for those that resided there only lived a shade above imprisonment. The streets were narrow. The row houses were ill-kept. Percy walked past children and rats digging through rubbish.

According to Lawless, Devlin lived with her family in one room in a row house on John's Lane, a house, like all the others in the Liberties, which had once been owned by wealthy Protestants. The house was now carved into many flats. As Percy climbed the four flights to Anne's dwelling, he encountered dozens of emaciated children on the steps. Clearly, many families lived in the house, now a graveyard for the Irish poor.

At first, Anne's cousin tried to turn him away but when he announced that he was a friend to the Irish, she escorted him over to Devlin, who sat in a rocking chair next to the hearth.

Mrs. Nugent had advised him that Anne had suffered so extensively that in three years in prison she had aged forty. She had been only twenty-two when they had incarcerated her. Which meant she was now thirty-one. Still, he was unprepared for the woman he saw before him. She looked like what the Irish call the Poor Old Woman of whom a song had been written. Her dark hair twisted in a bun was streaked with grey. Her face was etched with fine lines and crevices and, when she turned to Percy, her eyes were dull and cloudy, as if they were cast over with cataracts, just like the aged. She was missing several teeth, and several others were blackened as if they had rotted. Her limbs appeared swollen, and she looked crippled. A knobby cane was within reach of her rocking chair. And, next to her chair was a baby's cradle with an infant nestled in it. He assumed the baby must be her cousin's, for Anne looked too frail and old to have recently borne a child. Percy surmised that unlike the old woman in the song, Anne would never have her youth restored, even if Ireland were liberated.

Even though it was February, and it had snowed the previous evening, the room was fiercely cold; no fire was lit. The sole window was cracked, and, in the corners of the room, holes were packed with broken glass and dirty rags to keep the rats out. The floor was stone and one lone bed and another pallet were wedged into the corner of the room. The only other furniture was a small table surrounded by three chairs and a broken-down armoire. Under the table was a washtub and the hearth contained a kettle and a large black cooking pot. Over the mantle hung a tearful portrait of the Virgin Mary with her broken, bleeding heart exposed.

Certainly, their living environment was, although clean, sparse. Percy felt embarrassed that he had once lived in wanton luxury in Sussex, where his father owned a manor house, farms, hunting preserves, abundant woods, and a splendid pond on which Percy had leisurely rowed, while his manservant Niles waited on him. And his Grandfather Shelley, Sir Bysshe, had built a castle that he called "Folly" where he hid scads of money in couches, armchairs, and in the leaves of books. Percy felt ashamed that his fellow foolish Englishmen had created the conditions in which Anne Devlin lived.

This was how the poor Irish live, at least the ones who have the luxury of residing in a dwelling, he thought. *This is not right. I must help them somehow. I must exact justice. I hunger and thirst for justice. No idle rich should grow fat from devouring the broken hearts of the poor.*

Anne Devlin

I was rocking my baby in her cradle when I heard a man at the door tell Aoife that he wished to see Anne Devlin.

"Why do you want to see her? Are you from Dublin Castle?" she asked.

I heard the door creak as if she were closing it. After the way they persecuted me during those many years, Aoife knew to keep the castle authorities away from me. They were not welcome in my home.

"No, I'm a friend of Ireland," he quickly replied. I then heard Aoife shuffle across the floor and alongside her stood a young man.

My eyesight is dim from the many years I spent in the dark. I squinted to try to bring him into focus. It was no use. But what I could see gave me pause. Dark curly hair, fair skin, average height. Black waistcoat and white pantaloons. Could it be him? No, it's not possible. I saw him hanged on the gallows on Thomas Street. I saw the henchman hoist his severed head, dripping blood. I heard the crowd roar and jeer. I saw women hoping to heal the sick and ward off evil by dipping their kerchiefs in his blood. I saw dogs and pigs lap up the remaining pools of it. It can't be him. He is dead.

Even so, when the young man sat before me, I reached and touched his face, feeling the contours of his nose, cheek, and mouth. I touched the top of his head, and he let me do so and didn't say a word.

"Who are you? Are you my Robert, back from the grave?" I asked as I felt my heart tremble.

He took my hand in his. He hesitated, "No . . . surely not, madam. But I am his admirer who seeks to learn more about him and . . . you. I've heard about your patient forbearance. Your many years in solitude in gaol. How you never betrayed him or the cause. I wish to hear his and your story."

Why would this young man want to hear my story? I'm just an ordinary Irish woman. I'm not remembered. Like the stars, I live outside of history. I'm not a hero or a martyr; I'm not a leader or an orator. I'm not Robert Emmet.

"I never told my story or Robert's to anyone except the little I told Brother Cullen who invented much of the story and made me out to be a saint. Saint Anne," I said with disdain. "I work no miracles; I'm no saint, and neither was Robert Emmet."

The youngster paused. "I'm no saint either . . . I'm like John Milton's rebellious angel. I'm a poet who bows to no man or God. Like the fallen angel, I believe I can make a heaven of hell. I desire freedom and justice for all."

I wondered who this John Milton was but didn't ask, for I knew of and had often met Lucifer himself and his legions when I was confined in Kilmainham's abyss. I wondered if I should have any dealings with this self-proclaimed devil. Would I endanger my soul by conversing with him?

But I was curious, so I asked, "Are you a poet like Mr. Emmet?"

"Yes," he replied, squeezing my hand. "I came to Dublin to use art to help Ireland free itself."

Using art to free Ireland? That was foolhardy. I'd heard it before, and I wondered how that would serve us. I didn't express my opinion. Instead, I asked, "How did you learn of me?"

"My friend and yours, Mrs. Nugent, and I saw you yesterday at St. Michan's graveyard. You were standing near Emmet's grave."

"No, I was not there. I've never been there." Even though I had stood near the grave and brought flowers to it in remembrance of my friend, for whom God and I still wept, I didn't know whether I could trust this young man.

He continued to insist that I had been in the cemetery and left Deora Dé on the grave.

Again, I denied being there.

"But Mrs. Nugent recognized you."

For the third time, like St. Peter, I denied his claim. I thought I heard a cock crow.

In truth, I visit the grave regularly, a grave that I had a hand in creating. I usually go later in the day when I think the guards have buried themselves in the pub and hence will not follow me. They are always trying to find a way to imprison me once more; they falsely believe that I lead another revolution. They also follow anyone who visits me, so I suspect that they will be surveilling this young man. I considered telling him that he was perhaps in danger, but I thought he would soon discover that for himself.

"I'm surprised. We . . . Mrs. Nugent and I, were certain it was you."

"No, that's impossible. I rarely leave my home. It is difficult for me to walk." I picked up the cane next to my chair.

"Well, then, I believe that your spirit traveled to the grave. Perhaps Emmet instructed you to meet me."

This youngster was full of fanciful, mad ideas but before he could regale me with his supernatural beliefs, I said, "I've heard enough of fairies and elves in my lifetime; I've even encountered a few spirits myself, but you can be assured that my spirit was not traveling about Dublin on a magic carpet or on the backs of dragonflies but was instead sitting right here in this chair as I do every evening when my work is done."

He began to speak again, but I cut him off. "If you will, I would like to ask, not about spirits, but about Mrs. Nugent. She ministered to me when I was in prison. How do you know her? How did she find me?"

"She read one of my pamphlets and visited me. And I located you through your circle of friends."

"I'm aware of the circle; don't say anything more," I said. "Why do you call yourself a friend to Ireland? I hear your accent. You are not one of us, but one of our adversaries."

"No, no, I am kindred to you. I am done with my people, the British. I am ashamed of John Bull. I aim to fulfill Emmet's work and to carry it out across the globe, to free all oppressed people."

His aims sounded absurd and blasphemous. Did he think he was some sort of Messiah? Jesus Christ himself? Robert Emmet himself?

"Please, you absolutely can trust me. I will keep Emmet's secrets. I am no friend to the British government and its institutions. Like Emmet, I am considered a traitor."

"Who are you?"

"My name is Percy Bysshe Shelley."

He was no poet I had ever heard of. He was no Robert Emmet. And revolution? Again? Would this Percy Shelley, whomever he was, lead another failed attempt at freedom like Robert did? I felt my heart sink and wondered what he could gain by hearing my or Robert's story.

"Please trust me. I share your patriotism, even though I am by birth a member of the nation that has long oppressed the Irish. I wish to hear Robert's and your story and record them in the Irish history I intend to write. Perhaps through hearing these stories, one day soon my fellow Britons will understand the suffering they've caused and will soften their hearts and learn to love and admire their Irish cousins."

"Sure, you're mad. When were we ever cousins to the British? They never treated us like family, but like their underlings, their dogs, like slaves, especially us Catholics."

"Perhaps I misspoke. You understand what I intend though, don't you?"

"You must be careful with your words, Mr. Shelley. Words have power; they carry weight. I understand that you want to use our stories to help settle differences between us and the British. I doubt that knowing my story would quell their rage against or fear of us. And, if I tell you my story, how do I know that you won't betray me? That you won't betray Robert and the rest of us? That you won't be a bloody informer?"

"I would swear to God, if I believed in God, but I don't. Perhaps you'll trust me if I read you the poem that I wrote about Mr. Emmet."

He'd already said that, like Satan himself, he bowed to no man or God. I thought why would I want to listen to someone who doesn't believe in the Almighty? God might strike me dead for listening to this atheistic devil. But then I thought what harm will it cause to hear a poem about Robert? I wanted to hear what Percy Shelley thought of him.

"Go on," I said. "Read your verse."

"I can recite it from memory." He cleared his throat and began:

> No trump tells thy virtues—the grave where they rest
> With thy dust shall remain unpolluted by fame,
> Till thy foes, by the world and by fortune caressed,
> Shall pass like a mist from the light of thy name.
>
> When the storm-cloud that lowers o'er the day-beam is gone.
> Unchanged, unextinguished its life-spring will shine;
> When Erin has ceased with their memory to groan,
> She will smile through the tears of revival on thine.

I wasn't impressed by his poem, but, out of Christian kindness, I refrained from criticizing it. I thought Emmet a finer poet.

"You have read his speech on the dock when he was sentenced to death?" It was clear that he had. Robert did not want his virtues praised, at least not until Erin is a free nation.

"Yes, I have memorized it also. Do you wish to hear it? I can recite it."

"No, no, I also know the speech, Mr. Shelley." Even though he knew Robert's speech and seemed to admire Robert, Percy Shelley hadn't yet convinced me that he was a genuine friend to Ireland; after all, he was an Englishman and by the sound of his accent a wealthy, privileged one. And I feared that his plan to free Ireland might further destroy rather than liberate us.

My baby began to whimper. And then I felt my milk letdown. Aoife picked her up and handed her to me. I covered myself with my shawl and then placed the child on my breast.

"You think that because I'm Irish I'm a storyteller. I'm not. And I'm not a fool or a non-believer. I'm a God-fearing woman. I have nothing to say to you, Mr. Shelley. And my baby is hungry. Please go away and leave us alone."

Three

Outside of History

24 February 1812

Harriet walked to Merrion Square to find Mrs. O'Byrne, the girls' mother. Was she even aware that her girls were in the Foundling Hospital? Had their mother been searching for them? The problem now was how to find Mrs. O'Byrne. It seemed like a needle in a haystack undertaking. Harriet would have to knock on every door and ask if a Mrs. O'Byrne worked as a maid for them.

The fact that many of the homes were abandoned made the task less onerous. It was easy to see which homes were uninhabited. The curtains were closed. Weeds grew in the cracks of the stone walkways. The chimneys were smokeless.

Harriet approached several houses, but no one answered the doors, and several butlers told her that they never employed married women with children, for they could not be accommodated. Finally, at the end of the square, she approached a house that appeared to be lived in. A carriage was parked in the mews and the driver was hitching up a snorting horse. Harriet rang the bell. She heard dogs barking and someone ordering them, "Quiet, now."

The butler opened the door. "Are you selling something? The sign says, 'No solicitors,'" he curtly said as he pointed to the sign in the window.

"No, I'm looking for someone. A Mrs. O'Byrne who works in a house on Merrion Square."

"Is she in trouble with the law?"

Harriet's heart beat fast with excitement. Through persistence, she had found the girls' mother. "No, I wish to speak with her about her children. I have news of them."

"She has no children."

"Indeed, she does. I've met them. May I see her?"

He sucked his teeth and paused as if he were calculating whether to allow the interview. "She's cleaning a hearth right now, but, if you wait, I'll allow you to speak with her."

Harriet nodded. As she waited, she wondered how to tell the woman that her daughters were in the Foundling Hospital. How would she react? Would she weep? If so, how could she be comforted?

A few minutes later, a haggard-looking woman with ginger hair streaked with gray came to the door. She looked like a chimney sweep with her face blackened with soot.

She removed a handkerchief from her apron and blotted her face. "Sanders says that you have news of my girls, miss. How do you know of them?"

"I met them on the Liffey Bridge where they were waiting for you."

The woman shook her head. "That can't be. I haven't seen them in months. I'm not allowed to have me children here. They stay with me sister. She sends them out to the streets to earn their keep, and I give her some money when I can to provide for them."

Harriet paused. She wondered why the children had told a fabricated story rather than the truth. Now, she had to tell Mrs. O'Byrne the sad truth of where the children were. "I'm sorry to tell you that your sister is not caring for the children. Instead, they are confined in the Foundling Hospital. A policeman took them there after he told them to move along. I saw the younger one, Sinead, who is not faring well. The caretakers drug the children with laudanum so they will sleep." She waited to see Mrs. O'Byrne's reaction but noticed none.

"Me sister should have told me that they never came home." She took a breath. "What do you want me to do about it?" she said without expression, tears glistening in her eyes. "I have no way to get them out and no means to take care of them if I did. My sister has her own brood to mind. Maybe the girls are better off in the Foundling Hospital pretending to be Protestants and learning a trade. Then they won't have to be skivvies like me."

"I can help you. I'll write a petition to the Governors for you to get them released," Harriet said earnestly.

"I doubt it would help."

"But Sinead could die. She didn't look well. She was in a stupor."

The woman turned away from Harriet. "I must go now; I have work to do. I don't wish to lose my position."

"Please don't go. Where is their father? Perhaps he can help."

She turned back and laughed. "Kevin, that fool? He can't help. He's dead." She paused. "He was hanged after he joined Robert Emmet's failed rebellion." She shut the door.

Harriet stood dumfounded; the girls' father had been Emmet's colleague. She wondered how many other patriots lost their lives because of their connection to Emmet's rebellion and how many more might be persecuted in the future.

Anne Devlin

Once more that atheist came to our door. He is certainly relentless. I'll give him that. But so were Major Charles Sirr, the Dublin Chief of Police, and Dr. Edward Trevor, the superintendent at Kilmainham. Devils that they were, they never gave up trying to get me to talk about Robert and my other colleagues.

Aoife answered the door. "You're back. What do you want now, Mr. Shelley? Anne told you that she has nothing to say. She didn't speak of Robert Emmet for three years. What makes you think that she will ever convey her or his story to an Englishman, even if you deem yourself a would-be Irishman?"

"Of course, but as an admirer of Emmet, I hope to right the injustice perpetrated on both of them. If she tells me her story, I will protect her by using a false name. Her story, like Emmet's, will be inscribed in history."

I picked up my cane and walked to the door. "Perhaps I don't wish to be inscribed in history. I am an ordinary woman who has nothing to say of any import. If you are the gentleman you claim to be and a faithful friend to the Irish, you'll leave me and my family alone. I finally feel somewhat safe and at peace with my past and I don't wish to recall what happened to me, Robert, and the others." In truth, I'm often tortured by those memories, especially when I lay my head on my bed and try to sleep. I frequently have nightmares where I see Robert hanging from a noose and my body dangling alongside his.

The lad doffed his hat and bowed. "As you wish, ma'am. Surely, I meant no offence. I will comply with your request. If you change your mind, here is my card."

With that he left. I asked Aoife to toss his card in the hearth; we would burn it tonight.

Because I am an ordinary woman, my story is not recorded in the annals of history, for histories are written by the victors and they always speak of what men accomplish; they rarely speak of women's lives, unless a woman is a queen or saint, like Maeve or Brigid. I'm neither, even though Brother Cullen, a friend of my outlaw cousin Michael Dwyer, tried to make me out to be a saint. But I'm not a peasant or a demon either. I'm just a simple woman who loved Mother Ireland so much that I worked toward her liberation.

My love of Erin comes from my love of the Wicklow Mountains, the Garden of Ireland, where I spent my childhood. I was born in the Vale of Avoca, the very heart of Ireland herself that the poet Thomas Moore lovingly wrote about, near where my mother grew up near Glendalough, the valley where the monks lived.

From the time I was a child, I looked on the precious land on which we lived as a gift from God. With its rivers full of trout and salmon, its fields and glens blanketed with purple heather, its mountains verdant and majestic, its caves sacred, I knew it was the most blessed place on earth.

You see, St. Caomhán, or as the English call him, St. Kevin, the first abbot of Glendalough, consecrated this land. And the monks, who later lived along Glendalough Lake, managed to evade the Viking hordes, the invaders that tried to plunder its riches. As a child, when I sat in the ancient cemetery in Glendalough Valley, where St. Caomhán is buried, and near the lake itself, I often imagined myself as one of those monks saving the gospel and civilization from the barbarians as I climbed the round tower and pulled up the steps that prevented the Vikings from wrecking God's word. Even though I was a wee one, I knew that I would fight anyone who tried to destroy us, our land, and our culture.

Besides loving the land, I was proud to learn of my mam's family. In the evening, me brothers and sisters and I would gather around the glowing hearth and Mam told us of her ancestor, Feagh Mac Hugh O'Byrne, the Gaelic Chieftain and Lord of Ranelagh, a descendant of one of the High Kings. Mam told us that Feagh led the Clanne Uí Bhroin, the O'Byrne clan that resisted English Tudor invasion and settlement. Feagh wanted to keep the Garden of Ireland for the Irish, so he frequently raided the English settlements to try to drive the English out of our Eden. Mam regaled the stories of Feagh's exploits. She told us how he once helped the rebel Sir Edmund Butler escape from the notorious prison in Dublin Castle. And she recalled how Feagh was so powerful he could call up one hundred expert swordsmen to fight in an instant. Moreover, he and his clan sent one thousand Englishmen to their death at the Battle of Glenmalure in 1580, where he defeated Lord Arthur Grey de Wilton. Mam said that he knew that the English were invaders just like the Vikings had been, but Englishmen were even more treacherous because they wanted to force us to turn our backs on the true Church; they wanted to make us give up our love of Mother Mary and all the blessed saints and become heretics like themselves; they wanted to perversely morph us into English Protestants. Bah! Feagh wouldn't have it, and he kept fighting, playing cat and mouse with the British in the Wicklow Mountains.

The British despised Feagh and his tricks. He was such a troublesome chieftain that the English placed a bounty of £100 on his head. They called him a traitor to the Crown, which was true, but, like Robert Emmet, he never once betrayed Ireland. He spent thirty years making the Tudors squirm! Eventually though, an English captain, Thomas Lee, captured the Lord of Ranelagh. After torturing Feagh and then hacking him to death, Captain Lee further dishonored the Gaelic Chieftain. He severed Feagh's head from his shoulders with Feagh's own sword. Then he stuck Feagh's head on a spike and displayed it at Dublin Castle as a warning to other rebels. Afterwards, Lee carried O'Byrne's head back to Queen Elizabeth so that he could boast that he had defeated and murdered a notorious Irish rebel. And for this he was awarded the £100, a fortune at that time.

Much later in 1799, another of O'Byrne's descendants and my distant relation, Billy Byrne of Ballymanus, was hanged and beheaded at Wicklow for his role in the 1798 rebellion. And a distant cousin, Kevin O'Byrne, met Robert's fate in 1803 for participating in the uprising.

Even though I am a woman outside of history, I've always been proud that my blood runs green, not red; it comes from O'Byrne. My mother frequently reminded us that we were O'Byrne's legacy and that none of us were cowards nor would any of us ever betray Mother Ireland. One day I would prove that to her and my entire clan.

When Percy left Anne Devlin's, he saw an open door that had been shut when he had walked past it earlier. He glanced inside. Unlike Anne's abode, this room was in shambles. The walls were cracked; plaster lay in heaps on the floor. As if they were trying to become invisible, a woman and a boy cowered in a corner. They were shivering.

"What are you doing in here?" Percy asked.

The boy, who looked to be about fourteen years old, stood up as if to defend the woman and himself. He towered over Percy. His face was ruddy and light stubble graced his lip. Despite his height and manly attributes, he seemed a child to Percy.

"We mean no harm, sir," the woman said as the boy helped her rise. "We just came in from the cold. We'll be on our way, sir; we just needed to warm ourselves. Please don't summon the constable." She pulled her threadbare shawl over her head and moved toward the door.

Percy thought of Harriet's compassion and how she'd been recently disappointed by his uncharitable actions. "No, wait. I have no intention of calling for the constable. I'd like to help you. What are your names?"

"I'm Mrs. Lynch and this here's my boy, Johnny," she said as she looked away. It seemed, from her inability to look him in the eye, that she was likely telling a falsehood. It didn't matter. He didn't really need to know their true names. He only wanted to know how to address them.

"Mrs. Lynch, how may I be of service? Are you hungry? When did you last eat?"

"Yesterday."

"I'll fetch you a loaf," Percy said as he excitedly rubbed his hands together.

"That would be most kind of you, sir."

"Johnny, come with me and I'll buy you and your mother a loaf," Percy said as he gestured for the boy to follow him.

"We ain't done nothing wrong, sir. Don't take Johnny away. He's all I have."

Her fear was palpable. Percy realized that she had no reason to trust him. "Fine. Stay here and I'll return soon with some nourishment."

Percy hastened down the street and purchased a large loaf of brown bread and a wheel of cheddar cheese. He raced back, but when he returned, Mrs. Lynch and her son were gone. He placed the cheese and bread on the mantle, hoping that they'd find it before the rats did, and then he slowly walked back to Sackville Street, while snow softly fell on his shoulders.

Sitting by the blazing hearth, he ruminated on the hunger, squalor, fear, and mistrust he had witnessed on John's Lane. Anne Devlin didn't trust him, and the famished mother and son refused his aid. He thought that he should have taken a different approach with Anne. Perhaps he should have spoken to her about his *Address* rather than asking immediately about Emmet? Maybe he should have insisted that Johnny come with him, or he could have taken both of them with him so that Mrs. Lynch wouldn't have to fear that he was taking her son from him. Next time, he would refrain from impulsive actions.

When Harriet tried to speak to him, he told her that he was too disturbed to talk.

"What's distressing you?" Harriet asked. She had her own concerns but wanted to soothe her husband's suffering.

"I don't want to talk about it right now. Why don't you read to me? Perhaps that will ease my mind," he said as he leaned his head back onto the headrest of the armchair.

"What would you have me read?" Harriet ran her fingers across the spines of the books on their small shelf.

"Whatever suits you," he said as he closed his eyes.

So, after she put more turf on the fire, she pulled Mrs. Radcliffe's novel from her bag, thinking that Percy would appreciate it because he himself wrote Gothic tales. The section she read in which the protagonist Emily was forced to marry and was imprisoned in a gloomy castle resonated with Harriet as she thought of the little girls being held against their will. And Percy thought that the protagonist's troubles resembled the general state of Ireland itself, which was "wed" against her will to Great Britain. Harriet read the lines:

O! useful may it be to have shewn that, though the vicious can sometimes pour affliction upon the good, their power is transient and their punishment certain; and that innocence, though oppressed by injustice, shall, supported by patience, finally triumph over misfortune.

Percy silently trusted that Mrs. Radcliffe was correct; those treated unjustly would prevail and triumph over their oppressors. He had to believe that good would conquer evil or his work would come to naught.

25 February 1812

Harriet poked the fire and pulled her shawl closer and then settled down in the armchair to re-read the letter she had written to the Governors.

To the Governors of the Foundling Hospital, James Street:

I write to respectfully request that Sinead and Michaela O'Byrne be released from the Foundling Hospital and returned to their mother. Their mother did not abandon her girls. They were living with her sister temporarily while Mrs. O'Byrne was employed by the O'Sullivans of Merrion Square. The O'Sullivans did not allow Mrs. O'Byrne to keep her children with her, but they have now given their consent. The officer who brought the O'Byrne girls to the hospital believed they were foundlings, but he was mistaken. Their mother gravely misses them and will provide for them so that they can grow and become useful citizens. I will gladly transport the girls to their mother. I hope you will consider her case and return her girls to her loving arms.

Harriet Shelley
10 Sackville St.

Harriet thought the letter sufficient and persuasive. She actually didn't know who Mrs. O'Byrne's employer was, but she thought that O'Sullivan sounded like a reasonable name. Even though she noted she'd return the children to their mother, Harriet intended to mother them herself. Their mother had admitted that she had no way to care for them. Harriet showed the letter to Catherine that evening after dinner.

"You mean well, but I doubt that you will have any influence over the Governors," Catherine said after she read the letter. "Perhaps it would be best for you to seek a clergyman or priest or even your own husband and have them write the petition. Unfortunately, men have greater influence than women, especially one as young as yourself."

"I know no clergyman or priest. And I haven't discussed this with Percy," Harriet felt ashamed to confess.

"Sure, if you hope to bring the girls into your home, you must discuss it with your husband."

"How did you know that I intend to bring the girls here?" Harriet asked.

"You told me that their mother cannot care for them. She hasn't the means. The letter you've written stretches the truth."

"Sometimes it's necessary to stretch the truth, in order to achieve the result you wish for," Harriet replied. She knew that at heart Catherine agreed, for she had repeated a wee lie when they were at the hospital. "Care for more tea, Catherine?"

"No, I must go. I'm tired and have an early appointment tomorrow. Promise me that you will speak with your husband about the girls."

"Of course, you're right. I promise, Catherine," Harriet replied as she embraced her friend.

After Catherine left, Harriet revised her letter. She did not sign her own name, but signed it Sir Timothy Shelley, Esq. MP. She wasn't sure if a baronet would have the title of Esquire, but she thought it more influential than his name alone. She sealed the letter, walked to the General Post Office, and posted it. Then she said a silent prayer for success. The girls deserved a loving, stable home with a mother and father who cared for them, not a mother who couldn't care for them and a father entombed in a narrow grave.

The porter opened the door to the Foundling Hospital.

"Back again, miss."

"It's madam, sir."

"Beg your pardon, madam," he replied. "I assume you're not delivering a tot. What is it you want?"

"I wish to see the O'Byrne girls."

"I dunno know if they's still here. We've had a terrible bout of typhus."

"What do you mean that they may not be here?"

He opened the door and pointed toward fresh graves.

Harriet felt her stomach sink. Perhaps she was too late to save the girls.

"Kindly take me to the matron, please."

"As you wish, although I don't know if she can be of help or if she will see you. She's tending the sick children."

The matron looked skeptically at Harriet. "We are rather busy with the children. I'm sorry but I can't take you to see the girls. You aren't their parent anyways and the superintendent instructed me to send you away."

The matron had indicated that the girls lived. Harriet felt relieved but she wished to know why the superintendent wanted her to be sent away. "Is he worried that I'll report you all to the authorities for the lack of sufficient cleanliness?"

"You have no idea what it takes to run this hospital; you'd best keep your place. You ain't Irish," she said disdainfully. "And the governor doesn't tell me his business or his reasoning."

"I have a letter from Sir Percy Shelley, the baronet, that allows me to see the girls," Harriet said, as she waved the paper in front of the matron's face. "Do you wish to see it?" She hoped that she didn't because it was Eliza's shopping list, but for all she knew the matron couldn't read.

"Let me see it," the matron said.

Harriet handed it to her, and the matron glanced at it. "Fine. I'll escort you but you must be brief."

Harriet sucked in a relieved breath. The matron did not know how to read and was too embarrassed to admit it.

"Take me to Michaela first. I assume she's not working."

"The child's too sick to work. She's in the infirmary with her sister."

Once again, the matron locked the door behind her after they entered the infirmary. The room was crowded with more children than the last time and the stench was awful. Many children were crying. Harriet had never seen typhus up close, but now she witnessed children vomiting and coughing, and, even from a distance, she saw sores on the faces and bodies.

As Harriet drew close to the first bed, she recognized, in the throng of five children, Michaela, who held her sister in her arms. Sinead's face was scabbed and red, with sweat on her brow.

"Michaela?" Harriet whispered.

The girl looked up. Her face was drawn, making her look much older than her years. "How do you know me, miss?"

"I met you on the Liffey Bridge weeks ago. I gave you some money."

"I had to give that to me aunt."

"I wish to get you out of here. I saw your mother. I can help get you back in her care."

"Our mam ain't allowed to have us," Michaela said after a pause. "And my aunt doesn't like us cause she has her own bairns. We have nowhere to go if you did get us out of here."

Michaela pulled Sinead closer.

"You could live with me. I will take care of you," Harriet said tenderly.

Michaela looked at Sinead who nodded.

"We'd like that, miss," Michaela said.

"I'm Mrs. Shelley. I'll be back for you," Harriet said as she touched Michaela's arm and then stroked Sinead's feverish face.

The matron led Harriet away. "Don't make promises you can't keep. I seen what false promises can do."

"Promises are better than a narrow grave," Harriet said as she bid the matron good day.

Harriet returned home, removed her clothing, and asked Eliza to draw her a bath. She fretted that her contact with the sick children might lead to her own sickness. While bathing, she asked Eliza if she knew a treatment for typhus.

"I understand that it's wise to take a purgative. Why do you wish to know?"

"I heard that typhus is rampant."

"Well, we've had no contact with anyone with typhus so I wouldn't worry if I were you."

In the morning, Harriet visited the apothecary and bought a purgative and then went home and took it, telling Eliza a white lie—that she felt a little ill and needed to go to bed. By noon, she filled her chamber pot and then promptly threw the refuse out the back window into the garden. The Deora Dé and roses growing there would likely flourish.

26 February 1812

Percy wished to see where Emmet had been confined before his execution so as the sun was sinking, he, Harriet, and Eliza walked several miles west of Dublin to find Kilmainham Gaol, the earthly hell built on Gallows Hill. Harriet did not mention to Percy or Eliza that she and Catherine had visited the Foundling Hospital they passed on the way to the gaol. And she hadn't told him about the girls, as she had promised Catherine. As they passed the hospital, she visualized the girls in each other's arms and hoped that they weren't eternally sleeping in an unmarked grave.

Percy pointed to the five snarling stone dragons above Kilmainham's doorway. He asked the guard about the symbolism of the dragons.

"You must not be Irish," the young man said. "They stand for the five felonies: murder, rape, theft, treason, and piracy. Everybody knows that."

"So, the people brought through this gate have committed one of these crimes?"

"To be sure, sir."

They were interrupted by the commotion of an officer dragging a woman to the door of the gaol. The woman stumbled and fell to her knees. Percy bent to lift her and saw that it was Mrs. Lynch. Instantly recognizing Percy, Mrs. Lynch beseeched him with her eyes to do something.

"Which of the five crimes has this woman committed?" he asked the officer.

"Theft, sir."

"And what is the penalty?"

"Hanging or transportation to Australia or America."

She spat on the officer. "I only took a loaf to feed me son. I couldn't let him starve. We'd been eating nettles to survive." She looked with dismay at Percy.

"Perhaps there's been some mistake. I know this woman," Percy said. "I bought her the bread. She's no thief."

Harriet eyes grew wide. Was Percy actually doing the right thing on his own and helping the poor? Where did he meet this woman and why hadn't he mentioned meeting her? It didn't matter. It was more important to know that his heart had finally been opened and moved by the suffering and destitution that he saw around him every day.

"We have a witness who saw her take a loaf from a house on John's Lane," the officer replied.

"But that's where I left it. I fetched it for her and her boy." Percy's tone was tinged with anger.

"Take it up with the judge, sir."

"Have you no heart, sir?" Harriet asked.

The officer scowled. He touched his chest. "Indeed, I have, miss, it's right here and I feel for those I must arrest. But I have a job to do. I'm called out twenty times a night to carry out this order." He then ordered them to move along. "There's nothing to see here, gentlefolk. If you know what's good for you, you won't defend a thief."

Harriet reached toward Mrs. Lynch, but the officer pushed the woman ahead of him and warned Harriet not to interfere.

Eliza pulled Harriet back. "It will do no good for you to be arrested too, sister. Come away now. Perhaps Percy can help her at a later time."

They watched as Mrs. Lynch passed screaming through the portal as the dragons above silently assented.

Percy realized that the rich grind the poor into abjectness, and then complain that they are abject. They goad them into famine and hang them if they steal a loaf.

After witnessing the injustice of Mrs. Lynch's arrest, Percy felt more adamant about conducting Robert Emmet's work. Knowing that Anne would likely never speak with him, he wondered if she would be willing to speak with Harriet.

Percy settled down on the settee and put his arm around Harriet, who was absorbed in reading Mrs. Radcliffe's novel. "Darling, I'd like to discuss something with you."

"One second. I wish to finish this paragraph." She placed her bookmark in the book, closed it, and laid it on her lap. "What is it, Percy?"

"Do you recall Mrs. Nugent mentioning a woman named Anne Devlin? I visited her; she was Emmet's colleague. I wanted to learn Emmet's complete story, but she turned me away."

Harriet looked at Percy with a puzzled expression. "Why did she refuse to talk with you?"

He sighed and crossed his legs. "It seems she doesn't agree with my theological views."

"Percy, when will you learn to withhold your atheistic belief? That's no way to convince someone to listen to you," she said impatiently. Sometimes, even though he was brilliant he seemed such a fool.

"Never mind that. I think that she'd be more likely to open up with a woman. I'd like for you to approach her."

"But what would I talk with her about?"

"Just talk with her about women's duties; you know, children and householding. She has a baby. You could talk with her about her child. Perhaps, after you become acquainted, you can learn Emmet's story."

Harriet scoffed at the idea of women's duties; Percy didn't usually label certain duties women's or men's. Still, she bit her tongue. "But I know little of these things. I don't manage our household. Eliza does. And I've never taken care of a child; I know nothing about children." She thought again of the two girls she wished to care for, hoping that if she did become their guardian, she would learn how to properly care for them. Maybe, if she met this woman, she'd learn something about mothering. Still, that seemed dishonest and a poor motivation to meet with this Anne Devlin.

"Well, talk with her about sprites and fairies. I don't know. I just want you to make her acquaintance, strike up a friendship so she'll tell you about Emmet. I need to know what exactly transpired before the rebellion so I can avoid Emmet's errors."

"What makes you think that she'll speak with me? Perhaps she'll equate me with you and your atheism." Harriet didn't like the idea of being thought atheistic and of being used for Percy's purposes.

"That's nonsense. She'll see that you're sincere and that you have an Irish heart. That you consider yourself more Irish than English. That you detest Castlereagh. That will be all that you need to get her to talk. She'll trust you. You needn't discuss our atheism."

"I don't know. I'll think about it."

Percy was surprised that Harriet didn't immediately accept his proposition. Was she developing her own ideas and goals? Weren't they working together to free the Irish?

"As you wish, my love, but please seriously consider my request. If you do visit with her, please enquire about his story. That's what I need to know to do my work."

"Of course," she said, as she returned to reading her book.

Later that evening after they had made love, Harriet turned over on her side and brushed Percy's hair from his sweaty forehead. "I've thought it over, darling. I will try to speak with Anne Devlin, but I want to learn her story, not Emmet's."

"Thank you, but Anne's story is superfluous. I need Emmet's story," he said as he stroked her flushed cheek.

"If I learn anything about Emmet, I'll tell you, but I disagree about the importance of Anne's story," she said as she turned her back to him. As she tried to sleep, she fretted that his sense of equality was becoming warped. Why was he changing? Did he no longer believe in the equality of the sexes?

Harriet climbed the steps to Anne's abode and knocked on the door. No one answered, and she felt relieved and turned to walk away. A young woman opened the door and asked if Dublin Castle had sent her.

"No, no, I'm here to pay my respects to a fellow Irish woman. For, even though I am born English, my heart is Irish. And, here, I've brought you some bread," Harriet said as she extended her hands.

"You say you have an Irish heart," the woman said. "I don't know what that means. Who are you?"

Harriet saw what appeared to be an old woman sitting in a rocker, lovingly rocking a baby in her cradle. She surmised that this was Anne Devlin herself, for Percy had informed Harriet of Anne's aged condition. She looked at her with great love and pity. She was exactly how Percy had described her but, even though she was broken, Harriet was surprised that she remained whole, for she could see radiant light around her as if she were a saint.

"I'm Mrs. Percy Shelley," Harriet said as she stood in the doorway. "May I come in?"

"You're that Mr. Shelley's bride? You look like a child," the younger woman said.

"I'm married to Mr. Shelley. I'm not a child, I assure you. I'm nearly seventeen years old," Harriet said.

"I don't care how young or old you are," Anne said as she stopped rocking the child. "What I need to know is whether you are God-fearing. Or are you a heathen, a heretic, an atheist, like your husband?"

Harriet resented being equated with her husband and his beliefs. She was her own person. "Percy has his own opinions and beliefs. I have mine. Yes, I fear and love God. Why do you ask?"

"We wish to know who we are speaking with."

"My beliefs are likely aligned with yours. I've come in friendship to share my bounty with you."

"We don't take charity," Anne said. Her baby whimpered, and Anne used her foot to gently rock the child's crib.

"This is not charity. I wish to break bread with you and become your friend, because I have heard about your courage," Harriet said. "I recently visited the place where you were incarcerated. I didn't go in but from the outside it looked like hell itself. I don't know how you survived. I'd like to know how you became so brave and resilient. I wish to become like you." She felt her cheeks warm; she was embarrassed to have revealed so much to these two women. "Your story ought to be told, for women's history has always been ignored by the powerful who deem women inferior and subservient. I learned this from the great philosopher Mary Wollstonecraft. Do you know of her? Her mother was an Irish woman."

Anne looked at her thoughtfully. "I know of Mary Wollstonecraft. Someone lent me her book when I was young." She paused. "I am Mrs. Campbell now. Anne Devlin no longer exists; she died in Kilmainham and became a ghost that haunts the place. But you may come in. Aoife, put the kettle on."

At that moment, Harriet knew that Anne Devlin, now Mrs. Campbell, would become her second Irish friend.

Harriet hoped that once she began to tell Anne her own story, Anne would tell Harriet hers, for that's what friends do. For the time being, Harriet thought that she would not tell Percy what she learned from Anne. Perhaps he was right; only another woman would be able to learn her story and appreciate and understand her trials. After all, telling Percy what she learned from Anne was superfluous to his goals.

27 February 1812

To enter Fishamble Theater, where Percy was scheduled to address the Catholic Committee, it was necessary to walk through a foul-smelling alley overrun with beggars and drunkards who blocked the door as they extended their hands for coin.

"Please kindly allow my wife to pass," Percy said. The men moved aside, and Harriet distributed a few pence to as many of them as she could.

Once they ascended the rickety staircase, Percy and Harriet were stunned to see the grand theatre illuminated by ornate candlelit chandeliers that cast light on theatre boxes filled with ladies dressed in expensive furs and wearing the latest Parisian fashions. Below were stalls overflowing with hundreds of modestly, cleanly dressed Irishmen. The crowd was lively and eager to hear the speakers; they quickly quieted when the main speaker took the stage.

Lawless introduced the great emancipator, Daniel O'Connell. An elegant, persuasive speaker, O'Connell roused the audience to peacefully rise up and liberate themselves. The crowd roared its approval. Once O'Connell completed his address, he generously introduced Percy. "My fellow patriots, I have the honor of introducing to you a young man who advocates for all of us, but particularly for we Catholics. He's a poet, like our great Fianna warriors. He proclaims liberty for all. I entreat you to give him a warm and respectful Irish welcome."

Percy felt nervous as he mounted the stage and looked out at the sea of strangers. He knew he was no orator like O'Connell. To reassure himself, Percy searched for Harriet, whose face lit up as he began to speak. His voice trembled slightly as he said, "I thank Daniel O'Connell, John Lawless, and the Catholic Committee for inviting me to speak. Like O'Connell and the Fianna, I am your champion. I am here to tell you how you can liberate yourselves through the philanthropic society that we will establish and as I've outlined in this pamphlet." His hand shook as he lifted a copy of the pamphlet and began to explain its points.

Harriet had cautioned Percy once more to refrain from mentioning religion, because it was divisive and yet he once again spoke of Catholic acts against Protestants as barbaric. Apparently, he hadn't altered that part of the address. He was greeted with loud hisses and boos, and he raised his hand to try to quell the crowd. He turned and saw O'Connell cringe. He looked at Harriet and Lawless who also shook their heads. Fearing condemnation, Percy decided to quickly move on to his thesis about the nature of courage, perseverance, thoughtful reading and discussion, temperance, sobriety, charity and finally independence.

Someone in the audience shouted, "Care for a drink, lad? If so, meet me at O'Leary's." The crowd laughed.

Percy ignored the heckler and asked the audience, "Are you slaves or men? If slaves then crouch to the rod, and lick the feet of the oppressors, glory in your shame . . . But if you are men, a real man is free, so far as circumstances will permit him. Then firmly, yet quietly resist. When one cheek is struck, be like Christ and turn the other to the insulting coward. You will be truly brave; you will resist and conquer." This point seemed to resonate with O'Connell's speech, and Percy felt as though some of the audience understood the similarity in thought.

He continued to another theme. "Is war necessary to your happiness and safety? The interests of the poor gain nothing from glory, a word that has often served as a cloak to the ambition or avarice of statesmen . . . The poor purchase this glory and this wealth at the expense of their blood . . . It is horrible that the poor must give in taxes what would save them and their families from hunger and cold."

A few men rose to their feet and cheered.

Percy concluded by sharing this stanza from a poem he had penned:

> Bear witness, Erin, when thine injured isle
> Sees summer on its verdant pastures smile,
> Its cornfields waving in the winds that sweep
> The billowy surface of thy circling deep, --
> Thou tree whose shadow o'er the Atlantic wave,
>   its blossoms fade,
> And blighted are the leaves that cast its shade,
> Whilst the cold hand gathers its scanty fruit,
> Whose chillness struck the canker at its root.

Percy briefly and genuinely felt like Emmet in reciting his poem to his "fellow Irishmen," pointing out the cold hand of the British gathering Irish "fruit." And after his recitation, he called for peaceful political agitation.

He had spoken for nearly an hour, and his audience had dwindled.

Another heckler shouted, "Sit down, you bloody Englishman," and then they called for O'Connell to speak again. Percy received a scattering of applause.

Overall, he felt disappointed. He should have heeded Harriet's and Catherine's advice. Perhaps if, through some good fortune, he ever did get to learn Emmet's story, he would more fully understand the mindset of people who have long been abused by British tyranny. His goal remained the emancipation of all oppressed people through the development of their rational processes and through peaceful political protest. As such, when all men were liberated, as Godwin wrote, they would no longer need government but would be able to govern themselves through their rational faculties. Since Ireland was the most oppressed nation under British rule, Percy would continue to test Godwin's political theories there.

28 February 1812

Harriet returned in the afternoon to Anne's. She pulled her cloak closer, for it was quite cold in the flat. Anne was cradling her baby daughter wrapped in a shawl on her lap. It was an odd juxtaposition, since Anne looked more like a granddame than a mother. Anne said that the child's name was Catrìne, named after Mrs. Nugent, who ministered to her while she was in prison. Harriet told her that this was a worthy tribute. Harriet wondered if Catherine knew that Anne had named her child after her.

"Would you care to hold Catrìne?"

"I love children but have never held a baby before, may I?" She thought about how she tried to pick up Sinead and how the matron prevented her from embracing the child.

"Of course," Anne said as she handed the baby to Harriet.

Anne advised that Harriet support the baby's head and hold her close to her bosom, which would make the infant feel secure, for she would hear Harriet's heartbeat and feel the warmth of her body. Harriet unbuttoned her cloak and held the baby near her heart. The baby rooted around and tried to nuzzle Harriet's breast, which made Harriet laugh, but she also latched on to Harriet's finger with her wee hand and Harriet felt her own heart flutter. Even so, Harriet was a little embarrassed that the baby tried to nurse her, so she quickly returned her to her mother. Clearly, the child was hungry. Anne discreetly fed her baby while they drank their tea.

Afterward, Harriet pulled a small packet of turf from her bag. Anne thanked Harriet kindly and asked her cousin to put it away.

"Aren't you going to light it?" Harriet asked. "It's dreadfully cold in here, especially for the baby."

Anne frowned. "No, Mrs. Shelley, we never light the fire during the day. We must save the fuel for the evening so we can cook." She swaddled the baby tighter, while tying the baby's cap, and placed her in her cradle.

Harriet felt embarrassed that she had asked whether they would light a fire, and she felt ashamed that Anne and others experienced such deprivation, while she lived comfortably. Even though Harriet was not born to wealth, her father had prospered as a businessman and vintner who owned a successful and popular coffee house. He provided the family with a comfortable and commodious house near Hyde Park in London, and he employed many servants who took care of the family's every need. Her family even owned a summer house, Aberystwyth, in Wales, where they kept horses and ponies. Harriet had owned a favorite sable-colored pony named Ginger. Their summer house was surrounded by great natural beauty with a nearby beach and healing springs that were overlooked by castle ruins. As a child, Harriet played on the beach with her nanny Irene, and found amethyst, agate, and pink and white jasper. Her childhood was serene and secure. And even though Percy's father currently refused Percy his allowance, they always managed to retain sufficient funds so that they did not suffer from extreme hunger or the cold. Although small, their accommodation was comfortable with its four rooms, and aesthetically pleasing with its stone fireplace, paintings, and tapestries that depicted Irish heroes.

To change the subject, Harriet told her how Percy was laudable because he saved her from her controlling father who insisted that she continue to attend a frivolous finishing school for girls. Now, Percy was teaching her philosophy and Latin so that she could grow in intellect and knowledge, and thus become a more suitable companion to him.

Anne seemed shocked regarding Harriet's education. "You have not studied Latin? Many poor Irish know their Latin. My sisters and brothers and I learned Latin at our hedge school." With that, Anne told Harriet about her education, which in fact far exceeded Harriet's own. She also spoke whimsically of fairy forts that she and her brothers and sisters visited, where fairies protected the sacred land where the High Kings were crowned.

Even though Anne had told Percy that she lived outside history, Harriet felt certain that history must contain the stories of ordinary women. Besides, Anne was no ordinary woman, but an extraordinary one.

Harriet had promised to maintain secrecy in regard to Anne's testimony, but she did tell Eliza about her visits to John's Lane, thinking that Eliza would understand the need to learn women's stories.

"This seems quite foolish to me, but you've been rash before, so I shouldn't be surprised," Eliza said. "After all, you ran off with a penniless poet who endangers you."

Eliza had often criticized Harriet's choice of a husband. Sometimes Harriet thought that Eliza was jealous of her marriage and had perhaps thought that Percy would propose to her, not Harriet, for she and Percy had once been fond of one another. Eliza's remark wounded her, and she told her so. Even though she sometimes doubted Percy, she argued with Eliza in regard to his positive attributes: his brilliance, his passion, his noble goals.

"He will come to a bad end," Eliza said. "He will hurt you. Perhaps he will betray you, for he only seeks his own happiness and notoriety."

"That's simply not true. He is faithful and caring."

"No, he cares only for himself. He neglects and endangers you. I came to Ireland with you to ensure that you are safe. Your husband has his head in the clouds and doesn't recognize peril." Eliza warned Harriet again that she perhaps placed all of them in danger by speaking with a woman whom the British vilify.

"You don't understand," Harriet said. "Anne Devlin is a noble woman who has withstood tremendous suffering. I can learn much from her about how to be a stronger, more worthy woman."

She hastily donned her bonnet and cloak and headed out into the blinding snow. She walked to the GPO to see if she had received a response from the Board of Governors. She was troubled by Eliza's remarks. She and Percy were not in jeopardy. Anne did not endanger them. Percy's work was valiant. Harriet told herself that she must continue to believe in him. He would never betray her or his cause.

As soon as Harriet left, Eliza put on her cloak and bonnet and followed her, keeping a look out for the danger that threatened them.

Four

Green, Not Red Blood

28 February 1812

Harriet tore open the correspondence as soon as the clerk handed her the envelope.

> *Dear Sir Timothy Shelley,*
> *After learning of your son's scandalous reputation, the Governors must decline your offer to intervene on behalf of Mrs. O'Byrne. Foundling children cannot be associated with those who do not believe in the Almighty.*

Harriet, astonished, stopped reading. How would the Governors know of Percy's lack of belief? How had they associated Sir Timothy with his son? Had Percy's reputation been sullied all over Ireland? What could she do now that she had failed to adequately petition for the girls' release from their confinement?

Harriet hurriedly walked to the Foundling Hospital as snow continued to fall. The ground was slippery, and a foggy mist hugged the ground. It was difficult to see far ahead of her, but she finally arrived at St. James Gate and proceeded to the narrow door of the hospital.

Eliza watched from St. James Gate and wondered why Harriet was visiting this place, which resembled a prison.

Harriet spoke with the porter. "I wish to see Sinead and Michaela O'Byrne."

"I've been told no visitors allowed today," the porter said. "The children's sick and we don't wish to spread contagion."

"I was here before when the children were ill. Besides, I'm not afraid of contagion." Harriet pulled her cloak closer, for the wind had become sharp.

"Matters not, madam. You're not welcome today," he said as he started to shut the door.

"Wait, are the O'Byrne girls still sick? Are they well?"

"I don't know. I know there's a girl named O'Byrne in the Bridewell."

"Why? What did she do?" Harriet asked exasperated.

"I dunno. She probably spoke out of turn."

"May I see her?" Harriet asked as she started to step closer to the door.

"You would have to ask the matron."

"Then, may I see the matron?"

"No, no visitors today," he said. This time he firmly closed the door.

Eliza watched from behind a tree. Harriet looked crestfallen as she slowly walked away and then turned and passed through St. James Gate past many mendicants with outstretched hands whom she ignored. She ventured out into an open field covered with mist and snow.

Anne Devlin

I'm no storyteller like my mam but I told that Mrs. Shelley, the wife of the atheist poet, a tale or two. I told her about fairies and their forts, about the hedge school, and how we learned Latin and Greek, but not what happened to my teacher. Still, because I've been badgered to remember, I've been thinking about my young life while we lived on the farm.

I loved our farm life; the land that we rented was fertile and plentiful. Unlike others, we were never hungry. Oftentimes we ate our fill of blackberries, bilberries, nuts, and wild raspberries. Our landlady, Mrs. Darby, allowed my brothers and Da to hunt on her land, and Da ensured that we were well fed, for he would bring home rabbits, grouse, and partridges. When we weren't doing chores, my six brothers and sisters: John, Jimmy, Little Art, Mary, Julie, and Nellie and me would roam the woods, where we visited the ring forts where the fairies lived and where we allowed our imaginations to ramble. Our childhoods were indeed magical and abundant with love and fellowship.

But as I grew older, I wanted more than what farm life and dreamy fairy worlds could afford. I wanted an education, but the only school available was the hedge school. The penal laws forbid Catholics to be educated in the way that Protestants are in a proper schoolroom. Instead, we secretly attend school outdoors or in a barn, as if we are farm animals: cows, pigs, sheep, donkeys. In doing so, we break the law, for the English wish to keep us ignorant and powerless. They know that knowledge is power.

When I was a child, our school was a sod house scooped out of the bank on the roadside. We had no desks; we sat on round stones on the ground and propped our slates on our knees. We attended school each season except in harvest time, and we paid the teacher in potatoes, corn, or turf. In the winter, each young scholar was required to bring two sods of turf for the fire that was kept in the center of the house. A hole in the roof discharged the smoke. The lucky and best students were those who got to sit near the sweet-smelling turf fire and the school master in the winter. I was often perched there because our teacher, Mr. Mac Williams, told me I was the head of the class.

Our teacher was a righteous Welsh scholar. He taught us Latin, mathematics, reading, and geography, and he read to us from his classical books, his Ovid, Homer, and Virgil. That was until the authorities at Dublin Castle discovered his cache of books. They seized the books, lit a bonfire, and forced Mr. Mac Williams to throw his books one by one onto the funeral pyre; they intended to destroy his library. We heard that he wept as he cast each book into the flames. The ignorant Irish Yeomen who burned his books laughed at him. After that, our honorable teacher lost his wits, and we saw him wandering down the cow path near our home. I asked him what he was doing, and he said, "Why I'm looking for my friend Virgil. Have you seen him? I must find him before he's lost for the whole of Ireland." Poor Master Mac Williams was never the same after the English and their henchmen destroyed his library. You would've thought his library was Alexandria itself. I guess that it was to him.

Mr. Mac Williams was lucky that they only burnt his library. In Wexford, a schoolmaster had been tarred and feathered and another had been pitch-capped and went blind from the pitch that oozed into his eyes and his scalp was torn off when the cap was pulled from his head. He died and his body was thrown in a bog. Another teacher was flogged because he spoke French, for the British loathe the French and fear that their revolution will spread to the British Isles. (We Irish dislike the French too, but for different reasons, mostly because they are cowards and do not keep their promises).

So, we were left with no teacher until Father Sean Martin, a priest who'd been jailed for inciting riots, was finally released after a long incarceration. He said Mass and heard our confessions in one of the sacred caves in the mountains. He was a brave man, for the location of his altar was near the hanging tree where a priest had been recently executed for doing precisely what Father Sean was doing—fearlessly administering the Eucharist, the Lord's body, and blood, to us. Afterwards, Father Sean gathered us children together and taught us our Latin, but he also taught us, as Mr. Mac Williams had, reading, mathematics, geography, and history. He reminded us that, when the Viking raiders tried to stamp out civilization, the pious monks saved it. He said that in studying and gaining knowledge, we would be like those faithful monks and save civilization. He made us proud that we too could save civilization just by learning our Latin and our world history.

As I grew older, I became interested in studying the American Revolution, and I asked Father Sean if he owned a book that would help me understand the ideas behind it and the French Revolution. I didn't know it at the time, but Father Sean belonged, like my cousins, to the Society of United Irishmen, which had been deemed illegal. He asked me if I had ever heard of the English man who became American, Thomas Paine, and when I said that I hadn't, he said, "Here, read this," and he handed me his copies of Paine's *Common Sense* and *The Rights of Man.*

"Are you sure it's permissible for me to read these books?" I asked.

"And why shouldn't you?"

"I'm not certain my da would approve. He is against rebellion, because his nephews worked with Wolfe Tone and now they have to hide in the mountains. We never see them; they are always in danger. Besides, Da told me these books are banned here."

"Then hide them from him," he said. "If you want to understand what is happening in the world, you need to be acquainted with the current politics and not be afraid of the consequences. Don't let anyone tell you, even your da, what you have the right to know." I was astounded that a priest would condone me not honoring my da's wishes, for the fourth commandment tells us to honor our father and mother. I guess he thought that our greater obligation is to our fellow women and men.

I did what Father Sean advised and hid the books beneath a haybale in the barn. Reading Paine was difficult, especially because the ideas were complex but also because I read his books by candlelight on the sly, usually after everyone had gone to bed. I was intrigued by what he said about children and the future: "If we fail to act, we condemn our children to tyranny." I wanted a better future for all of us, but especially for Nellie and Jimmy, my wee sister and brother. This passage also moved me:

> When it shall be said in any country in the world my poor are happy; neither ignorance nor distress is to be found among them; my jails are empty of prisoners, my street of beggars; the aged are not in want; the taxes are not oppressive; the rational world is my friend; because I am a friend of its happiness: when these things can be said, there may a country boast of its constitution and government.

This was what we wished for our country, for our Erin. I further understood that these goals would not be achieved immediately but would blossom with time. I agreed with Paine that "all mankind are my brethren, and to do good is my religion." I understood also that

Paine claimed that the Rights of Man included life, liberty, free speech, freedom of conscience, security, and ownership of property. And from Paine's point of view, revolution is permissible when a government does not safeguard the natural rights of man. As I read, I wondered if those rights were extended to the female sex. Paine never said anything about females per se. Perhaps his idea of "man" was general, and it included those of the fairer sex. I knew I should ask Father Sean about this, and I intended to do so, but one afternoon my da caught me reading *The Rights of Man* in the barn when I was supposed to be cutting turf with John.

"What in God's name is this, Anne?" he asked as he grabbed the book from my hand. He looked at the title and shouted, "Don't you know that such writing is dangerous and will lead you down the wrong path? You could be arrested for reading this. Do you want to end up like your cousins who can never come home? Do you want to end up even worse than them?"

I cried and shook my head and said, "Please don't be angry, Da. I only wanted to learn about what is going on in the world."

"You're better off not knowing. Who gave this to you?" His tone was harsh, and he was growing red in the face.

"Father Sean lent it to me." I gulped tears.

"That damned priest should mind his own business." I knew that Da was angry because he never swore and he washed our mouths out with soap if we said, "Jesus, Mary, and Joseph," which he considered blasphemous.

Da confiscated the book and returned it to Father Sean. My brother John witnessed their meeting, and he said that Da cursed the priest, telling him that he had no right to encourage rebellion. Did he want children to be placed in danger by reading political tracts that the Crown believed treasonous?

Then Da forbade me and my brothers and sisters from attending Father Sean's hedge school. Even though Da wanted us to be educated, he didn't want the seeds of rebellion planted. Little did he know they were already safely sown and were already becoming seedlings that would eventually sprout into flowering trees. I had retained *Common Sense* and hoped to implement its goals.

Shortly after this, the British hanged Father Sean from that hanging tree for teaching us about how the British stole our land and made us their vassals, and for allowing us to commune with God and partake of His body and blood. The British hate the true religion and us Catholics. Father Sean had no trial and was not allowed to defend himself. So much for British justice. Even my da felt bad after that for the damned priest, who lost his life by speaking the truth.

1 March 1812

Percy wanted to meet the apologist for the United Irishmen to convince him to support his heroic cause. So, carrying with him a letter of introduction from William Godwin, he traveled to John Philpot Curran's home in Merrion Square. It was early morning, and the lamplighters were snuffing out the streetlamps.

Curran lived in one of the few well-kept Georgian mansions across from the park; there was a footman at the door and a carriage in the mews behind the house. O'Connell was said to be one of Curran's neighbors. Percy rang the bell, and a butler opened the door.

"Good morning. I would like to see Mr. Curran."

"I'm sorry, sir, Mr. Curran is not in."

"Do you expect him anytime soon?"

"No, sir," the butler said.

"As soon as he returns, would you please tell him that Mr. Percy Shelley, a friend of William Godwin's, wishes to visit with him?" Percy handed the man his card, feeling confident that this would ensure that Curran would grant him an audience.

"I shall inform him as soon as he returns. Good day, sir," the butler said as he shut the door.

When he returned to Sackville Street, Percy opened a letter from Godwin who told him that he had recently discovered that Curran detested the memory of Emmet, and it's likely that Curran had learned of Percy's revolutionary zeal and his attraction to Emmet, which he had mentioned in his speech to the Catholic Committee. Curran's loathing of Emmet was based on the fact that Emmet had been romantically involved with Curran's youngest daughter Sarah. When Emmet was arrested for treason, Dublin Castle authorities found letters that Sarah wrote to him. Curran believed that Emmet might try to implicate his daughter and him in the rebellion of which he wanted no part, even though he had vigorously supported Irish independence in the past. When Emmet was executed, Curran sent his daughter to convalesce with a Quaker family, for she experienced nervous collapse after Emmet's execution, which she had unfortunately witnessed. Curran claimed that Sarah did not return Emmet's ardor—that she thought of him as a friend, not a suitor. Godwin said, "Perhaps her letters to Emmet belied this supposed fact but that Curran was unwilling to acknowledge this."

Godwin explained, "For Curran meeting you would be like making acquaintance again with Robert Emmet, who, I believe, like yourself, was a man of pure mind, but respecting whom I could not have told, from day to day, what calamities he might bring upon his country."

Of course, Percy felt honored to have been equated with Emmet. However, if Curran saw Percy as a reincarnation of Emmet, he would inform Curran that, even though he personally admired Emmet and wished to carry out his rebellion, he did not condone Emmet's tactics. For, like Godwin, he did not believe in violent upheaval. Percy was a pacifist. And, naturally, he intended to bring no calamities upon Ireland. Even with this knowledge of Curran's hatred of Emmet, he was most eager to speak with Curran and would try again soon to obtain an interview with him.

2 March 1812

Aoife ushered Harriet into their flat. Anne was not in her chair but standing over a large washtub and next to her was an enormous pile of clothing.

"That's quite a lot of washing that you have to do, Mrs. Campbell," Harriet remarked. She noticed that some of the items were fancy shirts with ruffles and some were the latest fashion of ladies' corsets and other undergarments; surely Anne did not own such luxurious items.

"It's not our clothing, Mrs. Shelley," Aoife said. "Anne and I work as laundresses for the Gillespie family and have since Anne was released from Kilmainham."

"I must help support the family, for Mr. Campbell does not provide a sufficient wage as a day laborer at the docks. There now," Anne said as she rinsed and wrung out the collar she was scrubbing, "Is this sufficiently clean, Aoife?"

"Indeed, it is."

"Well, then, we're done for the day. The weather is not fair so we must hang the laundry inside." She handed the shirt to Aoife, who took it to the clean pile of clothes, and proceeded to hang the items on a clothesline along the wall.

Anne sat down in her rocker and lit a small clay pipe. Harriet noticed that her hands and arms were red and raw, probably from the rigorous scrubbing on the washboard. Harriet kept her hands hidden in her gloves because she didn't want Anne or Aoife to know that she'd never scrubbed a collar.

As Anne rocked Catrìne, she told Harriet about her family: her six sisters and brothers and her mam and da. "My mam told us many tales, especially of her ancestor who was a rebel during the Elizabethan era."

"Was he famous?"

"Yes, he was famous for being a thorn in the British Crown," Aoife proudly said. "And he and we are descendants of a High King."

"She doesn't wish to know about that," Anne said.

"Oh, but I do. I know a little about the High Kings; my friend the Duke of Norfolk told me about Brian Boru."

"We aren't Brian Boru's descendants. My mam was an O'Byrne, who was a direct descendant Bran mac Máelmórda, King of Leinster," Anne replied.

Harriet perked up. "Are there many O'Byrnes? Is it a common name?"

"It is, but we're all related."

Before Harriet had a chance to ask about the rebel O'Byrne who died helping Emmet, Anne recounted more about the Hill of Tara, where the High Kings were crowned and where fairies lived.

"There was once a girl named Kathleen possessed by a fairy-spirit that resided near the Hill of Tara. Kathleen became quite peculiar; she spoke a strange tongue that no one could comprehend, and she was often angry and violent; she was so odd that her mam and da had to lock her in a shed, for she throttled her sisters and spoke the strange tongue of the fairy language. Once night, she escaped, and they found her stealing a neighbor's baby.

"She ended up living in the shed for two years and after two years they took her to an old witch-woman in Drogheda who rid her of possession by fairies."

"Another person died after cutting down bushes where the fairies lived," Aoife added. "They retaliate against those who destroy their homes."

"You don't believe any of this, do you?" Harriet asked.

"Of course, I do," Anne replied. "Irish Fairies are not benign. They don't sprinkle fairy dust and goodwill, like fairies do in English stories. Or live among the toadstools and fly around on the backs of dragonflies. They seek revenge. They sometimes bring babies to families but then steal them. You should beware of the fairies, Mrs. Shelley. They are still with us, and they can cause great harm."

Even while knowing this troubling but somewhat dubious truth, Anne's young life sounded full of mystery and enchantment to Harriet. And despite the fact that she enjoyed Anne's tale, she wondered when Anne would tell her about her rebel life and when she might ask about Kevin O'Byrne's young family and what his role in the rebellion had been.

Anne Devlin

I tell the young lass whimsical tales about fairies and other Celtic nonsense, the kind of tales that the British expect us to tell. She sometimes asks me about my family and when we became acquainted with rebels, but I do not answer her questions; I act like I never heard them. I'm good at playing deaf.

The truth is we had always been a rebel family. Of course, we were descendants of the O'Byrnes, but my cousins, Big Art, and Pat Devlin, fought alongside the likes of Wolfe Tone and Thomas Addis Emmet, Robert's brother. When the United Irishmen were defeated in 1798 at Vinegar Hill, Big Art and Pat, experts in subterfuge, found their way back to the Wicklow Mountains and hid in a cave with their fellow rebels. They did not communicate with the family, except on occasion where they would appear in the dark of night and disappear before the first streak of orange kissed the sky.

One night, Da sent me to bring food to his brother, my Uncle Patrick, Art, and Pat's da, who lived alone and was suffering from a fever. I was a good horsewoman and, even though the night was creeping on, my eyesight was keen at the time, and I could easily find my way in the shadows over the fells. As I approached my uncle's farm, I became afeared when I saw smoke and flames jutting from the roof! My horse reared and nearly threw me, but I steadied her, jumped down, and raced toward the house. I shouted for my uncle, but he didn't answer. The smoke was billowing around me, and I began to cough. I pulled my kerchief from my neck and covered my nose. Seeing the door ajar, I ran in and found my uncle lying on his bed. I feared he was dead. I spied a pitcher of water next to the bed and I threw the water on him! He awoke with a start and shouted, "Jesus, Mary, and Joseph, girl! What in God's holy name are you doing? Are you trying to drown me, lass?"

"No, uncle, please get up. Your house is on fire!" I pulled at his arm and when he sat up, we saw flames licking the window. We crawled toward the door as we choked. I held my breath and placed my kerchief over my uncle's face, and we managed to find the doorway.

When we reached outdoors, we coughed and coughed and then finally caught our breath. Then we looked back at the house, and knew it was hopeless. Windows broke, the roof erupted in flames, and then the house completely burned and fell to the ground. Only cinders and smoldering ash were left by dawn.

As we gazed at the morning star, we were silent for a long time. I tried to hide my tears, but was overcome with great sadness, for I knew what my uncle was thinking—This is where my children were born and where my wife Bridget died in the bed upstairs where she gave birth to our boys. This is where I taught them their letters and read to them of the saints and scholars who inhabited and still inhabit our island. Somehow those Irish Yeomen aligned with the Brits and who burnt my house will pay. I felt his pain so hard that I wept openly and then he cried with me.

After a while, I asked him what had happened, how the fire started, but I had already suspected its origin, for others in our county had had their homes burned by the dastardly Yeomen, who did anything that the British wanted. My uncle told me that Yeomen had visited him the day before wanting to know where Big Art and Patrick were. They demanded to know if my uncle was hiding them. My uncle replied, "Do you think if I knew where they were, I would tell the likes of you?" Of course, that angered the Yeomen, and they warned him of consequences. After that, he went to bed and the Yeomen, being the demons they are, set the house on fire to make him pay for the way he'd reminded them that they were traitors.

I was seventeen at the time and, of course, I knew of Dublin Castle's violence towards the Irish, but until then I had never encountered it first-hand. Soon, I would see more atrocities. Dublin Castle tyrants torched more of our neighbors' homes and barns. They killed their cattle; they destroyed their crops, their only livelihoods. They falsely accused some neighbors of rebellion. Because of this cruelty and injustice, I knew that I had to steel my heart if me and my family were to survive.

Not long after that Yeomen paid us a visit to see if Da knew the whereabouts of my other cousins, the Dwyer Brothers. My da Bryan said that he hadn't seen them in over a year. That he had nothing to do with rebels; he was no Fenian. In truth, Da and Mam had assisted two rebels recently wounded in an attack on Newtonmountkennedy and had helped these rebels find shelter at our neighbor, Tom Halpin's farm. Mam even pressed a musket ball out of the shoulder of one of the rebels, and I helped her with the gruesome task by holding the young man's hand and telling him he would be grand. Afterwards, I dressed the wound, and then Da ferried the men to our friend's farm and hid them in the hayloft.

Even though Da was no rebel himself, he was a big-hearted man who hated to see anyone suffer. And since my mam was a descendant of O'Byrne, if she could have, she would have fought the British herself in the Wicklow Mountains, for she was as brave and grand as our legendary Queen Maeve herself.

The Yeomen refused to listen to his claim, saying that they had an informant who saw Da transport two known rebels. Then, they said they were arresting Da for harboring and aiding traitors. They dragged Da outside and bound his hands, pulling his breeches down around his thighs so he couldn't run.

My mam was crying and so were all my brothers and sisters, for we feared for our da's life and hated seeing him humiliated in such a manner. We knew that our cousin Billy Byrne had been confined in

Wicklow Gaol and then was hanged there. We didn't want our Da to meet the same fate. I blurted out, "What are you doing to him? You've no right! He's not a rebel. He's against rebellion. Stop. Let him go!"

"You'd best keep your mouth shut, you tart, or you'll share a cell with your da," the captain said, as he shoved my father toward a wagon that would carry him to gaol.

Da grew red in the face and glared at the Yeomen. I could tell that he wanted to speak out against the captain, but he feared that I would be harmed by more than vile words. He turned and calmly said, "Anne, do as the soldiers say. I'll be all right." He nodded to my mam and my brother John and said, "Winnie and John, you know how to run the farm. I'll be home soon. Don't cry and don't fret."

Mam wiped her tears with the edge of her shawl, and John stood tall and wrapped his arm around her.

Da was wrong though about returning home soon. They kept him in Wicklow Gaol for two years, five months, and two days and for two years, five months, and two days, I traveled to the gaol once a week to bring my da food, for prisoners' families had to supply victuals for them or they would starve, which is clearly what the British wished for us. They wanted all of us Irish Catholics and our sympathizers dead, so they could possess all of our four green fields.

Each time I brought Da food, I saw a new batch of bruises on his arms and legs. When I asked him about them, he wouldn't talk. He only said, "It's nothing, lass. Don't tell your mam though. She's not to worry. They will heal."

People talk about my time in Kilmainham. How I never talked about Robert Emmet, how I withstood all sorts of torture. They don't know that I learned to be silent despite the pain inflicted on my body, mind, and soul, through my da's example. He was the brave one, not I. And he had a more compassionate heart than I did, for I still harbor resentment for all that was done to me, my family, and Robert. Maybe Da was correct that we should have kept our distance from the rebellion, but one cannot rectify the past any more than be born again.

3 March 1812

Since Harriet had said that no one answered the door when she visited, Percy returned to the Liberties to try once more to see Anne, but first he made his way to Merrion Square to call again on Mr. Curran, for he was growing impatient to make his acquaintance and receive his support. Once more, Curran was not in. As he had previously, Percy left his card and kindly asked the butler to see to it that Mr. Curran was made aware of his address. He included a reminder that he was William Godwin's disciple, and he expressed his eagerness to talk with Mr. Curran. The butler acknowledged that once more his message would be delivered.

As he walked away, he began to wonder if Curran was deliberately avoiding him. He glanced at the house and saw someone pull back a curtain from an upstairs window and then quickly shut it as if they didn't wish to be seen. Perhaps Godwin was correct that Curran dreaded seeing him because he likened him to Emmet.

Walking away from St. Stephen's Green and toward the Liberties, he became intensely aware of the contrasting neighborhoods. Even though St. Stephen's Green was overgrown with weeds, it was populated with the most glorious oaks, willow trees, and wild rose-filled gardens. The Georgian mansions at Merrion Square needed upkeep, but they were far superior to the buildings and environment in the Liberties. No graceful oaks lined John's Lane. Windows were broken, and bricks and mortar had fallen on the cobblestones. People sat on their door stoops, and children played among the rubbish.

He entered Anne's building and was delighted when he found Johnny once again in the downstairs flat. He had been searching for the boy on the street but never thought that he would find him squatting in the same place.

"What is happening with your mother, Johnny?"

"She's still in jail. If she's lucky she might get transported and I could go with her."

"You consider that luck?" Shelley was incredulous. Perhaps the child didn't understand the ramifications of transportation. Still, it was better than being hanged.

"Yes, sir, we could start over."

"You and your mother would likely be indentured."

"What's that mean, sir?"

"You'd basically be slaves for seven to ten years. Your lives would not be your own." Percy thought that was a fate Johnny would rebel against.

"At least we'd eat, and we'd be together. She'd be alive," Johnny said tenderly.

Percy felt Johnny's pain and shifted the discussion to the arrest. "It's outrageous that your mother was arrested. She is no thief. I feel certain she'll be exonerated."

"What's exonerated mean?"

"Found not guilty."

Johnny looked at Percy as if he were a fool. Percy ignored his look, believing him to be too young to understand genuine justice and mercy.

Thinking that he should help the lad since he was unable to help the mother, he asked, "Would you like to earn some coin?"

"Of course, sir. What would I have to do?"

"Distribute these to the pubs on the north side," he said, as he handed him his new *Proposal* that Stockdale had printed for him.

"What are they?"

"See for yourself."

Johnny looked at the pamphlet on top and hung his head. "I'm sorry, sir. You'll have to tell me what it says. I'm ashamed to admit it but I can't read."

Percy was startled but hid his shock, for he did not want Johnny to feel greater shame. "That's nothing to be embarrassed of. You've just not had the opportunity to learn. You seem bright enough. I will teach you, and you'll become a young scholar." He patted Johnny on the back. He told him that he would return the next day with books and a slate, for he must also learn to write. They would begin his rightful education.

Now, Percy had a new activity and goal. He would meet Johnny (who confessed that his real name was Devin O'Donnell) every day at this house. He would teach the boy to read. This would also please Harriet who advocated for children, and it partially satisfied Percy's hunger for practical action for, after all, his hope was that every Irish person would become literate, which would lead toward their liberation. Even though Anne Devlin didn't answer her door, he felt encouraged. Perhaps he needn't learn Emmet's story to complete Emmet's righteous work, to make each Irish citizen worthy of living on the Isle of Saints and Scholars.

Five

Charity and Justice

4 March 1812
Anne Devlin

You'd think the lass would grow tired of hearing about the fairies and how they went underground to hide from the Brits, but she persists in coming here and listening to that drivel. One can't account for the whims of the British, who like to hear a good yarn and expect the Irish to spin them. I told that husband of hers that I'm no storyteller, but I do my best to mimic my mam and use her tricks to keep the listener attentive. Like Scheherazade, who told King Shahryar stories to keep him from murdering his wives, I tell a tale to keep the Crown from killing more of my comrades and myself. I create cliffhangers, which encourages the listener to return to hear what happened next. Even though I will never tell Mrs. Shelley my rebel story, I appreciate her company. She's a kind lass with a generous heart, one she claims is Irish, but that's impossible.

After she kisses Catrìne goodnight and leaves to return to her heretic, I return in my imagination to rebel times and recall vividly the horror in bloody detail. While my father was suffering in Wicklow Gaol, my crafty cousin Michael Dwyer, the captain of the Wicklow rebel outlaws, managed to escape arrest, just like our ancestor O'Byrne did centuries ago. The Yeomen had surrounded a house where they knew my cousin was staying and they ordered him to come out. When he didn't comply, they torched the house, just like they'd done to my uncle's house. At that point, a young man named Sam McAllister created a diversion by opening the door and shooting a blunderbuss. During the commotion, Michael climbed out a window and then onto a burning roof. A comrade riding on Michael's horse galloped up next to the house and Michael jumped onto the horse. Tragically, brave Sam was shot and killed when the Yeomen mistook him for my cousin. And sadly, twelve others burned up in the fire when the roof collapsed on them.

Because he was a Presbyterian, Sam was buried in Leitrim, in a different churchyard than the Catholic rebels who were buried in

Kilranelagh. So, my cousin Aoife, Sam's sweetheart, suggested that we disinter Sam and lay him to rest with his comrades.

"Do we dare?" Maureen asked. "It sounds gruesome."

"It would be more gruesome for him to eternally rest alongside heretics. Father Finn said that he'd bless Sam, just as if he were a good Catholic, a true believer. We would want his soul to go to God, wouldn't we?" Aoife asked.

"Of course, we will bury him where he belongs. We are used to handling the dead, as that's the duty of daughters. This will be no different. Truthfully, I fear the living far more than the dead," I said.

Maureen and Aoife nodded in agreement and so we hatched a plan to move Sam to holy ground.

A full moon and glistening stars helped us locate Sam's burial site. We went to work immediately with our shovels and picks and found poor Sam in a shallow grave. Even though I said that I didn't fear the dead, I quaked as we dug up Sam. The torchlight illuminated his face frozen with fear. His eyes were wide open, for no one had tended his body at death. I tried to shut his eyelids, but they were like stone. What had he seen at the moment of death that frightened him so? Could he foresee a terrible future? More rebellion? More death and destruction? His face continues to haunt me. I still wish I could have brought him peace.

The odor of the open grave was something awful and we wore kerchiefs around our faces as we pulled him out of the grave. Because of the stench, Aoife vomited after she embraced Sam. The wind blew like mad, and we had to secure the coffin with bricks so that it wouldn't blow away before we hoisted Sam into it.

I drove the horse and dray to the churchyard in Kilranalagh, and Father Sean's replacement and fellow United Irishman, Father Finn, was waiting for us near an open grave.

We lifted the coffin lid, and Father Finn raised a torch and blessed Sam's soul.

"God forgives you your sins. You were a brave man who gave his life for his brothers and sisters. There's no greater gift."

The priest anointed Sam with sacred oil, and then he took the green scarf from his own neck and wound it around Sam's. Aoife had fashioned a garland of Deora Dé, and she placed it around Sam's neck before we hammered the coffin shut and placed it in the grave. Maureen had to lead Aoife away, for she wept bitterly to see her beloved dead and paralyzed eternally in fear.

"He will now be at peace, Aoife," Maureen said. "He's in God's strong arms." Aoife continued to weep in Maureen's arms as they stood in the moonlight.

As Father Finn and I covered the coffin with dirt, I asked, "Will the grave be marked?"

"No, none of the rebels get a marker, for their names must remain unknown. Perhaps one day, when we're free, we can mark the grave."

I felt sad that no one would know where Sam was buried but understood the reasoning. "Father, did we commit a sin by robbing the grave?"

In the torchlight, I saw him shake his head. "No, lass. We moved the lad so that God would embrace his soul. Your graverobbing was an act of grace."

At that moment, I felt proud to be a graverobber. And I knew that I would do it again if I ever had to save the immortal soul of a righteous one once more. I returned later to Sam's grave and placed a garland on it to honor his memory.

While in gaol, my da said that as soon as he was released, he would move us away from the mountains. All of us were distraught at the thought of leaving our Eden, but I was especially unhappy. Knowing that we would soon move, I made one last trip to Glendalough, but later wished I hadn't. For while there, I observed three dead monks, one of them St. Caomhán himself, rowing on the lake and thus I knew that calamity would befall us, because it is said that anyone who sees those monks are dealt a bad fate. I wondered what further trouble could possibly find me and my family. I began to think that we were like Job himself. I asked God what we had done to deserve the suffering that we experienced, but He never answered. I didn't tell anyone my vision, least of all my mam and da, for I knew that there was no stopping fate once it had found you on that downward-turning Fortune's Wheel.

As promised, Da moved us away from the mountains, closer to Dublin. We exchanged the mountains for flat land at Rathfarnam. I was extremely sad to be exiled from the Garden of Ireland; I felt just like Adam and Eve being thrown out of paradise, but Da said that we must be removed from rebellion and discord. He thought that we would be better off if we could start over. Little did he know that by moving us closer to Dublin, we'd eventually become further embroiled in rebellion.

To help my family, I went to work as a scullery maid at a Great House owned by wealthy Protestants. I cleaned up after their galas attended by their fellow aristocrats. I had never seen women dressed in such fancy silk ball gowns covered with jewels or men decked out in tails and top hats. Each woman would sweep in as if they were Queen Charlotte herself, all of them wanting to be noticed. The men puffed on big cigars and drank whiskey by the gallon.

When free on Sunday afternoon, I was able to walk the grounds and look at the fine gardens, abundant with pink, red, and yellow roses, enormous fountains containing lotus blossoms, and naked Grecian statues, which I thought rather indecent but beautifully sculpted. I marveled at the talent that it took to make something so lifelike, even when I was embarrassed to see what men kept hidden under their pantaloons.

I walked with one of the other maids, Colleen, and one Sunday she said, "Anne, I have to show you something. You won't believe it."

We hiked into the woods and came upon a small cemetery. I thought that it was grand that rich folks kept their relatives close by when they had passed. It made me think better of the rich than I previously had. But what I saw next was incredible.

I looked at a large tombstone and inscribed on it was the name Magic, and then on the tombstone was a carved picture of a pony. They had buried their favorite pony here! And another tombstone was erected for their best hunting dog named Fanny. Another grave was that of another pet, a Jersey cow called Eugenie. The cemetery was for their pets not for people. Their pet cemetery was better than anything that I had seen for the Irish poor, where we are sometimes buried in unmarked graves, like Sam was and as many children to this day are. Poor people and poor and bastard children have no funds for a proper burial, or a fancy tombstone inscribed with epitaphs such as "Dear wee Magic, You were loyal and loving. We shall miss you."

I told the lass about the cemetery as a way to keep her attention and to tell her a bit about my life without revealing anything about Sam and his grave. Her checks turned crimson. I suspect that she or her family had such a burial ground at their home, but she never said so. But the lass admitted that she once owned a pony. She left shortly after, and then Aoife and I lit the fire, so we could make supper before the husband came home from the docks.

5 March 1812

Percy, Harriet, and Eliza were taking a constitutional along the River Liffey when they saw something white along the shore. At first, Percy thought it may have been some of the pamphlets that flew away from their balcony. But upon further scrutiny, it seemed to be a bundle that someone had lost from a boat. Percy climbed down the bank and fished out the bundle but then cried out because the bundle squirmed. He gathered the bundle in his arms and climbed back up to the street.

"What is it, Percy?" Harriet asked.

He peeled back the cloth covering the wriggling thing and found a naked newborn baby girl. Percy laid it on the ground. Her arms and legs were mottled blue, and she was struggling to breathe. Someone had recently thrown a newborn in the river. Harriet had heard of such things but to have direct knowledge of evil was another thing entirely. Someone had tried to drown the infant, like people drown unwanted kittens.

Percy looked under the bridge where he saw a body floating face down in the water. He handed Eliza the child, raced down to the water, and pulled the body over to the edge.

"Harriet, come help!"

"I can't. It's too horrible. I'm afraid of the dead." She felt quite ashamed, but she had never seen or touched a dead body before.

"Then, Eliza, hand the child to Harriet and you come quickly."

Eliza did as Percy commanded. She handed the child to Harriet, and the baby's little body felt frigid. Harriet pulled the wee thing closer, hoping to warm and revive her. The baby didn't nuzzle her breast.

Harriet watched in horror as Percy and Eliza tried to drag the water-logged woman's body up the hill.

"It's no use," Percy said. "She's too heavy. We'll have to notify the authorities. They will fetch her."

"Oh, Percy, we must save the child," Harriet pleaded. "How could anyone be so cruel?" She realized that women sometimes felt so desperate that they throw away their own lives, but a good woman would never kill her own child.

Percy didn't say a word but took the child from Harriet. He knew of a charity hospital nearby, so they rushed to the entrance.

As he handed the child to the nun at the door, he said, "We found this child in the river. And her mother's drowned body is nearby under the Ha'penny Bridge."

The sister uncovered the child showing the blue had spread to the child's face and that her tiny chest did not move.

"I will notify the constable," the nun said.

"What about the child?" Percy asked.

"This poor child is dead. Thank you for bringing it here."

"Are you sure? Can't you save her? Warm her body? Bring her back to life?" Harriet asked.

"No, look for yourselves; I can't perform miracles," the nun said as she held the limp child out to them. "'Tis God's will."

"What? God wills that a mother drown her child and kill herself?" Harriet asked incredulously. "If that's true, your God is cruel."

The nun looked contemptuously at Harriet. She began to close the door, but Percy put his foot in the doorway. "What will you do with the child?"

"We'll bury it along with the others. That's the fifth one this week. We have a special place for all the discarded, unbaptized babies, who cannot be buried on sacred ground and who remain in Limbo and cannot see God's good face. It's unfortunate, but it's as God wills it," she repeated, as she asked Percy to remove his foot from the doorway, and then she shut the door.

They walked home in shocked silence, but later, Eliza condemned the drowned woman for her selfishness. Harriet defended her because she was sure that the woman felt hopeless, and that God had nothing to do with orchestrating her death; yet she silently agreed that the woman had committed a grave error in killing her child. She might have merely ended her own life and given the child to someone who would care for it, for many women, like Sarah in the Bible, suffered from a barren womb. All night, she thought about the dead woman, the child's sweet face, and the nun's heartless remark. Her God is not mine, Harriet thought, for no good God would perform such cruelty. Percy believes in the perfectibility of humanity. But how is perfectibility possible when such evil exists?

Harriet attempted to put herself in the woman's shoes. Did the woman's husband betray her with another? Leave her while she was pregnant? Was she unmarried and thus considered by her society to be a grave sinner? Had her family ostracized and condemned her? Was she penniless? Did she have no one to care for her?

6 March 1812

Harriet had been badgering Percy to help the unfortunate, especially children, so he asked Devin to stay with them on Sackville Street, but Devin refused the offer, saying that he was fine squatting in the house where Percy met him. Besides, he thought that, if his mother were released from Kilmainham, she wouldn't know where to find him.

Percy told Harriet that Devin had declined the offer.

"He needs someone to care for him in his mother's stead, Percy."

"I understand, love, but I can't force him to stay with us," Percy said as he shuffled through a pile of papers on the table.

"You could entice him by telling him that we eat a substantive dinner each evening. I'm sure he remains hungry," Harriet said as she handed Percy some soda bread.

"I doubt that would mean much to him; I provide him with food every day."

Harriet frowned. "I didn't know that. Why didn't you tell me?"

"It slipped my mind. You know that I've been working on my *Declarations of Rights*. I can't always remember to tell you everything I do. But be assured that Devin and his generation are frequently on my mind and inspire much of what I write. Listen to what I've written," he said as he found and picked up his recent writing.

"Wait," Harriet said. "I hope that you'll tell me what you're doing to help Devin and others. I have the right to know. After all, we must work together to achieve the goals we share."

"I shall try to do so from now on, my love. Now, please listen to what I've written, which will help effect broader change than feeding one boy. This writing will help feed many." He lifted a paper and read, "'No man has a right to monopolise more than he can enjoy; what the rich give to the poor, whilst millions are starving, is not a perfect favor, but an imperfect right. No man has a right to be respected for any other possessions, but those of virtue and talents. Titles are tinsel, power a corruption, glory a bubble, and excessive wealth, a libel on its possessor.' And, particularly for the Irish in general: 'Sobriety of body and mind is necessary to those who would be free, because without sobriety a high sense of philanthropy cannot actuate the heart, nor cool and determined courage, execute its dictates.'"

"Sometimes, you think too much," Harriet said. "Physical action is necessary to create change,"

"It is impossible to think too much. And physical action without adequate planning can lead to disaster."

He wanted the last word, but she knew that this argument would likely continue. She thought his quest Quixotic. Like Don Quixote, Percy tilts at many windmills but misses the mark.

Anne told Harriet about Margaret King and her lover. Harriet listened attentively but she didn't want to know about this woman, even though Anne said that Margaret was important to her own tale.

"Mrs. Shelley, Margaret King left her husband, Lord Mont Cashell, and eloped with the man that she genuinely loved."

"I understand. Perhaps that made her happy; did she have children?"

"I don't know. She never said." Anne knew the truth but thought it better not to tell the young lass that women sometimes abandon their children. Besides, Anne believed that Harriet, like other English women, enjoyed romantic tales.

Harriet grew frustrated with Anne's storytelling and her avoidance of her own rebel story.

Anne Devlin

I told Mrs. Shelley a romantic tale of love between Margaret King and George Tighe because, when I asked her what she reads, she tells me that she reads such tales, like Mrs. Radcliffe's *The Mysteries of Udolpho*. I haven't read it, but I've heard that such novels portray venomous villains and imprisoned women who are tortured in dungeons and castles. Why would anyone wish to read such horrifying tales? Isn't the world bad enough without reading about and dwelling on evil?

I did tell her that Margaret King was important to my own story, but I didn't tell her why or to what extent. The truth was that Margaret King ushered me into rebellion.

A friend of the Wingfield family, Margaret King who became Lady Mont Cashell, was an Irish republican, but also a member of the governing Protestant Ascendency. Lady Mont Cashell attended several grand events that the Wingfields hosted and at which I served. Unlike the other Protestant women who attended these events, she dressed soberly and did not seek vain attention, for she followed the instruction of her former governess, Mary Wollstonecraft.

One day the Wingfields held a fox hunt and Lady Mont Cashell, like some of the other ladies, rode with the men. The youngest Wingfield boy, Ralph, was participating in his first hunt and when the guests were returning to the house, young Ralph was thrown from his horse when another horse kicked his horse. Lady Mont Cashell rushed into the kitchen with Lord Wingfield who was toting his son. The boy's lower leg was broken, and the bone protruded from his flesh. Young Ralph cried so hard that he shuddered as he screamed for his mam.

My stomach turned as I looked at his leg, but I had no time to be sick because Lady Mont Cashell ordered me to go into the garden and fetch some willow's bark and devil's claw and to quickly grind it. I knew from my mam that these herbs were used to subdue pain, so I did as I was told, and Lady Mont Cashell quickly administered the concoction mixed with whiskey to Ralph. His screams eventually turned to whimpers and then he grew quiet. Clearly, Lady Mont Cashell knew the healing arts. All the while she patted his head, telling him he would be grand. She would take care of him. She called him love and my pet. She asked Lord Wingfield to leave. At first the nobleman refused but with reassurance that all would be well with Lady Mont Cashell caring for the boy, he left. Then she pulled a green silk scarf from her bosom and wiped Ralph's tears. The scarf was like the one that Father Finn tied around Sam's neck. United Irishmen wore these scarves! I nearly blurted out my knowledge of what the scarf signified but Lady Mont Cashell raised her eyebrows and looked at me as if to say, I know that you know the meaning but now is not the time to discuss it.

While she continued to tend to Ralph, I wondered why a wealthy Protestant lady would own such a scarf. Surely, she wasn't aligned with the secret society. If she was, didn't she put herself at risk with those who may wish to turn her in to Castle authorities?

Once Ralph's long leg bone was realigned and his wound cleaned and dressed, she wiped Ralph's face once more and then she returned the scarf to her bosom. I now knew that Ireland contained some powerful Protestant women who perhaps loved Ireland as much as I did. I told myself that I would be bold and speak with Lady Mont Cashell at some point and learn her story.

I didn't see her again until a long weekend that my employers hosted. While I was cleaning up after afternoon cocktails, I overheard some of the rich folk talking about and disparaging the rebels who were hiding nearby. They were worried about an impending attack on their estates.

The men swirled the whiskey in their glasses and one of them said, "Those Fenian devils are animals; they're not fit to live."

"We ought to firebomb their caves," another man said.

My hands trembled and my heart ached because they were talking about men that I knew, including my courageous cousins. I wished to rush to my cousins and inform them of the plan.

Lady Mont Cashell was in the group and when she heard the gentleman speak of violence and murder, she grew pale and walked away with her friend Lady Moira. They retreated to an adjoining parlor and closed the door. However, they had neglected to close the side door, so I ambled over and stood by it, while picking up crystal that guests had placed on a table near there. I kept my head down as if I were minding my own business.

"We must move some of the rebels into a safe house," Lady Mont Cashell said. "Moore House is a perfect place, for our cellars are deep and no one would suspect that I would harbor fugitive rebels. My husband is currently in London so the men will be safe from those who would do them harm. Then we can help them move to another safe haven."

At that point, I knew that I needed to contact my cousins to let them know that Lady Mont Cashell was their friend. She was a United Irishwoman, a Protestant woman who sought Irish independence from England, a Protestant woman who did more than tolerate Catholics and dissenters. She was our friend and our collaborator. I later learned that Lady Mont Cashell had lived near the Emmets in St. Stephen's Green and knew Robert's sister, Mary Anne, a pamphleteer, and rebel, and was a friend of John Philpot Curran. Clearly, the former Margaret King was deeply aligned with the rebel cause.

7 March 1812

Percy finally secured an audience with Dr. Curran. After Godwin wrote to him to encourage him to meet with Percy, Curran sent him a message inviting Percy to dine with him.

Percy was escorted into the dining room. Curran graciously told him that he and Godwin had long known one another and, if Percy was Godwin's friend, then they certainly were comrades. Percy was much encouraged by this and after they had finished their dinner, where Percy declined the rack of lamb, saying that he ate no animal flesh, they retreated to Curran's study.

Curran rang a bell, and a young woman entered the room. "O'Byrne, we'll take our coffee in here."

Harriet had mentioned a man named Kevin O'Byrne in reference to meeting a young woman who was married to an 1803 rebel.

"O'Byrne? Do you know someone named Kevin O'Byrne?" Percy asked the woman.

The maid turned crimson. "He was my husband. He's dead."

"Did he work with Robert Emmet?"

"Mr. Shelley, we don't mention that name in this house," Curran said. "He caused much trouble and sorrow for me and my family and for this woman here. He's an anathema to me. And I hate to say it, but you remind me of him."

"Although I admire him, I am not like him. Dr. Curran, I aim for a non-violent, patient uprising, not like Emmet's. I am a committed pacifist," Shelley said as he clenched his fists.

"Please do not mention his name again. You misunderstand that man," Curran said solemnly. "He was as young and idealistic as you. He did not advocate outright violence either. But his poorly planned plot threatened my family. His ignorance and cowardice ruined my daughter's health and life. I will not speak of him any longer or of your proposals. If you wish to speak about other topics, I shall engage with you, but otherwise, we have nothing further to say to each other."

Percy didn't know what to say, for his entire aim in meeting Curran was to discuss plans to help free Ireland.

"I regret that I've taken so much of your time, Dr. Curran. I wish you a good evening. If you change your mind, here is my card."

"I possess a pile of your cards, Mr. Shelley. There's no need for another. O'Byrne, please escort Mr. Shelley to the door."

At the door, Shelley said, "I'd like to talk with you about your husband."

"Whatever for?" Mrs. O'Byrne asked.

"He was a brave man. I want to know more about the 1803 rebels. Emmet and his friends."

"No, sir, he was a fool who sailed on a ship of fools commanded by Robert Emmet. Kevin ruined our lives. I have nothing to say about him."

After Percy left, Curran asked O'Byrne to throw Percy's calling cards in the fire. As she did so, she pocketed one in her apron.

As Percy walked back to Sackville Street, he reflected on Curran's change of heart, which reminded him of Southey's. Both men had been idealistic when young and now had abandoned their youthful ideals. It was exceedingly disappointing to see what some people become as they age. Percy vowed again to never abandon his ideals but to foster them and bring them to fruition. Still, he fretted that if he couldn't get one of the apologists of the United Irishmen to align himself with his cause, he feared that he would make no real headway in Ireland. And he wondered if he could learn more about Kevin O'Byrne, who may have been a fool to some, but even Jesus was considered a wise fool, at least according to Erasmus.

8 March 1812

Harriet heard a gentle knock at the door. She opened it to find Devin O'Donnell on the steps with cap in hand. He asked for Mr. Shelley.

Although she had never met the lad, Percy had described him accurately as a tall, lanky boy with sandy hair and freckles.

"Are you Devin O'Donnell?"

He nodded.

"My husband has told me of you. He's not in but you are welcome to wait for him. We're about to take tea."

"No, Mrs., thank you kindly," he said as he turned to leave.

Harriet insisted, saying they had plenty to share. He hesitantly came in, and Harriet escorted him to the table. He sat with Eliza and Harriet and gobbled up the tea cakes. He seemed ravenous. Harriet asked about his mother's welfare, and he had little to say. Then he appeared quite sleepy, and Harriet noticed he was shivering.

She asked Eliza to stoke the fire, and she said that it was a bit early.

"The boy is tired and cold; we should warm him up," Harriet said.

Eliza reluctantly agreed and as the fire roared, Devin's head nodded. Harriet led him over to the settee, laid him on it, and covered him with a counterpane.

"You're too soft-hearted," Eliza said.

"And you're too hard-hearted."

Eliza appeared miffed. She took her book and retreated to her room.

Harriet sat by Devin, watching him breathe softly.

Feeling content that Devin was nearby, Harriet went to bed and quickly fell asleep. She felt someone gently awaken her.

"Love, I have news," Percy said.

Harriet tried to focus her eyes. "Can it wait until morning?"

"I think you'd like to know now. I met Curran. The woman you told me of, Kevin O'Byrne's wife, works for Curran. I tried to ask her to tell me about him, but she refused to speak about him."

"Are you sure? I'm confused. I wasn't aware that I visited Curran's home." Harriet sat up and was fully awake now. "What else did she say?" Harriet said as she rubbed her eyes.

"Sadly, she said that he and Emmet were fools." Percy laid his head on the pillow. Before long, Harriet heard soft snoring.

Harriet wondered if she should try to speak again with Mrs. O'Byrne? Would joining the Society of United Irishwomen help her secure the girls and prove that she was Irish at heart? Harriet tossed and turned. She got up, lit a candle, looked in on Devin, and adjusted the counterpane around him. He stretched and then relaxed. He seemed content. She then returned to her room, blew out the candle, and waited for dawn.

When sunlight fell on the floor, she stepped into the parlor to check on Devin. He had disappeared as if he had never been there.

Anne Devlin

I didn't tell the lass that Margaret King had left her seven children when she ran off with her lover, for I fear that Mrs. Shelley would think less of her. Truth be told, the lass should know that, according to the law, children belong to their father and mothers have no right to them.

Although she has no experience with them, the lass seems fond of children. She even asked me about the welfare of children in the Foundling Hospital, but I said that I know little of it, even though one of my sisters ended up there.

After she left, I spent some time thinking about Lady Mont Cashell and her interest in saving rebel men. I decided to be bold and tell Lady Mont Cashell about my cousins. Of course, it turned out that she already knew of them and that they were in grave danger.

"Would you run a message to them?" she asked.

"Of course. I wish to help them. They are my kin and comrades."

She told me that it would be best for me to dress as a boy, in order to act as a courier, for that is what she did when she was a messenger; it would grant me liberty in moving about. No one questions a lad as he runs errands. From that time on, I wore a boy's breeches and cap as I ran messages for the United Irishmen and women. Before I began this work, I had to be initiated into of the Society of United Irishwomen, which was something I actively desired.

First, I learned the following from the United Irish Catechism: "What have you got in your hand?

A green bough.

Where did it first grow?

In America.

Where did it bud?

In France.

Where are you going to plant it?

In the Crown of Great Britain."

After that, Lady Mont Cashell administered the oath to me.

"This is a solemn pledge. Once you swear to God, there is no turning back," she said.

Of course, I knew that swearing an oath was a point of no return, for I was and am a God-fearing female. I didn't wish to be damned to hell's eternal flames.

Before I assented, she said, "Death may find you—the struggle may not succeed. It may be generations before Ireland is free from perfidious Albion. Are you still willing to take the oath?"

"Yes, of course. I do this for my generation and for those that follow and for my sisters and children in the struggle."

In her presence, I vowed:

> In the awful presence of God, I, Anne Devlin, do voluntarily declare, that I will persevere in endeavouring to form a sisterhood of affection among Irishwomen of every religious persuasion, and that I will also persevere to endeavour to obtain an equal, full, and adequate representation of all the people of Ireland. I do further declare, that neither hopes, fears, rewards, or punishments, shall ever induce me directly or indirectly, to inform on, or give evidence against, any member of this or similar societies for an act of expression of theirs, done or made collectively or individually in or out of this society, in pursuance of the spirit of this obligation.

I said all of this even though I believe that Protestants hold heretical beliefs but that did not prevent me from working with them toward liberation. After all, the Society had been founded by Protestant gentlemen from Belfast.

When I had finished taking the oath, Lady Mont Cashell tied a green silk scarf around my neck. I was now a member of a forbidden, secret society that wished to topple the illegal British government ruling Ireland.

From that time on I was fully committed to the Society and its aims. I took the oath before God for the love of Ireland, not for any love of man or woman, but for the love of all my fellow Irish women and men. And because my da feared revolution, I assumed he never knew that I, like my cousins, was a rebel, at least not until we met Robert Emmet.

9 March 1812

Harriet knocked on Dr. Curran's door. A light snow had fallen overnight and as she waited; she stamped her shoes on the steps. Her feet were like ice.

The butler opened the door and stared at Harriet. "If you're looking for O'Byrne, she's no longer here; she's been dismissed."

Harriet was bewildered. "Why? What did she do?"

"To put it simply, she lied about her family situation."

"Did Dr. Curran let her go?"

"How do you know of Dr. Curran?" The butler stepped back farther into the foyer.

"My husband visited with him and met Mrs. O'Byrne."

"Are you Mr. Shelley's wife? Dr. Curran wants nothing to do with him and I should not speak with you lest Dr. Curran overhears us," he said as he started to shut the door.

Harriet felt that it was unfair that Percy's maligned reputation hindered her practical work. "Wait, I am not like my husband. I have different objectives. Do you know where she's gone?"

"She didn't share her destination with me," he replied. "But she may have gone to her sister in the Liberties."

"Do you know the address? Or her sister's name?"

"I recall she said her name is Seona Fitzgerald. But I have no idea where she lives, and the Liberties is a warren of houses. You may have trouble finding her."

"I found Mrs. O'Byrne. I'll find her again. I know someone who lives in the Liberties. I shall inquire of her. Good day," Harriet said.

Walking home, she wondered if she was somewhat responsible for Mrs. O'Byrne losing her position. Harriet had never intended to create trouble for the woman; she had only wished to help.

Percy agreed to accompany Devin to see his mother at Kilmainham. As he approached the house on John's Lane, a constable was pulling Devin out through the door. Devin was in chains.

"What's this all about?" Percy demanded.

"This rapscallion has been stealing food from the greengrocers," the constable said. "He's going to gaol."

"How can that be? I provide him with food. I'm his friend. His guardian of sorts, not legally, of course."

"We have evidence, sir. Kindly stand aside."

"Please help me, Mr. Shelley. I'm innocent," Devin cried as the constable dragged him away.

"Where are you taking him?"

"Why to the place that all thieves go," the constable said. "Kilmainham. He will see the judge tomorrow, for our justice is swift."

Percy's heart fell as he recalled the image of Devin's mother being hauled into gaol.

Percy traveled to Kilmainham and asked to see Devin O'Donnell. The interior smelled strongly of urine, and Percy fetched his kerchief from his pocket and held it to his nose. He tried not to gag.

"Who are you?" the guard asked.

"I am his guardian," Percy said.

"His legal guardian?"

"No, not yet, but I will be soon. My wife and I are inquiring about the process." Percy held his breath and then exhaled.

"Unless you are his legal guardian, you are not allowed entrance."

Percy thought about writing a note but knew that Devin's reading was rudimentary. "Will you pass a message to him?"

The guard frowned and looked around. "I will see that he gets it."

"Tell him to be as courageous as the hero Cúchulainn and that Mr. Shelley will help him. I will not allow him to be prosecuted for a crime that he did not commit. After he is exonerated, I will adopt him."

The guard gave Percy a skeptical look but reiterated that he would deliver the message.

Catherine Nugent was waiting outside for Harriet when she arrived back at the flat. They climbed the steps, hung up their cloaks, and removed their gloves and bonnets. Harriet wondered where Eliza was, for she seldom went out.

Once they sat down, Harriet told Catherine that Mrs. O'Byrne had been dismissed from her post and that she wished to find her.

"She may not wish to be found," Catherine said softly.

"Why would that be?"

"Perhaps she'd like to try to start over, to begin again."

"Without her children?"

"She's already separated from her children; nothing is different in that regard now that she lost her position. If anything, she's worse off."

Catherine seemed to know quite a lot about Mrs. O'Byrne.

"Do you think that I interfered?" Harriet asked. "I feel somewhat responsible for Mrs. O'Byrne's dismissal; if I hadn't told the butler about the girls, Mrs. O'Byrne would still hold her position."

"You can't control what others do. I don't think you intended to interfere. I think you have a good heart, but your quest may not yield the results you wish for. It's a bit Quixotic. You wish to help the children, but what are your intentions regarding the mother? Do you still wish to bring the girls here?"

"Yes, I could provide them with a home. She can't take care of the girls."

"Have you finally told Mr. Shelley your intentions?"

Harriet looked directly at Catherine. "Not yet but I will soon. I promise."

Harriet asked Catherine to tell her more about the Society of United Irishwomen. Catherine explained the organization's history and objectives in detail.

"How can I become a member?" Harriet asked.

Catherine frowned. "Why would you wish to do so?"

"To prove that I am Irish."

"But you're not," she said. "You have noble intentions and great compassion for us, but you cannot become one of us, for you haven't lived the same experience as we have. Besides, one cannot become Irish or prove one is Irish. You're either born Irish or you're not."

Harriet felt humbled by Catherine's attitude and correction. Catherine was somewhat correct, for who ever heard of someone becoming British? Even so, Harriet wanted to find a way to join the Society.

Still, she wondered if she was brave enough to join a secret, forbidden society. And did she possess sufficient courage to confront evil and injustice?

Was she true kin to the Irish, to Anne Devlin? Was she as courageous as Anne?

Eliza walked in, removed and shook out her cloak.

"Eliza, we wondered where you were," Harriet said.

"Not to worry. I went to the market."

"I thought I saw you up near Merrion Square earlier when I was leaving work," Catherine said.

"No, I don't shop in that area. I stay on this side of the river."

"What did you buy?" Harriet asked.

"I saw nothing that was worth buying. Is there tea?" Eliza asked. "Or do I need to make it?"

Anne Devlin

Mrs. Shelley possesses a romantic heart, for she's constantly telling me that she's Irish, which is pure nonsense.

Being Irish is far from being romantic. In fact, it is dangerous, especially if you're a rebel.

My cousin Big Art visited our house late one night and said he was helping a young Protestant man, a member of the Society, who had a plan to finish Wolfe Tone's rebellion and bring down the illegal government at Dublin Castle. Did we know of any place where he could stay?

"Who is this man?" Da asked.

"His name is Robert Emmet. He's the brother of the exiled Thomas Addis Emmet; his brother intends to take Thomas's place. He recently met with Napoleon in France where the Society sent him as an emissary because he speaks French and many other languages. Napoleon has agreed to help us. The French will invade England to distract the British, while we storm Dublin Castle."

"Arthur, my lad, do you know how unsafe and irrational this plan is?" Da asked. "You know that the French failed us in ninety-eight."

"Of course, I do, uncle. But we have Napoleon's pledge to assist us, and I'm not afeared. I've been in danger most of my life. I can't stand by while the English and the Protestants deny us our rights and our land. I demand justice."

"Does your father approve?" Da asked.

"Yes, you know he does. Please, uncle, will you help us?"

Da hesitated but then said, "Alright, son, I tried to keep my family safe, but God must have had other plans for us. There's a house on Butterfield Lane that's empty. I know the owner who is a sympathizer. Your Mr. Emmet could reside there."

"Grand. One more thing—he needs to appear legitimate. He needs someone to take care of the house and the men who will live there. He needs a housekeeper."

Da looked toward me and said, "Anne will do it, Michael. She's already involved."

I felt my skin redden. "How'd you know, Da?"

"I'm not blind or deaf, lass. I know when you sneak out to dig up the dead, deliver messages and the like. I see you scurrying away wearing John's cap and breeches."

"Are you angry?"

"No, Anne, I'm proud that you have principles and a courageous soul. You're like your mam's kinfolk, the O'Byrnes."

"Thank you, Da. When and where can we meet this Mr. Emmet?"

"Now. He's right outside," Art said. "He's just been waiting for an introduction."

Robert Emmet looked young. We had been told that Emmet was twenty-five, but, to me, he looked like a fresh-faced lad, wet behind the ears. He was of average height and was dressed in gentlemen's clothes: white pantaloons, a black waistcoat, black boots, and a bicorn hat in the fashion of Napoleon. He was rather unremarkable, and I secretly wondered if this lad, who wasn't much older than me, could lead a revolution. I remembered reading that an American Revolutionary, Alexander Hamilton, was only twenty-one in 1776, but Hamilton wasn't the outright leader. Would the boyish Mr. Emmet evoke respect from his older Irish peers? How was he qualified to lead the United Irishmen?

"I am pleased to meet you, Mr. Devlin and Miss Devlin," he said as he tipped his hat.

"*Cead mile failtes*," I said.

Emmet gave me a quizzical look, and his face turned pink.

"A hundred thousand welcomes," Big Art translated

I was not impressed. Although we didn't speak Irish at home, all of us knew this traditional greeting and a few other common phrases. Our new leader spoke French but didn't know Irish. I thought perhaps he'd inspire the French but how would he inspire the revolutionaries if he knows no Irish?

Even though I was initially doubtful, I moved into the house that Mr. Emmet rented. Mr. Emmet began to call himself Mr. Ellis and posed as an importer. With my cousins' help, we quickly established a household. I was in charge of the meals and cleaning, but that was a ruse, for I was also still acting as a courier. One evening Mr. Emmet sent me into Dublin to rent space in a warehouse near St. Patrick's Cathedral. I continued to don my brother's clothes and tuck my hair up into my cap whenever I ran a message. When I wore this clothing, I was able to move about more freely than when I wore a dress and shawl. I liked the feeling and the freedom that accompanied me while I wore men's clothing. It made me feel powerful.

To rent the space, I was first to meet with a fellow rebel. I would know the person by exchanging hand signals. As I approached the designated meeting place, I spotted a fellow leaning against the cathedral, and I noticed a green scarf poking out from his turned-up collar. I lifted my right hand and drew it down the right side of my face. My comrade lifted his left hand and drew it down the left side of his face. Then we shook left hands, and I asked, "What do you know?"

"I know U—What do you know more?"

"I know N."

At that point, I knew that I had found the correct person.

When I returned, Mr. Emmet asked if I knew anyone who was expert at explosives and I said that my cousin, Kevin O'Byrne, was quite proficient. He had served with Tone and, fortunately, was not captured.

"Would you ask him to meet with me?"

"Of course, I will send him a message."

Soon after, Kevin came to the house, and they discussed Emmet's plans to create fuses for explosives that they would use to alert various groups around the city that the rebellion had begun.

Kevin regularly spent time at the house, where he was most welcome, for he and his wife Kathleen were members of the Society. Sometimes Kathleen, who was pregnant at the time, came to Butterfield Lane to help me with my duties as housekeeper and she brought along her toddler Michaela who enjoyed chasing the hens in the yard.

Two other men moved into the house—Russell and Hamilton. The men slept in the upstairs rooms, while I kept a room near the kitchen. Of course, there was no impropriety. I was not a lover of any of these men or anyone else. I remained chaste; I was not a "housekeeper" in the euphemistic sense.

I soon learned that, although he seemed a mere lad, Mr. Emmet was an inspiring leader and a poet. He read his poetry to us at night and shared his thoughts about our future government. I have one of his poems by heart that he said he wrote as a youngster:

> Brothers arise! Our country calls—
> Let us gain her rights or die:
> In her cause who nobly falls,
> Deck wreaths shall lit;

And freedom's genius o'er his bier
Shall place the wreath and drop a tear.

Long by England's power opprest,
Groaning long beneath her chain,
England's ill-used power detest;
Burst her yoke; your rights regain;
The standard raise to liberty—
Ireland, you shall be free!

Brothers, march, march on to glory—
In your country's cause unite:
Erin's sons, for freedom fight:
England's legions we defy
We swear to conquer or to die.

He sometimes talked about art as a way to bring about change. Mr. Emmet's poetry rang true for us, and we were moved to action. To me, that is the function of poetry. Mr. Emmet's poetry evoked the aims of the great Fianna Warriors. Like Mr. Emmet and Fianna, we all swore to conquer or die.

We often met at the home of Leonard McNally, a friend of Mr. Curran's and an avowed United Irishman. While there, Robert read us the beginning of the proclamation that he was writing: "This solemn declaration we now make. We war not against property . . . We war against English dominion . . . If we are to fall, we will fall where we fight for our country." Even though I believed and still do that the Roman Catholic Church is the true Church, I asked that he amend the Declaration by inserting that we war against no religious belief. He agreed as did my fellow comrades.

His words reminded me of Paine's opinion that an unjust government has no right to govern. Even though he was young and didn't appear to know our native language (I understood later that he spoke some Irish but didn't comprehend the accent), I began to believe in him as a righteous leader of men and women because he reached our hearts and minds. He inspired us and the men looked to him as their general, just like the men in America looked to George Washington to lead them in their revolution.

One night I asked him where he drew his inspiration from and how he had become a fine speaker. He told me about his life and schooling at Trinity College where he was a champion debater. And then he mentioned his parents' influence.

He said that his parents expected much from him because his mother had given birth to seventeen children, but only four survived and three of those that died were also named Robert after their father.

"Your poor mother's heart must have been shattered, until you survived."

"Indeed, my mother was finally able to love a son named Robert who did not die in infancy. I thrived. Because of this, I could not let her down. I vowed to make something of myself, especially after my older brother Christopher Temple, a great leader, died in his twenties. My father spoke frequently about the success of the American Revolution and how we needed to get the foot of England off our necks. He even harassed our own members of parliament before it was dissolved. Father was a thorn in the side of the parliamentarian Mr. Henry Grattan.

Through my father's influence, my brother Thomas joined the United Irishmen and worked with Wolfe Tone. Afterwards, Tom had to hide beneath our home so that the Redcoats would not find him. He tunneled his way out but, nevertheless, was eventually arrested and exiled. I followed in Tom's footsteps and joined the United Irishmen when I was at Trinity. While there, I refused to pledge my faith to George III, for I considered him an illegitimate head of the Irish nation and for this reason, I was expelled. Because of my expulsion, I could not further my education and become either a physician like my father or a barrister like my brothers. But I still desired to finish what Tone and my brother Tom started, so I took up revolution as my profession. And my dear father, who died last December, wished for me to fulfill his dreams of Irish liberation."

"So, you're leading a revolution to impress your mam and your brother and in memory of your da?" I asked.

"No, Anne," he said gravely, "I'm leading a revolution to save us all from English treachery. I suppose, if I succeed, I will impress my mother who deserves to be a free Irish woman. And perhaps my father in heaven and my living brother, who is not so easily impressed."

Robert Emmet seemed the perfect man to me. Capable, loyal to his family and cause, a man with a just, charitable, and stalwart Irish heart, even if he was a Protestant heretic.

10 March 1812

"How is your heretic husband? Is he still rabble rousing, trying to be another Robert Emmet?" Anne asked Harriet.

"I'm not sure what you mean, Mrs. Campbell." Harriet felt defensive regarding her husband. No matter what, she disliked hearing criticism of him. "Percy writes pamphlets to arouse the common person to seek liberty through peaceful means. He's not trying to be Robert Emmet."

"Robert desired to use peaceful means too, but it did not turn out as he planned. Your husband should be aware of the consequences of poor planning."

"That's why he wished to speak with you about Emmet. Would you tell me what he should know to prevent catastrophe?"

"He should be sure to align himself with those who can carry out the work without flaw."

"And who failed to carry out the work flawlessly?"

"I can't answer that," Anne said as she drew on her pipe.

"If you can't answer that, may I ask you about Kevin O'Byrne? I met his wife after I befriended her children who are now in the Foundling Hospital." Harriet felt relieved that she had finally brought up Kevin O'Byrne, whom she recalled was Anne's relative.

"What do you know about Kevin O'Byrne and his wife?" Anne seemed surprised. She frowned as she puffed on her pipe.

"I know that he died helping Emmet," Harriet said softly.

"You know more than you should."

"Perhaps so, but I wish to help his girls. Now, Mrs. O'Byrne has lost her position because of me. I need to find her. Do you know her sister, Seona Fitzgerald?"

Aoife walked over to us. "She lives two doors down, and is separated from her rebel husband, but I doubt that she'll help you. She never approved of Kevin or her sister."

"And why would she not approve of her sister?"

"Her sister had been one of us. That is, until Kevin was arrested and hanged," Anne said. "You'd best keep your own counsel and not interfere in Irish business. That's all I'll say on the matter. Now, let's return to the story I was telling you of Finn McCool. Where did I leave off?"

As Harriet listened, she was distracted. She wondered why Catherine hadn't told her that Mrs. O'Byrne had been a member of the Society. And she already knew the story of Finn. She wished that she could be like Finn and eat the salmon of wisdom.

The courtroom was overflowing with prisoners and their solicitors as well as the prisoners' families.

The judge took his seat and adjusted his wig and robe. "Let's get on with it. Who's the first miscreant I'm to rule on today?"

Percy felt great foreboding, for it appeared that the judge was already prejudicial against the accused.

Devin's was the first case. He looked pale and rather sheepish, and Percy tried to get his attention, but he stared at the floor as if by doing so he could crawl under the wood and disappear. Percy wished that he would hold his head high to demonstrate confidence and to enable Percy to cheer him on.

The prosecutor announced the charge of theft, and the judge asked, "How do you plead, boy?"

"Not guilty," Devin whispered.

"What? Speak up, boy."

"Not guilty, Your Worship."

The people in the courtroom erupted in laughter. Harriet nudged Percy; so, to stifle their laughter, he spoke up.

"I wish to speak on this young man's behalf, Your Honor," Percy said.

"And who might you be, sir?"

"I'm his friend, Your Honor. His guardian of sorts."

"You may proceed," the judge replied, as he adjusted his wig that had fallen forward on his face.

Percy told the judge that he was teaching Devin and that he was an honest young man. Everyone deserved the right to learn to read in order to learn about the world in which they live.

"Is the boy a papist?" the judge asked.

Percy didn't reply. He suspected he was but did not know with certainty.

The judge turned to Devin. "Are you a papist, boy?"

"What's a papist?"

"A filthy Catholic heretic who bows to the Bishop of Rome."

"What's a heretic?" Devin asked.

The audience bellowed in laughter.

"A denier of the true religion, the Church of England or, in this case, the Church of Ireland. You truly are an ignorant boy," the judge said, without acknowledging how ironic his statement was in light of the prohibition to formally educate Catholics.

"I suppose I am a papist, Your Worship," Devin said reluctantly.

Once more the audience chortled.

The judge turned his attention to Percy. "Are you not aware, sir, that the law forbids papists to attend school?"

"He was not attending school. I was merely teaching him to read. The young man endeavours to improve himself, Your Honor. It wasn't as if I was teaching him Philosophy or the Law."

The judge snickered. "Nevertheless, your attempt to teach the child is still an infraction, but I will overlook your ignorance, since, based on your accent and demeanor, you appear to be an outsider."

Before Percy could further defend Devin, the judge enquired about witnesses for the prosecution.

The prosecutor called two witnesses who testified that they had seen Devin in the act of stealing. "I seen him grab a handful of potatoes, Your Honor. He stuffed them in his jacket pocket." Another claimed that Devin purloined a couple of apples. And a third announced that they saw him steal a loaf of bread from a house on John's Lane.

That was enough for the judge. He was eager to move on, so he pronounced Devin guilty.

Once more, Percy was about to speak but a woman was dragged into court. She cried out when she saw Devin.

The judge called for silence. "Order. We'll have no outbursts here," he said as he banged his gavel. "Who is this woman?"

"Why she's the boy's mother," Harriet said.

"And who are you, madam?"

"I'm also his guardian," Harriet replied.

The judge turned toward the prosecutor. "Why is she here?"

"Do you mean the guardian or the prisoner, Your Honor?" the prosecutor asked.

"Are you a dunce, man? The prisoner. I have no use for this guardian whomever she is."

The prosecutor looked embarrassed. "The prisoner is here to be sentenced, Your Honor."

"So, this is a family of criminals, is it? What's the charge against her?"

"She stole a loaf, first offence, Your Honor," the prosecutor replied.

"Hmmph, a family of thieves then. Well, I could sentence her to hang, but, since this is a first offence, I deem that she'd prefer the wilds of Australia."

Devin's face fell as his mother cried out.

The judge ignored the reaction. "Now, as for the boy, I could hang him, but I feel generous today. Boy, instead of three years of hard labor, I'll give you the option of joining the military. They won't teach you to read, but they will transform you into a proper British subject, not allow you to continue to be the scalawag that you are."

"Can't I go with my mam?"

"You wish to be exiled, to be transported?"

"I wish to be with my mam."

"No, if you had wanted to be with her, you and she shouldn't have become common thieves."

"We were hungry, Your Worship," his mother yelled.

Again, the audience laughed at their ignorance, for the boy and his mother didn't know the proper way to address the judge.

"That's no excuse. Which is it, boy?"

Devin hesitated but then looked at his mother in her rags and she shook her head, as she wept.

"You give me no choice, Your Worship. I will join the army, at least I won't go hungry."

"Then, put your X on the papers handed to you."

"I know how to sign me name, Your Worship," Devin said as a clerk handed him a sheet of paper.

Percy recognized the irony of the moment in that he had taught him to sign his name but now his signature relegated him to become a soldier in King George's army.

"I object. The boy is a child," Harriet blurted out.

"If he's old enough to work, he's old enough to be a soldier," the judge replied.

"But, Your Honor, the boy is innocent. We can prove it. And we know important people. My husband's father is a baronet, Your Honor, and a Member of the British Parliament."

"What's his name?"

"Sir Timothy Shelley."

"And your husband's?"

Percy looked at Harriet. "My name is Mr. Percy Bysshe Shelley."

"The court has heard of you, Mr. Shelley, son of an MP. If I were you, I would refrain from interceding in Irish affairs and your wife should do the same," he said as he beat his gavel. "If you speak up again out of order, I shall hold you in contempt. Next case."

Percy tried to get Devin's attention, but he didn't look up as he signed the paper and then was escorted from the courtroom. His heart stung for the boy who had lost his mother and now had lost his homeland. Harriet wept, for they had failed to save Devin and now he would become a British soldier, which was more than ironic, given his birth and upbringing.

Percy thought, This is how justice is dealt with among the poor and the hungry. This is what the powerful do to the disenfranchised and those who speak out against injustice. No matter how hard I try, I fail to engender the justice and equality that I seek. Perhaps my quest is Quixotic.

Six

Dreams of Failure

12 March 1812

Harriet and Percy's failure to aid Devin weighed heavily on them. The next morning at breakfast, Eliza scolded them. She told them they had been foolish to try to intervene in the life of the young boy.

"What were you thinking? You haven't the resources to care for a child. You're always scrambling for money and borrowing from Peter to pay Paul. And what court would allow you two to parent a child not much younger than you?"

Percy scoffed. "Resources may be tight now, but I will eventually inherit my grandfather's estate of £6000. That will more than adequately provide the means to care for a child or two or even three as well as help us establish our utopian community."

Harriet thought once more of the O'Byrne girls. She was desperate to get them to safety. If she succeeded in getting them released, she and Percy would indeed have two children to care for. She would be a mother, and Percy would be a father. Of course, she would need to discuss this with Percy, but even though she promised Catherine that she would speak with him soon about her plan, she thought she'd wait until she saved the girls.

Percy shifted the conversation. "Perhaps it's time to move on to Wales to start our communal project. I am making no headway here. I feel that I've failed in this Irish project."

"Yes, you have failed, but now you are making sense," Eliza agreed. "Ireland was never right for us. You might return us to England, reconcile with your father and the university, and perhaps enter parliament as your father wishes."

"I will never do that. We will go to Wales as planned, where my cousin owns an estate, Cwm Elan; we will stay with him until we find our own haven."

Harriet didn't like the way the conversation was going. She wished to remain in Ireland, her true home. She needed to squash this plan. "Percy, perhaps you just need more time. Don't despair and give up too soon. Your cause is noble, for, as you've said, you wish to complete Emmet's work, who desired to complete Wolfe Tone's rebellion. Besides, didn't we agree that Ireland is our home now?"

Harriet noticed that Eliza frowned.

"You're right, my love," Percy said. "I shouldn't act hastily and move on too quickly. There is still work to be done here and this country feels more like home that England ever was. I shouldn't despair. There must be some way to continue with my quest, our quest, that is."

Harriet was relieved that his tilting at windmills permitted her to remain in Ireland.

That night Harriet dreamt that the girls were gravely ill and that both of them were buried alive. She had failed to rescue them. When she woke, she told herself that it was just a dream that would compel her to complete her plan. She would prove she was Irish at heart.

Anne Devlin

I continue to fear that Mrs. Shelley has romantic notions of what it means to be Irish. In truth, it's not romantic in the least. It's perhaps a curse to have been born here, even though we live on this green isle full of saints and scholars.

Even though he was a Protestant, Robert Emmet seemed one of those saints. And, he was indeed a scholar, who had studied history and previous rebellions and their failures. Still, his study and plan needed to be questioned, and I did so whenever I could. I attended each rebel meeting. At one meeting, I spoke up when we discussed French intervention.

"Why should we trust the French? They failed us in ninety-eight. My cousins told me how they vowed to help Wolfe Tone, but never arrived."

Kevin O'Byrne agreed with me. *"In ainm Dé."*

Emmet looked puzzled so I translated. "In God's name."

Kevin seemed startled that Emmet didn't understand this common Irish phrase. "Thank you, Anne. In God's name, I personally witnessed the Frenchies' fickleness and do not trust them."

Robert raised his eyebrows and paused. "I understand your concern, Anne and Kevin, but I personally spoke with Charles Talleyrand, Napoleon's Foreign Minister and diplomat, and he assures me that French forces will invade at the moment of our rebellion and thus distract the British."

Robert insisted that we had nothing to worry about. The French were on our side. They would not let us down; they would not abandon us again. And they would not occupy us as the English had. French intervention would lead to true sovereignty. We must trust their good intentions.

I looked at Kevin, who said nothing. I still felt that we were correct. The French had always proven themselves cowards, unless they were acting on their own behalf. I hoped that I was wrong, but that night I dreamt that a French fleet sailed into Kingston and Kinsale and was sunk just like the Spanish Armada had been near Galway. I didn't tell anyone about my dream because I didn't believe at the time that dreams foretell the future. I later realized that I should have spoken up; I should have trusted myself and been a Cassandra. My dream prophesied doom.

After I cleaned up each evening, Robert and I often sat in the small garden behind the house. We gazed at the big sky with its field of faraway stars; they looked like halcyon lights giving us a glimpse of another, a better world. But for now, I asked about our world and what Erin would be like once we were free. How would rights be restored?

"As I've argued, drunkenness, hunger, and ignorance will vanish once we oversee our own country. Men and women will act rationally and with good consciences. And, of course, we will once again have our own parliament; we will elect members and build coalitions to choose a Prime Minister, a Chieftain."

"A Taoiseach? Will that be you, sir, since you are leading the rebellion?"

"I will serve if the people choose me. And please call me Robert. There is no formality or class distinction among colleagues."

I hesitated, for I had been raised in a strict tradition regarding social class but then said, "I think that you will make a noble chieftain, Robert." I had come to understand that his leadership was essential if we were to succeed as a free nation but wondered how women might also serve. "Do you ever think that a woman could serve in the parliament or as our chieftain?"

"I don't see why not. You recall Queen Maeve, don't you? So, there's a tradition to draw on. Are you an advocate for women's rights?"

I was pleased to learn that, even though he didn't know all Irish vocabulary and phrases and its various accents, he knew our ancient history when a woman ruled. "Of course. I believe that women can do whatever men can do, and I know in my heart that we are just as patriotic and loving of our country as men are." I told him that I had read Thomas Paine, but I was disappointed that Paine did not say anything about the rights of my sex.

"Hold on," Robert said. He went into the house and returned with a book in hand. "Read this." The book's title was *A Vindication of the Rights of Woman*, by Mary Wollstonecraft. It was written by the woman who helped Margaret King become a rebel.

I thanked him and told him of my meeting with Margaret King, her relation to her governess and mentor, Miss Wollstonecraft, and how Margaret herself swore me into the United Irishwomen, a fact that pleased him very much. That evening, I read and took to heart the entirety of Miss Wollstonecraft's treatise about the rights of women to be educated and to be treated as full human beings. She had expertly articulated my thoughts and desires.

I continued to run messages for Robert. Most of the messages were about securing arms but one day he asked me to take a message to John Philpot Curran's country house, the Priory. "Are you going to solicit his help?" I asked eagerly.

"No, the message is not for him," Robert said. "The message is for his daughter Sarah. It's important that she alone receives the message. Do you understand?"

"Of course," I replied, as he handed me a thin envelope. I noticed before I tucked my hair into my cap that the envelope was not properly sealed.

Even though they say that curiosity killed the cat, I wished to know why Robert was writing to Sarah Curran. I wondered if she was a co-conspirator, a fellow United Irishwoman. I was eager to be in contact with more of my women comrades. So, when I reached the woods, even though I knew it was wrong to read his private message, I sat down, removed the letter from my cap, and carefully opened the envelope. As I unfolded it, I was astonished to see rose petals and Deora Dé fall onto the ground.

The letter began, "My darling Sarah, I can't get you out of my mind. I have never had time for love before and likely do not now, but your image appears whenever I close my eyes . . . I dream of you and us . . . I wish to help you flee from your father who, as you said, does not cherish you. Please meet me tomorrow at half five at our rendezvous spot."

So, this is what he was planning. He was planning a tryst with a girl. He was love struck. I had never known love, but I knew that Cupid's arrow can cause a type of madness that can lead to catastrophe.

I was shocked, disappointed, and worried. Instead of mooning over a girl, instead of planning to free a young girl, he should be focusing his mind on liberating Ireland.

Sarah Curran was not at all as I imagined her. If she was his great love, she should have been as serious and impressive as him. She seemed frivolous with her ringlets and her bosom pushed up in her dress for everyone to gawk at. She was exactly like the pretty human doll used for male amusement, a coquette, that Mary Wollstonecraft denounced. Miss Curran was singing to herself when her sister Amelia escorted me into their room. Amelia appeared much more sober than her sister, and during our short conversation, she sat by the window sketching the hills behind their home. Amelia told me that if I had a message from Mr. Emmet, I must be careful, for their father did not care for Mr. Emmet and his politics.

"Oh, you've a missive from Robert. I'm so pleased," Sarah said. "What does it say?"

I didn't confess to reading the letter but merely handed it to her and she read silently, giggling as she read it.

"Do you wish to reply?"

"Tell him that I will see him at the appointed time. Tell him that I am his if he wants me. That is all," and she brushed me away like I was an annoying gnat.

After I took my vow as a United Irishwoman, I was willing to die for Erin just as the men were. But now, I was running messages, not to fellow patriots, but to a vain and silly child. I worried that Robert was distracted by a ringleted pretty thing unworthy of his attention, the exact opposite of what Wollstonecraft envisioned for what a woman ought to be. I hoped that Miss Sarah Curran would not be his undoing.

When I returned from my errand, Robert was eager to speak with me. He took me to the garden and sat with me on the bench.

"Were you able to deliver my letter, did she reply?" His brow was furrowed with worry.

"Indeed, sir. She told me to tell you that she's yours. She will meet you as you instructed."

He sighed and seemed relieved.

I piped up. "She's awfully young, sir, and not what I expected."

"What did you expect?"

"Someone as serious and dedicated as you are."

"Looks often belie what's in the heart. And her heart has been ravaged by her father," he said quietly.

"How so?"

"He has neglected Sarah and her sister ever since their mother ran off with their minister and made Mr. Curran a cuckhold."

I was astonished to learn this, but only said, "Oh, I see. That is unfortunate. How sad for her and her family."

"That's not all. Her father blames Sarah for her sister Gertrude's death," he said. "Gertrude fell from a window and broke her neck, but Sarah had nothing to do with Gertrude's accident. Sarah is a broken young woman, but she is a woman of many talents; I have known her all my life. I worship her."

I paused and felt odd to question his feelings. "Is it wise to give your heart at this time, with so much at stake?"

"I can't help it. One can't control what one's heart feels. Have you ever been in love?"

I shook my head no. "I only love my country."

"Well, someday you will feel great love of another human, and then you'll understand that it's impossible to tell the heart what to do," he said as he squeezed my hand. "Once the revolution is over, Sarah will be my bride. And if I fail, at least I will have loved someone in particular, not just my country."

I had grave misgivings but didn't say more. I hoped that Sarah Curran would prove herself worthy. And I was stunned that he spoke of the possibility of failure. I was sorely disappointed with Robert's choice as a mate. I was more suitable but clearly he saw me as a colleague, a fellow rebel, and not a woman at all.

13 March 1812

The ginger-haired woman who answered the door seemed a replica of Mrs. O'Byrne.

"What do you want? You're not one of those church ladies, are you? If you are, I haven't time for you," the woman said as a horde of children swirled around and tugged at her skirts.

Harriet was taken aback by the brusqueness of the woman's demeanor, which was nothing like the welcome she expected of Irish people.

"No, I'm looking for your sister."

"Which one?"

"Kathleen."

"Is she in hot water? What trouble has she caused now?"

"No, no, she's caused no trouble. I wish to assist her in fetching her children from the Foundling Hospital and I will help her find a new job." Harriet thought Catherine could possibly help Mrs. O'Byrne obtain a seamstress position.

"She lost her job? That's news to me. I haven't seen her in weeks. Ever since her brats got themselves carted to the Foundling Hospital."

Harriet felt dismayed with the woman's attitude. The girls were not brats. They were sweet children.

"Do you know where I might look for her? Does she have friends nearby? Is there anyone she'd seek for assistance besides you?"

"And why should I tell you? I don't know you from Adam."

"I was responsible for her losing her job."

"Typical British bleeding heart you are," the woman replied. "Well, you might try asking Anne Devlin, who lives close by. She and me sister were once fast friends."

Was Anne hiding Mrs. O'Byrne? Harriet thought. If so, why didn't she tell me? Why did both Catherine and Anne keep information about Mrs. O'Byrne from me?

Anne Devlin

While I acted as a courier, the men secured weapons and stored them at the depot that I had rented across from St. Patrick's. When Robert wasn't daydreaming about and pining for Sarah Curran, he was busy engineering small rockets with fuses, which he planned to use to alert his fellow rebels. Kevin O'Byrne helped him with those rockets, for that was his role in our rising. He often tested new techniques and enjoyed doing so.

One evening, Kevin was experimenting with new fuses and one of the rockets accidentally blew up in his hand. I heard him scream, "Jaysus! What the hell." I came running and found Kevin on the ground with his right hand hanging by some tendons and skin. There was blood everywhere and I quickly realized that I needed to stop the bleeding. I lifted my skirt and tore the bottom of my petticoat to create a tourniquet and then tied it around Kevin's forearm. Even though he was severely injured, he tried to calm himself.

"Find Russell," he said, wincing. "He's medically trained. He needs to sew my hand on."

At that point, Robert rode up on his horse.

He jumped off the horse. "Anne, help me get Kevin in the house. Kevin, I'm going to hoist you up. Can you stand?"

Kevin cringed. "Yes, I'll be grand. I can walk on my own."

He stood and gathered his dangling right hand in his left and walked slowly into the house.

Once inside, we laid him on the table and Robert looked at the wound. "Kevin, my father was a doctor. I watched his surgeries. This cannot be repaired. The hand needs to be removed."

"Jaysus, no, I'll never be able to work. Kathleen will murder me. We're about to have another bairn. I need to work."

"I'm sorry, Kevin. Look for yourself," Robert said soberly. He held Kevin's right hand up. It had already turned alabaster. Nerves and sinews dangled from it. The nails had turned blue.

Russell walked in at the that moment and confirmed Robert's assessment. "It's got to be removed, and we need to close the wound soon or gangrene will set in. Anne, fetch me the largest knife in the kitchen."

I fetched the knife but, once I handed it to Russell, I had to leave the room. I heard my cousin scream in terror as he recited the only prayer he knew, "Christ almighty, save me." He said this repeatedly until he passed out.

Later that day, I rode to Kathleen and Kevin's home. When she answered the door, she said, "What foolishness has Kevin done now?"

I told her, and she fainted. Later that night she went into labor and delivered a stillbirth.

The date for the uprising was set as 23 July 1803. It had been moved up because Robert was impatient and because he had heard from the French, who wished to wait until autumn for the uprising to occur. Just as I had predicted, the French failed us once more. They were not trustworthy. I hoped that Robert knew what he was doing and that, in the end, we wouldn't need the help of the false and fickle French.

As the day of the rising drew nearer, Robert sent daily messages to Sarah Curran. I couldn't help reading his messages to her, for I feared what might happen to him if he made plans that the others didn't know about. I wanted to ensure his safety, because he would likely continue to be our leader after the rising and, of course, he had a place in my heart. But I became a little disenchanted with him based on what I read in those letters to Miss Curran. Their love sounded like what my da called "puppy" love, not the love between a woman and man. Even so, I had to agree with him that we cannot control who one loves any more than we can control other feelings that arise from one's heart, such as resentment or jealousy, even if our Christian faith instructs us to do so.

Around this time, we had a major setback. There was an explosion at the depot where we hid weapons within the walls. Robert and Hamilton worried that authorities would investigate and would somehow learn of the planned uprising. One rebel was killed and another wounded. I was happy to hear that it wasn't Kevin's fault and that he was not further disabled. Luckily, Dublin Castle authorities did not investigate, and the arms stashed there were safe. Even so, I told Robert to be careful, especially with the messages that he sent to Sarah, for I had dreamt that she had betrayed him.

"Do not tell her when or where the rising will occur," I cautioned.

"You worry too much. I am careful," Robert said. "And dreams are just dreams. The sign of an anxious mind. They don't predict the future, just like the stars don't seal our fates."

Yet on July 22nd I was to relay a message that did spell out the rising's time and date and laid out a plan, if the rising failed. Robert told Sarah that they would flee to Cobh and then to America and that she should have her satchel packed and ready to go.

I was angry that he relayed the particulars of the plan, and that he felt the need to have an alternative. It was as if he knew that he'd fail. Because of this, I decided not to deliver this message. In my view, planning for failure was just as bad as failure itself.

Instead of delivering the letter as promised, I burned it and threw the ashes on the ground. I would not help him fail.

On the day of the Rising, I met with Robert early in the evening, and we said farewell until the morrow. I felt excited and sorrowful at the same time, for I wished for success, but I feared that our leader might be injured or killed. I also feared catastrophe. I recalled my Cassandra-like dream and hoped that it was only the result of an overwrought mind. Nevertheless, when I spoke, my voice quivered, even though I meant to bolster his courage.

"I wish that I could come along and walk beside you."

"No, Anne," Robert said, "it's best that you stay here and keep the men in the countryside advised."

"Are you sure?"

"Indeed I am."

Before I knew what I was doing, I touched his face. "God speed to you, Robert."

"And God keep you as well, dear Anne," he said as he removed my hand and kissed my palm. He bowed to me and then climbed onto his horse and galloped away. I watched as long as I could until he rode over the hill and then was lost to me.

The other men, Russell, Hamilton, and Kevin had left early to station themselves around Dublin as planned. Fellow rebels from Kildare and Wicklow were also waiting for the signal to enter the city. The rebels had secured ten depots filled with arms and ammunition around Dublin and they were ready to strike.

My da had brought my little sister Nellie to stay with me so that I wouldn't be alone while the men were leading the rebellion. I told Da that I didn't need her but still it was good to have company while I impatiently waited for word that all had gone well and that we now controlled Dublin Castle. Nellie distracted me by playing with her hoop in front of the house, and I sat on the porch and watched her until a misty dusk settled in. I knew that, if all went according to plan, Robert, Hamilton, and Russell, and Kevin would be sitting in the Privy Chamber by midnight.

It was twilight when Robert Emmet led the rising. I waited nervously for the word from my contacts that all went well, that the Union Jack had been lowered and the green Irish flag embroidered with a harp and the words Erin Go Brah, (Ireland Until Eternity), had been hoisted at Dublin Castle. Nellie had fallen asleep on the settee, so I sat in the parlor, and I tried to occupy my mind by imagining myself a soldier ready to dutifully follow Robert Emmet into battle.

I had retrieved my pike from the White Bull Tavern next to the depot where it had been hidden with all the other weapons. I heard the first signal; the church bell rang at half nine and I ventured onto Thomas Street. I heard rockets explode, alerting the other troops to enter the city. Then, I saw Robert, our chieftain, in the street gathering his troops. He looked dazzling in his white breeches, shiny black boots, and green waistcoat decorated with golden French lace and epaulets. The white shirt I had washed and ironed for him gleamed in the twilight. His bicorn hat with a plume sat atop his ebony locks. He looked to be the general that he was, not a love-sick boy who fancied a silly girl. After he boldly read his "Proclamation" to his soldiers, I fell in line along with hundreds of others, all carrying their pikes and blunderbusses, standing tall and moving forward like a grand army, an Irish army liberating itself, not an army taking the fall for our conquerors. Our general shouted, "Come along, men," as he shot his pistol into the air. "Turn out, my boys, now is our time for liberty."

We marched down Thomas Street while someone played a pipe, another a penny whistle, another a bodhran drum. People cheered us as if we were George Washington and his rebel comrades come to liberate us from perfidious Albion. People waved homemade republican flags that had been hidden for decades. As we marched down Patrick Street and then to Dame Street toward Dublin Castle, many more republicans left their houses and pubs and joined us, until we were a vast army that would easily enter the gates and take the Viceroy and the Privy Council hostage.

My heart swelled with pride as I walked. I was an Irish republican. I believed in the Rights of Man and Woman. I knew that our leader, Robert Emmet, did too and that when he was established as our Prime Minister, our Taoiseach, our chieftain, he would ensure that women would have equal rights, just as Mary Wollstonecraft had advocated.

I must have nodded off, for I recall that I dreamt that Robert Emmet had failed and that he stood on the gallows with a noose around his neck and then his face became my own. I woke up terrified. I screamed Robert's name and Nellie came rushing in. Just then, I heard the thunder of horse hooves, and the front door banged open. Robert and

          Kathleen Williams Renk

his deputies, Russell, and Hamilton, stood in front of me. Robert's green jacket was torn; the French lace hung by threads, and his plume was askew.

"Anne, all is lost," he said. "We must leave before the British arrive and arrest us."

"What have you done? A bad welcome to you. You cowards. Did you leave the innocents to get slaughtered?" I shouted. "Where's Kevin?"

"He was captured," Russell said.

Robert hung his head in shame; he turned away from me. "Don't blame me. It wasn't my fault that we failed."

My disappointment with Robert was profound. He had failed Erin and me. Before the rising, I had felt my heart flutter with love for him. I felt attached to him, but afterwards, he had been diminished in my view. He was not a true leader, for no one followed him. Even so, my heart felt bound to his, despite his love of the frivolous girl.

14 March 1812

"I found Seona Fitzgerald, but she directed me to you. She said you might know where Kathleen O'Byrne is," Harriet said. She felt odd asking Anne about the whereabouts of Mrs. O'Byrne who had sent her to Seona Fitzgerald in the first place.

Anne was smoking her pipe. She seemed undisturbed. "We haven't seen Kathleen O'Byrne in years. She never comes around here. She has deep animosity towards me now because of what happened to her husband."

"Did you have something to do with his death?" Harriet broached a subject that she knew was off limits, even though she had every intention of learning about the rebellion's details.

"You give me too much credit, Mrs. Shelley, and I never wished for Kevin to die. He was my relation, and he was devoted to the cause. I don't wish to speak about this further. I was telling you about Robert and Sarah Curran and their puppy dog love. I have more to say about that."

After Anne spent more time recounting Robert and Sarah's love affair, Harriet felt disappointed once more. She did not wish to hear about a love affair; her thoughts centered on Kathleen O'Byrne and how she must find a way to locate her. Surely, she didn't disappear when her children were still in Dublin. Harriet knew that Mrs. O'Byrne loved her daughters, for she had seen tears in the woman's eyes when she tried to hide her love.

Anne Devlin

Mrs. Shelley asks too many questions about my past. I don't wish to talk about my cousin Kevin and his wife, who used to be my friend and a stout member of the Sisterhood. She was angry initially because Kevin lost his hand, and she was sure that he would need to become a beggar to earn money. Then, once Kevin was executed, she blamed me for bringing him into Robert's inner circle. Losing her husband soured Kathleen O'Byrne, soured her toward me and all of the other rebels. Even so, in taking her own oath, she had to have realized that death might come calling at any time.

After the failed rebellion, Mr. Emmet felt sorry for himself and even sorrier for those he failed. We sat in the garden with the stars peering down on his confession, and he told me that he began the rising with eighty men and then another two hundred followed him, but many of them were drunk. The group spread out and he had no way to control those in the rear of the army. They used their blunderbusses to shoot out the gas lights along the streets. They were rowdy and ungovernable. By the time, they reached Patrick Street, his troops were diminished to around fifty men.

"Everything that could go wrong went wrong," he said. "The fuses for the rockets that Kevin had engineered were mixed up and none of the rockets were viable, so we had no way to alert the rebels waiting for our signal. One man, Quigley, was standing watch on Marshalsea Lane, and erroneously believed that British soldiers were aware of our rebellion and were on Queen's Bridge headed toward us. That caused some of the men to turn out too early. Our organization fell apart. Later, some drunken men dragged Lord Chief Justice Kilwarden and his nephew from their carriage and piked them to death. I tried to stop them, but I had no effect on subduing their violence; I could not control them. Anne, this was not supposed to have happened, and I shouted at them, for those ignorant men sacrificed one of our stalwart allies. It was then that I called the rising a failure and Hamilton, Russell, and I withdrew. Kevin continued on toward the Castle alone, like a madman, and we saw him dragged away by Yeomen. The rebellion lasted less than an hour. I'm sorry, Anne. Now that it's over, I don't know what to do other than for Sarah and me to escape the country. Meanwhile, we have to contact your cousins so that we can seek sanctuary."

I wasn't ready to forgive him, for he had errored in his planning and his predictions of failure had come true. "You failed us, you failed Erin. I thought you were a true leader, a man, not a boy. You promised no outright violence, no murder. I trusted you; I thought you had a steadfast soul. You have let all of us down."

"I know, but please, you must forgive me. I've written a message to your cousins but also one to Sarah. I beg you. I need you to intercede on my behalf. I need you to act as courier once more. Will you help me?"

I don't know why I complied, but I did. I remembered I was bound to him and our cause. At that point, I felt like it was my job to salvage what I could and that included Robert Emmet. And I would do what I could for my cousin, Kevin, even though I had no idea what that would entail.

Robert went into hiding, first in the mountains and then at Harold's Cross in Dublin, while he waited to execute his plan to escape with his love to America. I didn't want him to go but I did want him to be safe, so I continued to pass messages to Sarah Curran, even though my intuition told me otherwise.

Initially, I stayed behind at the house to warn others who might appear, like my cousins who didn't know of Robert's failure. Even though I was furious with him, I was glad that I had secured Robert's life, and I often traveled back and forth to Dublin to meet with him and sometimes he disguised himself and came to Butterfield Lane. I learned later that Sarah Curran had written to him to warn that the authorities were about to raid Butterfield Lane, but he never received the message her sister carried for her. Amelia turned back when a troop of soldiers blocked the bridge leading to the house. For that reason, I was subjected to a visit from the Yeomen and a magistrate on July 26th.

I was in the middle of burning the remaining papers that detailed the rising's plan, when I heard the door being battered and broken down and I saw four Yeomen, an officer, and a magistrate standing in the foyer.

"Where's Robert Emmet?" the magistrate asked.

"I don't know anyone named Robert Emmet, sir. I work for Mr. Ellis."

"And who are you?"

"Anne Devlin is *ainm dom*."

"What did she say?" the magistrate asked.

"She said her name is Anne Devlin," one of the yeomen replied.

"These Fenian types ought to speak English. Well, Anne Devlin, stop the playacting," the magistrate said. "We know that you know Mr. Emmet's whereabouts and that he calls himself Ellis. Now tell us where Emmet is."

One of the officers grabbed my arm. The officer in charge called me an awful name—a filthy c-nt—and my little sister Nellie cried as the men laughed and poked me with their bayonets.

"Stop hurting my sister. She's done nothing wrong."

Of course, Nellie was not aware of my involvement in the rising and even if she had known, she understood, even though she was a child, that freeing Ireland from English tyranny was not wrong but righteous.

"You'll soon tell us everything you know about the Mr. Emmet alias Ellis," the officer said, twisting my arm.

One of the men dragged me out of the house and then pushed me to the ground.

Now I stated what would be true from then on about my knowledge of Robert Emmet alias Ellis. "You may murder me, you villains, but not one word about Mr. Ellis will you ever get from me."

Clearly, the officers understood that I was referring to Mr. Emmet but I had briefly lost my head and then remembered that "Mr. Ellis" was not guilty of anything and I should not suggest that his actions needed to be protected.

The officer, who I later learned was Major Henry Sirr, the Dublin City Chief of Police, proceeded to tie a rope around my neck.

I was terrified; he intended to hang me. My prophetic dream flashed before my eyes; I felt my knees buckle and my heart flutter in fear. But I vowed to keep my oath, which I silently repeated to give me courage, remembering all the souls whose lives depended on me. Major Sirr then threw the end of the rope over his shoulder. He pulled on the rope, yanking me up. I felt my body being hoisted as the rope tightened.

"Lord Jesus, have mercy on my soul," I pleaded, for I believed that I was about to die.

"Lord Jesus won't have mercy or help you," Major Sirr said. He intended to sow doubt that anyone, including God's son, would save me.

I dangled from the rope and felt myself choking. Then he let me down and asked me again, "Where's Emmet? We know that you know everything, you miserable wench. That you helped hide him. We know that you called him a coward after his rebellion failed."

I coughed, trying to catch my breath. "I know nothing." I felt my heart in my throat. How had they learned my reaction to the failure? Obviously, there was a traitor within our group.

He hoisted me again and I heard Nellie screaming. "You'll kill her, stop hurting my sister." Those were the last words that I heard before I blacked out.

I woke up and found myself on the ground. I was confused and couldn't remember what had happened. I couldn't catch my breath. My neck was sore, and my skin was raw.

Nellie told me that Major Sirr had tried to hang me. "Why did he do that? You've done nothing wrong."

"Never mind, Nellie. They thought I was someone else. Don't worry, love."

I knew but didn't tell her that this half-hanging was a torture method the British used against the ninety-eight rebels. Nellie said that they repeated the hanging several times. She tried to stop them because she thought they would kill me. But they pushed her to the ground and called her filthy names too, which she didn't understand, for she had never heard such words. They finally gave up and left me on the ground. After regaining my ability to think cogently, I told Nellie to help me into the house.

Once indoors, I quickly changed into John's clothes and then ran into the barn. With Nellie in tow, I climbed onto my horse and rode away. Even though I ached all over and my neck had nearly been broken, I ignored my physical suffering, for I knew that I needed to hide. I returned Nellie to my da. I didn't tell him what had happened other than that the Yeomen had visited me. He saw that my neck was raw, and he told me that I should go into hiding. I then made my way to Dublin and concealed myself at our friends the O'Neills, where it was agreed that I would pose as their boy cousin. I knew where Emmet was, but I had managed to convey nothing. I had kept my vow for the first but not the last time. I only hoped that Robert had stayed put and had not gone to find Sarah Curran. I prayed that he was safe.

Seven

Worse than the Black Hole of Calcutta

18 March 1812
Anne Devlin

I've tried to spice up the story by telling Mrs. Shelley about Robert and Sarah Curran, because Mrs. Shelley seems rather akin to Sarah Curran despite her efforts to demonstrate that she's a serious grown woman. And she had mentioned that she and her heretic eloped to Edinburgh and were married by a dishonest minister who lied and said they had been living in Edinburgh for a sufficient amount of time before the marriage. They did not have to announce the Banns. I figured she would identify with Robert and Sarah's puppy dog love, since she and her heretic are rather callow.

Despite our efforts, Robert wasn't safe. I'd arranged for him to hide at a friend's home, Mrs. Palmer's, but he continued to visit Sarah. I couldn't say at the time that she was the reason he was eventually captured, but it was possible, for he continued to plan their escape to Boston, what was beginning in Ireland to be called "the next county over," where they'd find refuge among the Irish immigrants. Robert planned that he and the Curran girl would be smuggled out on a ship in Cobh on August 26th.

Unfortunately, someone had informed on Robert's location, and Major Sirr arrived at Mrs. Palmer's on that date, just as Robert was readying himself for his escape. He had disguised himself in a powdered wig and sported a mustache, ironically looking rather like a posh British gentleman. Mrs. Palmer tried to persuade Major Sirr that her lodger was a Mr. Hewitt visiting from Liverpool, not a Mr. Ellis, but the Chief of Police was not convinced. He posted a guard at Robert's door. But Robert overpowered the guard and then climbed out the window and ran to the barn to mount his horse. However, Major Sirr tackled Robert and pinned him to the ground, and Robert's wig fell off. He then declared Robert a traitor and arrested him for high treason; he dragged him in chains through the streets and confined him in Kilmainham Gaol. I learned later that, at that point, Robert knew that his dissembling would no longer work. He confessed he was Robert Emmet.

After Robert's capture, on September 3rd, the Yeomen found me at the O'Neill's, who testified that I was their male cousin helping with chores, but Major Sirr recognized me, despite my male garb, and told me that he had already arrested Emmett and that I was also being arrested for high treason. I told him that I knew no one named Emmet and that I had never betrayed my country, a remark that made him smirk and then laugh.

After he pulled the cap from my head and my long dark hair fell down my back in waves, Major Sirr tied a rope around my waist and dragged me through the streets, but not to Kilmainham. Instead, he took me to Dublin Castle and threw me into a cell that smelled of mold and urine. He left me there overnight in total darkness, hoping that one night alone listening to the screams of my fellow prisoners, some of them my colleagues, would break me.

"Catherine, do you know Kathleen O'Byrne? I learned that she is or was a member of the Society," Harriet said as soon as Catherine folded her cloak and placed it on a chair.

"Yes, I know her."

"Why didn't you tell me?"

"I told you that she may not want to be found."

"Was that your way of saying that she doesn't want me to intercede for her?"

"It may have been. I know that you still wish to help her girls, but perhaps she is doing that herself," Catherine said as she removed her gloves.

"Do you know where she is?"

"I do but I'm not at liberty to tell. She is angry with you and wants you to leave her alone. She can take care of the situation herself. She has told me that she has visited the girls and is seeking their release."

"And what will she do if she gets them released? She has no livelihood." Harriet paced the room.

"Neither do you, Harriet."

Harriet stopped and stood in front of Catherine. "I could take them in and care for them. Will you please tell her that?"

"I'll consider it, but you need to truly consider whether bringing the children here is in your and their best interest. You may be moving along to Wales soon and the children would not be able to accompany you, you realize this, don't you?"

"I'll find a way. You said when we first met the girls that you would help get them out. Please, Catherine, talk with Kathleen O'Byrne and assure her that I will adopt the girls. They will have a loving home."

Eliza walked into the room.

"Are you staying for dinner, Catherine," Harriet asked. "If so, shall I fetch another murdered chicken?"

"Catherine Nugent told me that you are looking for me. What is it you want?"

Kathleen O'Byrne stood in the doorway; she held Percy's calling card. Wrapped in several shawls, her hands were red and raw, and her face looked drawn and tired. Harriet wondered if she had been living on the street but worried that if she inquired, Kathleen would leave.

Harriet stepped out onto the landing and shut the door.

"Mrs. O'Byrne, I still want to fetch your children. I am willing to take them in, but I would need your help to get them released."

"What do I get from this?"

"Get? What do you mean? Your children would live in a secure and loving home."

"Can you pay me?" Kathleen's face was pinched, and she shifted from foot to foot. She seemed eager to move on.

"I have some funds, yes." Was this woman so venal that she would in a sense "sell" her children? Was she that desperate?

"Right. Let's go then."

"Now?"

"Yes, but give me the money first."

Harriet fetched her bag and pulled out a handful of pound coins. She dropped them into Kathleen's hand, and they silently walked to the Hospital.

"You again?" the porter asked as he opened the door.

"We are here to see the O'Byrne girls and we won't be denied. I have a letter from a Member of Parliament. And their mother, Kathleen O'Byrne, is with me."

"I'll take you to the one, but the other is gone."

"What do you mean? Where has she gone?" Kathleen asked.

Harriet's heart raced as she recalled her recent dream.

They followed the porter who directed them to a row of graves.

"I don't know where the older one is exactly, but her grave is one of these."

Harriet saw a fresh mound of dirt that indicated a recent burial. And next to it was a black hole ready to be filled with the next victim.

Kathleen fell on her knees. "What happened? She was well the last time I saw her. She was happy to see me and eager to get out of here."

"She escaped in another way," the porter said quietly. "All's I know is the older one wanted to be with and take care of her sister who had the typhus. They was sleeping in the same bed, and the older one passed away."

"So, the hospital that was supposed to save the children killed Michaela? Is that right?" Kathleen angrily asked. "Take me to Sinead now."

The porter escorted them to the matron who said that Sinead was still in the infirmary. When they entered, Harriet noticed that the sores on the child's face had healed. She was sitting up. As soon as Kathleen walked in, Sinead cried out and reached for her. Kathleen immediately swept her into her arms. Sinead clung to Kathleen's neck.

Harriet handed the matron the letter from Sir Timothy, which was really something that Harriet had written, and the matron said, "There's no need. I've been given approval to allow the mother to take her child. We need the room anyway; we just received a new batch of children on the wheel. Many people are abandoning their babies." Harriet recalled that babies were often stolen from their parents and women were paid to do this.

As Kathleen and Harriet left the hospital with Sinead in her mother's arms, they passed Michaela's grave once more. They stopped and Kathleen bent down and touched the earth. They heard children crying in the Bridewell, and Harriet thought of Michaela who had been incarcerated there. How sad that the poor child went from prison to a narrow grave. Once they were outside, Harriet turned to Kathleen.

Harriet reached for Sinead. "I'll take her now. I have a room, clothing, and toys ready for her. Here's one of the dollies that I bought for her." She held the doll out to Sinead. "We will adopt her and give her a loving home. She will go with us to Wales."

Sinead reached for the doll, but Kathleen swatted her hand. Sinead cried. Her mother pulled her closer.

"I'm sorry but I can't let you have her. She's my daughter. I'll find a way to take care of her." Kathleen turned quickly and rushed toward St. James Gate. Sinead looked at Harriet and continued to reach for the toy.

Harriet followed them.

"Leave us be. She's mine, not yours," Kathleen said. "She's an Irish lass, not a Brit. Besides, your husband doesn't believe in God. I can't have my daughter raised by a heathen heretic."

Harriet returned home and said nothing to Eliza as she headed straight into her room. Percy followed her, and she bitterly wept.

"What's wrong, love?"

"I'm deeply saddened," Harriet said between sobs. "One child is dead, and another is now on the street and it's my fault."

"How could you be at fault for the death of child?"

Harriet told Percy the complete story of her quest to save the girls.

"It was not your fault," he said. "The child died because the Protestant Ascendency that oversaw the hospital failed her. They treated her like a criminal just because she is poor and Catholic rather than a child that needed its protection. And the Brits have ensured that all of Ireland's Catholic children are poor. When Ireland is free, all children and families will be cherished."

"But that's in the future. Right now, her mother hasn't the means to care for her and we do."

"No, now is not the time to bring a child into our lives. We must be patient, my love. One day, we will have our own children. In the meantime, we will continue to strive to help those who suffer. Her mother has every right to her. We do not."

He held her close, and she cried as they made tender love. His comfort assuaged her heart somewhat, but she still thought of Michaela in her narrow grave, a victim of British injustice.

And she thought of Sinead, who no doubt was now living and begging on the street with her mother, the former member of the Society and the widow of a "foolish" rebel. If Harriet joined the Society, would she also be deemed a fool?

19 March 1812
Anne Devlin

I told the lass that I needed to work so I declined her visit, but now sometimes my work seems to be to record my history. Perhaps she's correct that there ought to be a full account of the horror of Kilmainham, Ireland's Black Hole of Calcutta.

The next morning Major Sirr interrogated me.

First, he told me that they had arrested Mr. Ellis, and that Mr. Ellis had confessed to being Robert Emmet. And then he said, "We have also arrested your family, including your cousin Michael Dwyer, and you know we captured your other cousin, Kevin O'Byrne. Your mother and father have admitted to aiding rebels, and they have turned evidence on you."

I knew that these were bold-faced lies. Mam and Da would never betray me, even though they hadn't sworn an oath, like I had. Their oath was loyalty to their family. And I knew that Dublin Castle would never find and arrest my cousin Michael, who was as sly as a feline; they'd tried to locate him for years, but he always evaded capture. He was far different from Kevin O'Byrne who was not as wily as Michael.

"Because of your parents' useful information, we have let them go, but we have retained your cousins and your brothers and sisters. Now, Anne Devlin, if you tell us what you know about Robert Emmet and your fellow conspirators, I will personally give you £500. Surely, a lass like you could benefit from that fortune. You and your family could depart for Boston, as Emmet intended to do with his fiancé. Did you know that he intended to flee and leave you behind to suffer, to make you his scapegoat?"

Of course, I was gravely concerned about Major Sirr's detailed knowledge of Robert's plans, but I didn't let on. And Robert never intended to make me his victim. I was good at keeping my face still and not letting it betray me and Robert.

"I know nothing about this Robert Emmet, whoever he is. I worked for Mr. Ellis at Butterfield Lane, not someone named Robert Emmet," I replied. "And you can't tempt me in any fashion. I know devils when I see them; I am like Jesus while in the desert; he withstood the devil who tempted him with worldly goods."

Major Sirr laughed. "So, you compare yourself to Jesus? What a foolish, brazen hussy you are; I thought you were smarter than that. Wouldn't you like to go to America as a rich young woman? I hear that Boston is a fine place for you Fenians." He smirked. "You should reconsider. Perhaps another night or two in the dark will enlighten your mind. Take her away. She is to have nothing to eat or drink. And remove her slop bucket; let her stew in her own filth. Let's see if she believes she's Jesus then."

I learned later through a kind guard that my mam and da were still prisoners as were my brothers and sisters, including my little brother Jimmy who suffered from smallpox. The only one in my immediate family who had avoided capture was Nellie but who was nevertheless found in the barn hiding under a haybale and was sent to the Foundling Hospital, a fact that made me both happy and sad. I was glad that she was not imprisoned, but the Foundling Hospital is just a step above that. I worried that she would be forced to become a Protestant and would never be reunited with Mam and Da, that she would be an unloved orphan and that she would, in time, forget us. I would have to trust that Providence would see that she would be returned to us, and that justice would prevail. I knew from then on to never trust anything that devil Major Sirr said. Once a liar, always a liar.

The cell that they placed me was basically a broom closet. I used one corner of it to relieve myself, although I had little human waste, for I had not imbibed or eaten in days. Still the stench of my waste and the odor of others' waste nearly overpowered me. I tried to ignore my senses and my circumstances and, to save myself from the horrors, I thought about the comforting scents of home.

In closing my eyes, I often transported myself there to sit in the fields of heather and lavender. Or I imagined sitting near the fragrant peat fire with my mam and da and listening to my mam recount stories of her brave ancestors, of Feagh and the High Kings. Or I assuaged my heart by imagining sitting atop Lugnaquilla, the tallest of the Wicklow Mountains, with my dear ones as we watched the stars beating their ancient rhythm. In reality, my family members were somewhere in this castle or worse still in Kilmainham. I was sorry that they were being persecuted for my deeds, and I asked for God's forgiveness for harming them, but I did not regret nor seek forgiveness for my role in the rising. Like Robert and the others, I did not pursue paradise in an afterlife; I hungered for paradise here, for a free Ireland.

Still, I fretted about my brothers and sisters, whose fate was unknown to me at the time. Was Dr. Trevor trying to bribe them also? Luckily, they knew little of the United Irishmen's plans, so they had nothing they could reveal. And yet I worried that Trevor was so evil that he might torture or abuse my brothers and sisters and force them to make false statements.

Even so, I felt steadfast because I had faith in my fellow United Irishmen and women. We swore an oath before God Almighty that we would never divulge each other's names or provide information about each other. We were not informers like some devils—devils like Tom Halpin, who sold his soul to Satan himself when he turned in my father, which we learned long after his perfidy.

One question kept coming to mind—How could Major Sirr think that I was so weak and cowardly that I would be a Judas and betray Robert and the others? I wouldn't do it for £500 or £5000 or even £5 million if there is such a thing.

Mr. Emmet had let me down, but I would not let him down or any of the other fifty souls who supported the rising and loved Ireland as much as I did.

19 March 1812

Harriet returned to the Foundling Hospital but didn't go in, for it was no use at this point. All that was left was an unmarked grave with a darling child sleeping in it.

She walked through St. James Gate and saw a tree ladened with knitted baby booties, a baby's cap, ribbons, and bows. She asked a passerby why such things were tied to the tree.

"It's a fairy tree, miss. Everybody knows that. You must not be Irish. Irish folk tie baby items to the tree and the fairies bring them a baby."

Harriet thought briefly about what Anne told her about fairies. How they trick people and sometimes effect catastrophe. Despite this knowledge of treacherous fairies, she pulled a ribbon from her bonnet and attached it to the tree. Then, she walked past the hospital and headed home to await the delivery of her fairy baby.

Anne Devlin

After several days in dark solitude, a guard opened my cell and told me to get up. I had been dreaming of fairies stealing babies and their souls, and so it took me a minute to realize that someone was standing in my cell and that I was being addressed.

The light from the torch the guard carried momentarily blinded me, and I struggled to get to my feet. The guard offered no help.

"What's happening? Am I to be hanged? Will I not receive a trial?" My mind flashed on the half-hanging that had been inflicted on me. Inside my heart quivered. I kept my face still.

"Dr. Edward Trevor wishes to speak with you," she replied.

My heart raced with anxiety, for I had heard of Trevor who was known as The Devil's Partner. What would that devil want from me? What would he ask me? What might he do to me? When I heard that I was to go to the notorious Kilmainham, I wondered if they were taking me there to skip the half-hanging and hang me outright next to the fearsome dragons that guard the entrance and mock those who pass through its portal.

During my visits to Kilmainham to provide solace for prisoners, I had witnessed its horrors: the filth, the wretched odors, the wails of those being tortured and I now wondered what my fate would entail once I arrived at the gaol. Would they try to break me as they did others? Would they torture me with more dark solitude? Would they starve me? Would they try to make me relent by hurting my family? Would I even see a judge? Would I see Robert? What about my family? Would they allow me to visit with them?

I rode in the back of a wagon to the gaol; every time the wagon hit a bump, my body lurched forward, but I had no way to protect myself, for my hands were manacled behind my back. I had not eaten for God knows how many days and my stomach ached from hunger, but I did not express my needs to my captors. They knew I was famished, thirsty, and rank, for I had sat in my own filth in the cell that I had been confined in. At least in the wagon, I could gaze at the horizon, which was a glorious pink, for we were travelling as the sun kissed the sky. I saw the morning star wink at me, letting me know that no matter what darkness lay ahead, there would always be stars watching and protecting us, for, even though the stars are outside of human history, we ourselves are akin to stars.

When we arrived at Kilmainham, the wagon stopped in the courtyard and my guard pulled me onto the ground. I looked up and saw the stone dragons entwined above the entrance. I knew I had not committed murder, theft, rape, or piracy. According to British law, I had committed treason, but, like Robert, I believed that our rulers were illegitimate, so I discounted treason. Like Robert, I had never betrayed my country. Even so, the dragons seemed to breathe fire at me, as I entered the gaol, mocking me as if to say, "You're in our lair now. You have no free will; you have no rights. You're entering hell on earth. Abandon all hope." Master MacWilliams had taught us about Dante's hell, and I felt as though I was about to enter his Inferno. I wondered which circle of Hell I'd be placed in. Perhaps I would be placed in the fifth circle due to my anger and disgust with Robert.

As I walked in, I was struck by the darkness and rancid, putrid smell of unwashed bodies, urine, and other human waste. Of course, I had smelled these odors before but knowing that I would be kept in such an environment made me sick to my stomach. I retched but nothing came up. I gained my composure as my captor dragged me to the desk, where they asked for my name and then assigned me a number. I was labeled number 98, which made me wonder if I was deliberately given that number because of my membership in the United Irishwomen and its association with the failed ninety-eight rising.

After the jailer ordered me to remove my clothing, something that I had never done in front of strangers, the female guards mocked me for wearing male garb, asking me if I was a tommy girl. (I didn't know what that meant until later when I learned that tommy girls prefer to dress like men, something the sumptuary laws prohibit. For according to the Bible, women and men are supposed to dress only according to their own sex so the sexes can be differentiated from one another). The guards left me standing naked for the longest time as they taunted me with various names—hoyden, tribade, strumpet, tart, filthy whore. Even though it was August, I shivered because of the dampness as I tried to cover my breasts and my lady parts with my hands. When I didn't respond to their offensive names, they gave up and finally pulled what felt like a rough burlap sack over my head; this was my prisoner's uniform, which I would wear for weeks at a time, until I was given another, and then made to scrub the first one at a sink in the common area, where women felons also laundered their own, the matron's, and the guards' clothing.

After that, a guard grabbed my hair and with blunt scissors cut it all the way down to my scalp. "We'll make you look like the lad you tried to imitate," she said. Once more, I mustered my strength and didn't cry out, even though I felt like I was getting scalped. My mam had always said that a woman's hair was her glory. The guards meant to destroy my glory and shame and belittle me, but I would not be shamed. I held my head high, and when they called me more names, I merely stared at them until they were forced to look away.

Then the matron explained the rules to me. Because I had acted and dressed like a man, she was placing me with the men who were also state prisoners; I would be the only woman among them. All prisoners, whether state or criminal, were to maintain absolute silence; we must reflect on our sins. If I were compliant, I would be able to walk in the yard for one hour a day, otherwise I would be confined to my cell. If I were a submissive, good girl, I would receive a daily ration of stirabout, which was bread, water, and milk. Occasionally, I would receive a little meat and a few potatoes.

"Do you understand the rules?" the matron asked.

"I do, but when will I see a judge?"

"You'll learn that in due time. Now here's a candle, a Bible, and a slop bucket. This is what you may have in your cell."

A guard walked me down a long hall that had open windows on the right and a row of cells on the other. I looked through the windows and saw an enormous wall that was likely fifty feet high. At one end, there was a guard tower where the guards could peer down on all the prisoners in the yard at once. I knew from the size of it that I could never scale that wall. I would have to hope that there was another means of escape.

"Here's your cell, Devlin. This is your new home. That is until you're hanged," my guard said.

I peered inside at a cobblestone floor and a pile of straw, which I assumed was to serve as my bed. There was also one small, barred window near the ceiling. Along the hall was a stream of water that smelled like a privy.

There was no light, except for the daylight that fell on the floor of the hallway. I wondered what good the Bible would do, if I had no light by which I could read. I wondered how often I would be able to light my candle, for they had given me only a handful of matches.

Once I stepped inside, the guard slammed the door shut, and then I heard her lift a slit from the outside.

"We can watch you whenever we want. We're like God Almighty. Don't do anything you wouldn't want God to know about," she said as she laughed.

I thought, No, you're the devil incarnate; even though you're Irish, you work for our oppressors. The sound of the spy hole being dropped reverberated throughout my cell and left me with an eerie feeling. I knew that they could watch me whenever they wished, but I vowed then to always maintain my composure, to never let on how I felt inside, where I felt a great fear and foreboding. I placed my candle, Bible, and slop bucket on the ground, and then crawled onto my pile of straw. It was soaked through with urine.

I fought hard not to retch once again.

As I lay there, I thought about my brothers and sisters once more. I wondered if I would be allowed to see them. I wondered if they had been fed. I wondered if they were also sleeping on sodden straw. I wondered if they were crying out for our mam. I worried about Jimmy, who suffered from smallpox. He had a fever the last time I saw him. I wondered if Jimmy had survived.

I didn't contemplate my sins, as I had been instructed, for I didn't think I had committed any in working for our liberation. Instead, after beseeching God to enter this damned place and keep my family safe, I thought about the sins of my oppressors, and wondered whether God would punish their wicked ways. Exhaustion set in and I felt my head nod as I was about to fall asleep.

It was then that I heard a pounding on the floor over my head and I heard a voice whisper, "Anne, is that you?"

20 March 1812

Harriet reflected on Anne's story. She tried to concentrate on what Anne had told her so she could eventually write the story, which she had not learned in full. In addition to the fanciful fairy stories and bits of romance, none of which were actually Anne's story, Anne only told Harriet of her young life and nothing of her rebel story. Harriet had done her best to ensure that Anne trusted her, but Anne may have deemed Harriet untrustworthy because of her husband. Harriet still wished to know what Anne truly experienced, so she asked Percy if anything had been written about Anne's story.

"Why do you want to know?" Percy asked. "We have nothing to do with her and she did not speak to you."

Harriet looked away; she didn't want to give away the fact that she had visited Anne. "I'm merely curious. And I'm interested, as you are, in Irish history, since we feel more Irish than we do British."

"Anne mentioned in passing that someone named Brother Cullen recorded her story. She disliked what he had said because he made her out to be a saint." He picked up his cloak. "I'm meeting Lawless to work on our history. By the way, we are also writing about the history of Irish folklore— I'm learning more about fairies, giants, and heroes, which is utterly delightful. Eliza, don't wait dinner for me," he said as he pecked Harriet's cheek.

As soon as he left, Harriet decided to find this Brother Cullen and ask him to fill in the missing pieces. Even if Anne refused to reveal her story, her history, Harriet intended to learn the truth.

She visited Anne briefly and brought a small doll for Catrìne, the one she had intended to give Sinead. Harriet asked where Brother Cullen lived, and Anne told her that Brother Cullen could be found at St. Patrick's Cathedral. Harriet thought this odd, since the cathedral was a Protestant house of worship, but perhaps Cullen had denounced Catholicism and had joined the brethren of the Church of Ireland.

Eight

Save Yourself, I'm a Dead Man

21 March 1812
Anne Devlin

I probably shouldn't have but I sent that lass on a wild goose chase to find the good brother. I sent her to a Protestant cathedral where no one will know Brother Cullen. I don't want her to speak with him, for I did tell him some of my story, and I told it truthfully. She is as persistent as her heretical husband. She'll soon understand that I am not sharing my history with her, and, if she wants to continue to visit, she'll continue to receive half-truths mixed with nonsense. I hate to be dishonest, but I must in this case, for my true story should not be revealed until Erin is free.

The last time I reflected on my imprisonment, I had thought about how I'd heard a voice from above my cell. I thought I was likely hearing things, for I felt a bit delirious from not having eaten and having slept poorly. If the voice were real, how could someone communicate with me anyway? I looked around the cell, dimly lit by a trickle of sunlight coming into the top of a barred window near the ceiling. I looked up and saw the outline of a narrow crack along the top of the wall. Then, I heard the voice again. "Anne, is that you?"

My voice shook as I whispered, "Yes, it's me." The voice was Robert's, but I did not mention his name for fear that I would betray him if someone were listening.

Then I heard a loud clanging that sounded like a heavy door were being shut. Then nothing.

I wondered if they had planned to place me in a cell directly below Robert's. If so, why? Did they want us to acknowledge each other? Did they want me to be a turncoat by enabling our communication? I didn't believe that Robert confessed his identity.

Days passed and I heard nothing. Then, when I received my daily stirabout I found a note under the bowl of prison gruel. I lit a match.

    Kathleen Williams Renk

My hands trembled as I read the note. "Our comrade Russell intends to help me, you, and O'Byrne escape. Wait for instructions. Burn this message. RE."

Was Robert Emmet truly communicating with me or was this a ruse to get me to betray him? I recognized his handwriting but wondered whether he had been forced to write this note. I didn't wish to get caught with this message and thus further endanger Robert or Kevin, so I quickly burned the note and swept the ashes into the corner.

I was unable to sleep because I knew that there was a plan to get me released from this horror. Furthermore, my bed straw remained wet and scratchy; I couldn't get comfortable. I was cold and they had given me no blanket. I still possessed the candle and a few more matches. I thought it best to save the candle for the times that I knew would come when I was frightened or needed the solace of light.

In the dark, I heard rats racing across the floor. They chittered away as if they were conversing with each other about how they would nibble at me. I was not accustomed to rats or mice; we kept our home clean and tidy. Sometimes the rats brushed against my feet, as if they were sniffing whether I was edible or not. When I felt them sniff me, I kicked them away, sat up and pulled my legs up to protect myself.

Awake in the dark, I heard inmates arguing with the guards. Even though they were supposed to remain silent, some of the men cried out for their mothers or the Virgin Mary or Jesus himself. Some screamed and sobbed as they were flogged. If they flogged me, I decided I would not make a sound. I would not show weakness even if I were crumbling inside. I knew that a show of weakness was deemed a victory by the Brits.

Finally, after a week or two (it was difficult to keep track of the days), a new guard was assigned to my cell. She told me she was in contact with Emmet and that she would help me.

"I don't know anyone named Emmet."

"Come now. Well, then Mr. Ellis wants to help you escape," she said.

She produced a note written in Robert's script, but I still wondered if it had been written under duress. I didn't respond but she continued to explain the plan to me.

The guard said that Russell was paying her to smuggle in disguises for "Mr. Ellis," Kevin, and me and that when I visited the exercise area, I should request to use the necessary and in it, I would find matron's garb to don. She would distract the other guards, and I would be free to walk out of the prison. Likewise, Robert and Kevin would receive and wear guard's clothes and do the same. We would be free, and a coach would be ready to take us to Cobh, so that we could flee to America. I wondered, if we did escape, what would happen to Kathleen and if she and Michaela would be able to run away with us.

I asked the guard why she was helping me, and Robert Ellis.

"Sure, my brother was a rebel who was hanged right here as I watched. He and I never let on that we were related," she replied.

I cringed at her revelation and thanked her for her compassion. I told her I was sorry for her and her brother, but didn't ask his name, for it was better not to know too much about the two of them.

I was naturally excited to learn this plan, but I also feared it, worrying that something would go wrong. Yet I hoped that Providence would prevail and be on our sides. Surely, God would not abandon us.

Because I had acted as a submissive prisoner, a different guard told me that I would receive one hour of exercise in the yard the next day. I was eager to exercise my limbs, for they were growing stiff from being immobile and knew that if all went well, I would be a free woman by the next evening, and then I would be able to walk among other people once more and feel the sunshine on my face and gaze at the canopy of stars. Robert and I (and perhaps Kevin and Kathleen and their bairn) would sail to America, where we would be safe, and we would be free to live among our fellow Irish and their descendants. We could then raise money to foster another rebellion, for it's said that America hosts as many Fenians as Ireland itself. That night I dreamt of Robert and me walking arm in arm through Boston's streets. And Kevin and Kathleen were with us. Together, we knocked on doors and solicited funds to send home to raise another revolution. We were happy.

The next morning my beneficent guard, like a guardian angel, opened my cell and told me to follow her to the exercise yard. As soon as I entered, I looked around and saw many women with their heads bowed walking like slaves in a circle as if on a treadwheel, and some men were playing with a ball and racket. I quickly asked if I could use the necessary, since I had only been allowed to use a slop bucket and that I was having my curse and needed more care. The guard excused me and directed me down a short hall to the privy. My heart beat wildly as I walked to what I believed to be my freedom, but when I entered the necessary, I was nearly overpowered by the horrific smell. The room was rank with human waste overflowing the seats. I had to hold my breath, as I quickly looked around the room. I searched frantically but found nothing. No clothing had been left for me, no matron's cap, apron, or dress. I thought perhaps I had misunderstood the instructions. Perhaps my matron's garb was somewhere else in the building or perhaps we had been found out. Perhaps we had been lied to and would be further punished for our escape plan. I felt confused and deflated and wondered what to do. I didn't have time or the freedom to search another area of the prison. So, I returned gravely disappointed to the exercise yard.

Immediately I saw a man with dark curly hair hitting a ball against the wall. I was stunned to see that it was Robert playing with a ball as if he were a child with no care in the world. I sought his attention by retrieving the ball on the ground.

He crouched down and whispered, "We've been found out, Anne. Save yourself. Tell them what you know about me. Kevin should do the same. I'm a dead man."

I felt my heart sink, and I wished that I could reach out and comfort him but knew that would be a sure way to condemn both of us. I wanted to say but couldn't, Sure, we can escape to America. Our friend will still find a way to help us. I dreamt that we were free and together in America.

But instead, all I could say was, "No, sir. I'm no scoundrel, no rotten informer. And neither is Kevin. We have O'Byrne blood."

He said nothing but took the ball from me and bowed his head. I noticed tears in his eyes. Then he left the exercise yard when a guard called his name.

That's the last time I was face to face with Robert Emmet. Days later, I saw him hanged and beheaded.

Harriet visited St. Patrick's Cathedral and asked a woman in the front pew how she could speak with the Vicar, and the woman kindly told Harriet to wait, for he would soon begin evensong. Harriet walked around the church and saw in a glass case the death mask of Jonathan Swift, whose *Gulliver's Travels* delighted Percy and her. Swift had been rector here. Percy had told Harriet that Swift often wrote satirically and that he once wrote that the Irish should eat their children as a remedy for famine and some readers believed he was earnest. Harriet recalled that with especial horror, given her love of children, particularly starving or hungry ones.

Harriet saw a young man in cleric's robes lighting altar candles, and she quickly approached and asked him if he knew the whereabouts of a brother by the name of Luke Cullen.

"We have no brothers here, miss. We are a Protestant Church."

"I know that you are, but I was directed here by someone who knows Brother Cullen. She was sure that someone could help me locate him," Harriet replied.

"Hmm, well, I think that you'd be best to seek help at a Catholic establishment. Perhaps St. Mary of the Archangels or St. Michan's. I don't know anyone at either place, for we don't communicate with papists. I'm sure you understand?" he asked. "Our rector distrusts them, you see."

Harriet said that she understood. What she didn't understand is why Anne sent her to St. Patrick's. Did Anne deliberately lead her astray? If so, why?

22 March 1812
Anne Devlin

The lass came here today and seemed displeased. I suspected she was peeved with me. She told me that her visit to St. Pat's was unsuccessful in finding Brother Cullen, but she said that she intended to go to St. Michan's and try to locate him. I didn't respond, for I didn't want to let on how much I hope she will not find the good brother. I must send a note to Brother Cullen and ask him to withhold information from the lass. I shall do this today and send Aoife to the monastery. Brother Cullen must not inform on me.

As I considered informants, I recalled that the real reason that Robert had been captured is that we had a spy in our midst. It turned out that one of the United Irishmen had been our informer all along. Leonard McNally, whose house we frequented, was the traitor to our cause. He was also a friend of the Curran family. And, as a friend of the family, he convinced that frivolous, foolish girl to tell him where Robert was hiding. McNally persuaded her that he would rescue Robert and help him and her escape Ireland. Instead, she accidentally betrayed them.

Knowing this, I realized that Robert's rebellion never had a chance. All along, McNally was conveying to Dublin Castle Emmet's plans. Emmet was followed, as all of us were. McNally was the real traitor; he was disloyal to Mother Ireland; he was a loathsome Irishman in league with the devil. And the self-absorbed, silly girl enabled Dublin Castle to capture Robert. Unknowingly, she had let down her lover. She had been his undoing, just as I feared from the beginning. She was unworthy of him. I should never have run messages to her after I realized how vain and thoughtless she was.

Later Catherine Nugent told me that Robert had worried that Sarah Curran would be charged as a co-conspirator; he sought to protect her, so, in order to keep her from being charged, he did not defend himself; instead, he admitted his guilt but still gave an hour-long speech at the dock, berating the British for their occupation of Ireland. In it, he said he did not fear death. I have what he declared by heart: "I do not fear to approach the omnipotent judge to answer for the conduct of my short life . . . Let no man dare, when I am dead, to charge me with dishonor; let no man attaint my memory by believing that I could have engaged in any cause but of my country's liberty and independence.

The proclamation of the provisional government speaks my views . . .
My lords, you are impatient for the sacrifice. The blood which you seek
congealed circulates warmly and unruffled through its channels, and in
a short time it will cry to heaven . . . My race is run. I am ready to die."
Such valiant words were never before expressed by any Irishman who
stood before a British tribunal. I later learned from Mrs. Nugent that
Robert had written to his brother Thomas, "I am just going to do my
last duty to my country. It can be done as well on the scaffold as on the
field." Of course, when she told me that, I wept.

23 March 1812

Harriet hurried after a priest leaving the confessional and walking back to
the rectory at St. Michan's. "Do you know a brother named Luke Cullen?"

The priest looked perplexed. "Yes. Why are you asking, miss?"

"I need to see him. I'm a friend of Anne Devlin's. I have a message from
her. Do you know where Brother Cullen lives?"

He hesitated. "You know Anne Devlin? I won't ask how or why you know
her, but it's not necessary for you to meet with the brother. You could give
me the message and I can relay it."

"No, Anne expressly said that I should only give the message to Brother
Cullen." Once more, Harriet felt terrible lying, especially to a man of cloth,
but she knew that this may be the only way she could speak with Brother
Cullen himself. She wondered why the priest was reluctant to have her talk
with the brother. Would speaking with him put her in danger? Would she
jeopardize his safety?

"In that case, you will have to find your way to Mount St. Joseph
Monastery, where Brother Cullen lives."

"Is it far?"

"It's a good way to the West of town center, about seven miles."

"I'm not afraid to walk."

"Would you like me to accompany you?"

"No, thank you. I'll go by myself." She thanked him, nodded good day,
and set off on her journey to learn the truth about Anne.

Along the way, she walked past where Emmet had been hanged. She
felt a shiver as she recalled what Percy had told her of his execution. Many
children who looked half dead were gathered in front of the church.

Eliza watched from afar as Harriet distributed a handful of coins to
the waifs. She wondered where Harriet was going as she followed her out
of Dublin City. Was Harriet finally coming to her senses and leaving her
reckless, slightly mad husband?

Anne Devlin

The lass didn't visit today. I hope that trouble hasn't found her in the same way it found me. While I waited for her visit, I thought further about the final time I saw Robert.

The days passed slowly. Every day, I fretted about Robert and his fate. It wasn't supposed to be like this. If all had gone well from the beginning, he would be reestablishing our parliament and he would be the prime minister, our Taoiseach, who believed in human rights, including women's rights. Instead, he was in the cell above me awaiting his trial, where he was sure he would be found guilty and then hanged from the gibbet. I prayed that somehow, he and I would be released. I prayed that God would intervene and save Robert (and me) from the noose. I didn't think that I could bear the thought that the British and the traitorous Irish at Dublin Castle would hang him. He was not a traitor to Ireland, his home.

I wondered what he was doing but could not ask; we had obviously been found out. And the guard who had promised to deliver us from this earthly hell had informed Dr. Trevor of our plan and then Trevor imposed further strict restrictions on my mobility. The guard had lied about her brother; she didn't even have a brother, and she only promised to help us because she was paid. She did not care about our freedom, and Trevor paid her even more to turn on us.

Trevor ordered that I remain in my cell; I was to receive no exercise, and my slop bucket was once again removed. I was being punished for Russell's attempt to free us. I wondered if Robert was receiving the same treatment and learned later from Mrs. Nugent that his cell was commodious and comfortable. His cell contained a bed, a writing desk, and a hearth. He was allowed to use a chamber pot and often the privy designated for first-class state prisoners. He was allowed visitors, while I was not. I thought this unjust, but, of course, could do nothing about it. These are injustices built into the class system. Occasionally, I could hear several visitors in his cell. I later learned that those visitors, including ministers, attempted to persuade Robert to seek forgiveness, to confess to treason, to seek absolution from the government. He refused. If he had, his life may have been spared. Sometimes, I wished that he had sought forgiveness, but he was too honorable for that.

Unfortunately, he also learned that his mother had died because of the stress of his rebellion, incarceration, and the government's plan to execute him. Her only bairn named Robert who survived childhood would not live to maturity; his life would be shortened because he was a patriot, true to his greater matron, his Mother Ireland.

In the meantime, Dr. Trevor continued to badger me each day to tell him all I knew about Robert and my fellow conspirators. Trevor was merciless. Like most of the guards, he called me all sorts of filthy names, which being the good woman that I am, I hesitate to repeat but for veracity's sake I will. He also accused me of sexual impropriety with Emmet and all the other men who had lived at Butterfield Lane.

I continued to deny that I knew anyone named Emmet. I was Mr. Ellis's housekeeper.

"Come now, Anne, give up the pretense. We know that you worked for Emmet. We know that when he returned from his insurrection, you said to him, 'A bad welcome to you.'" Trevor smirked.

I kept my face blank, even though I was shocked that Trevor knew the words I had spoken. I said nothing.

"You were angry with the men who had let you down, especially since you had relations with them and felt close to them. You felt betrayed. We all know what a housekeeper does. She cleans the house and prepares victuals, but she also obliges and services the men in the house if you know what I mean. She satisfies male urges by presenting her feminine wiles to the men. Even though you now wear your hair like the boy you pretended to be, you're a fine-looking colleen and the men thought so. They told me. Emmet told me. I know that you did this. We have other witnesses besides Emmet," he claimed. "In fact, your cousin Kevin is one of the witnesses."

"No, sir, you are a liar," I replied. "I am chaste; I remain a maiden. I would never degrade myself in the way that you imply. Besides, I know no one named Emmet."

"Hmm, eventually you'll speak the truth, you slutty vixen, I do believe that you remain loyal to Emmet or Ellis whatever you want to call him, because you wish that he loved you and had asked you, not Sarah Curran, to run away with him to America. Isn't that correct?"

"No, sir. I know no one named Robert Emmet. I have never had a lover. I love my country. I love my kinsmen and women."

"You think that you're capable of being a silent Sphinx. But, when I'm done with you, you rebelly bitch, you'll betray, like St. Peter, your very own Messiah, whom you claim loyalty to."

"Take her back to her cell; this time manacle her hands to the wall. She'll likely do anything that I ask after being shackled."

"Oh, and no food for you tonight, Devlin. We'll starve the truth out of you."

24 March 1812

On the day of Robert's trial, Trevor visited my cell. I was still chained to the wall and was sitting in my own filth. He bent down and spoke directly into my face, laughing as he said, "Bad luck to you, Anne Devlin, bad luck to you, you rebelly bitch; I hope that you may be hanged. I never saw but one woman hanged in all my life, and I hope that I shall see you hanged; and if there was nobody else to hang you, I should hang you myself. And now, for your comfort, your pet, your Robert Emmet, your favorite, Mr. Ellis, is to be executed tomorrow and I will gladly take you there so that you can see your pet disgraced, and so you can witness your own fate."

My mouth was dry, but I was able to gather enough moisture to spit on his ugly face. For that, I was whipped. I prayed for strength and made no sound as I was lashed fifty times. I bit my tongue so hard that it bled. That night I dreamt that Emmet stood on the scaffold with the noose around his neck. I stood next to him with the executioner about to lower the noose around my neck. I woke startled, for I could not bear to witness our deaths.

As promised, Dr. Trevor took me to Thomas Street. My back felt like it was on fire from the whipping I received, and my dress was in shreds barely covering me. My hands and feet were bound, and I sat in the carriage in front of St. Catherine's Church, where the gallows had been constructed and where the drunken rebels had murdered Lord Kilwarden. Redcoat soldiers sat on each side of me with their bayonets drawn. Hundreds of people had gathered to witness the execution, young and old, some of whom I noted were among those patriots who had supported the rising.

Trevor pulled me out of the carriage and put me on display as if I were a circus animal. Soldiers stood on either side of me with their bayonets pointed towards me. When those I knew looked up at me, I did not acknowledge their stares; I did not wish to betray anyone associated with the rebellion and bring them to the circumstances in which I found myself, a type of living death. I looked around the crowd and spied Sarah Curran standing in front of the crowd next to her sister. Sarah leaned against the gallows platform as her sister held her up to keep her from collapsing.

I stood motionless as I watched as Robert was escorted up the steps and onto the platform. His head was covered by a black hood and his hands were bound. He stood tall and did not cry out. My heart was beating furiously. I wanted to shout out to him but knew that, if I did, I would betray him and me. Yet I wished for him to know that I was there, so I did scream out to him, not caring if I would be reprimanded nor that Trevor would know that this Robert Emmet indeed was my employer and colleague, my friend. Yet the noise from the crowd was so loud that Robert didn't hear me.

Trevor snickered. "Lucky for you, Anne Devlin, that your Mr. Emmet can't hear you. Scream all you want. You can't save the traitor."

The crowd grew silent as the executioner removed the hood from Robert's head. He looked calm. He looked noble. He did not tremble. He asked to speak to the crowd. He was denied the request, but just before the executioner lifted the noose over Robert's head, Robert shouted, "My friends, I die in peace and with sentiments of universal love and kindness towards all men and women. I may have betrayed England, but I never betrayed Ireland." Then the noose fell to his shoulders, the plank was kicked out from under him, and he dropped. I closed my eyes, but Trevor shouted at me to open them. I kept my eyes shut but I heard some in the crowd cheering while others wailed. I opened my eyes and saw Sarah Curran collapse into her sister's arms and then to the ground.

I wept while Trevor laughed. "Your pet will soon be dead, and he will meet the devil face-to-face."

"You're the devil incarnate, Dr. Trevor, for you side with our tyrants." I knew that my outburst would have consequences, but I didn't care.

We waited a long while before Robert's body stopped jerking, for Dublin Castle had forbidden anyone to break his legs. I thought after he was dead that perhaps they would leave him hanging to warn other rebels or potential rebels. But, at last he was quiet, and the executioner cut him down and then lifted an axe and severed Robert's head from his body. My head swam, and I nearly fainted as I saw the lynch man raise Robert's head, dripping with blood, and proclaim, "Here is the head of Robert Emmet—the traitor." Immediately, women came forward to dip their kerchiefs in his blood, some of the scarves were green, and I saw several of my fellow United Irishwomen cross themselves before they dipped their scarves. I looked away with tears flowing down my face.

"You're next, you know. You're as guilty as he was," Trevor said. "You'll not evade the noose for long. I'll gladly hold your severed head aloft so that your followers can spit on it. Beware, Anne Devlin, you'll soon follow that traitor into hell."

I was not afraid, but that night, instead of dreaming of our escape, I dreamt of Robert's execution. I could not control how the nightmare repeated itself over and over in a great loop in my mind, where I saw the dogs lap his blood and the young women, including Sarah Curran, cut off a scrap of his clothing or his hair, thinking that such a tribute would ward off evil or perhaps save them from the noose. I never saw myself dipping my scarf, for I knew that this was folly. Evil would surround us as long as the British remained on our shores. And I had no way of preventing the hangman from coming for me. I could only hope that Providence would somehow eventually save me from Robert's fate and that I would not be the first woman hanged in Ireland.

Nine

The Oubliette and Female Felons

25 March 1812
Anne Devlin

I paid for having cried out at the hanging and for calling Trevor the devil that he is. Trevor told me that I had betrayed Emmet; that I was a coward and then he continued to threaten me daily with hanging, but I told him that I wasn't afraid to die, for I had done nothing wrong. Unlike him, God would not condemn me, for my God was a just and good God.

Even so, in the dark, I did feel afeared. I sometimes lit my candle to dispel the darkness and feel less alone. I thought over and over about Robert's end and whether I could be as brave as him or whether I would scream and beg forgiveness when they were hanging me. Whether I would cling to my executioner's legs and plead with him to spare me. I felt terror whenever I remembered the half-hanging that Major Sirr had executed on me and recalled what it was like to feel my throat constricted so that I couldn't breathe. It's the worst feeling ever to try as you might to breathe, but then get no air. I barely survived the half-hanging. And I began to feel unprepared to die; I hadn't earned the right to die for our cause. I hadn't done anything that truly advanced Irish freedom. All I had done was support Robert and run letters between him and that foolish girl. If I were to die, I needed to earn my death.

That night I dreamt for the first, but not the last time, that Trevor himself dragged me out of my cell and pulled me up to the gallows. He chortled as he called me every vile name he could think of, as he placed the noose around my neck. He then sharpened the axe that he would use to decapitate me. I was so afeared that I woke myself up and felt that my straw bed was warm, and I realized that I had wet it. I lay there until dawn, too frightened to return to sleep. Somehow, I eventually slept but was startled when I heard the latch of my cell door lifted.

When I arose, I found a copy of Robert's speech at the dock thrown on the floor of my cell. I didn't know who threw it at the time but learned later that Kevin had found a way to bring it to me. Like Robert, I would desire no epitaph be written on my grave until Ireland liberated herself. And reading his brave words gave me hope. It was as if he was reaching out from his grave to touch me. I was not alone. I would try my best to be as honorable and valiant as Robert. I silently thanked my benefactor for sharing Robert's words with me.

A guard told me that Trevor allowed a conjugal visit between Kathleen and Kevin. I wasn't sure why. Maybe such an act was like a last meal that prisoners are offered, a sort of moment of normality and tenderness, a feast for the senses. Afterwards, they also allowed Kathleen O'Byrne to visit me. I suppose they hoped that Kathleen would harass me for getting her husband Kevin involved with Robert, which she did.

"You know what you did, Anne? You ruined my life, Kevin's, and Michaela's."

I looked at her with pity and compassion, for I knew that she needed someone to blame. If not me, she would need to blame herself or Kevin, for they both had joined the Society. I said nothing.

"He will die," Kathleen said. "It was bad enough that he lost his hand working with Emmet, and would have to become a beggar, but now, we will have no one to take care of us."

"Kathleen, love, I'm sorry for you but Kevin joined the cause of his own free will and so did you. You had to have known that this could happen. That we might fail, that he could get captured."

"I want to know why you aren't going to the gallows. Are you confessing and betraying the others?"

How could she think me a miscreant? "I vowed to never speak about my colleagues. I'll die before I ever say a word about Kevin, Robert, or any other rebel."

She pulled her shawl over her head. "I'd rather you die, you know. You and all the rest are fools, including Kevin. God forgive me for hating you and all of them, but my heart has been torn from my body. I shall never be whole again."

I understood her feeling. I also felt as though my heart had been ripped from my body when I witnessed Robert's execution. I didn't acknowledge my empathy but merely said, "I'll do what I can for you and your daughter." Afterward, I found a way to get her hired as a maid at the home of Dr. Curran.

I knew in my heart that she loved Kevin and that she was lashing out at me because of fear and great sorrow.

Later I heard that Kevin had been given a reprieve of sorts and that he said he would confess. I didn't believe it. He was descended from O'Byrne. He did not possess a coward's soul.

Their conjugal visit resulted in a pregnancy. Baby Sinead was born nine months and five days later.

In addition to that devil Trevor, we had an equally evil jailer by the name of Dunn. Word spread that many of the rebels would be executed without a trial, for habeas corpus had been suspended. One by one I heard men removed from their cells. The row of cells down my hallway became as quiet as a mausoleum, for most of the men had been taken away to be hanged and have their heads placed on pikes outside the jail. I wondered if my cousin Kevin was among them. Soon after the executions, Dunn opened my cell door and came in brandishing a knife. He came close to me and held the knife to my throat.

"This is the knife that severed the head of Felix O'Rourke, one of your fellow conspirators."

I didn't back off as I faced this devil.

I summoned all the courage that I could. "Go ahead. What are you waiting for? Just remember that you'll burn in hell along with all he other devils for the wickedness that you do and the sins that you commit in threatening pure souls. What kind of Irishman are you? You side with our enemy. I curse you, Dunn. You'd best watch your back."

He quickly retreated, for he must have thought that I was some sort of witch, for he didn't move closer to me. In truth, I know that if you curse a person nineteen times, they die. My mam taught me this. I personally have seen others use it to defeat their tyrants.

After a short while, I was surprised that Trevor allowed me to have another visitor, perhaps his scheme was to learn, through the visitors, more about our rebellion. The guard told me that a Carmelite nun, Sister Benedicta, wished to visit me and that Dr. Trevor had granted the request. The good sister came into my cell bearing a candle, and she blessed me before she pulled some food from her cloak. She handed me a warm loaf and a pork pie. I was so ravenous that I bolted the food; she advised me to slow down before I vomited. Then she turned her back to the door and whispered, "I'm not what you think," she said as you pulled her veil back. "My name is Mrs. Catherine Nugent; I know U." She was here to help me, just as I had aided other prisoners before the rebellion.

My heart swelled. I replied, "I know N."

She smiled. "I'm here to give you strength and for you to know that all of us pray for you daily."

We knelt in the corner of my cell and prayed the Lord's Prayer. We kept our backs to the door. She stopped praying and told me that twenty-one of Emmet's comrades had been hanged, which I already knew, but she said that I must not join them. She told me that Kevin O'Byrne remained alive.

My heart overflowed with happiness. "He's my distant cousin, you know. Is Kathleen well?"

"Her health is fine but she's quite angry now that Kevin is jailed. She wants him to turn evidence, but I saw him and advised him to keep mum."

"I know she's angry. She visited me and told me that she wished I would die. I don't blame her. Sometimes I wish it too," I confessed.

"You can't mean that."

"Oh, but I do. I sometimes think it would be best, for this is like living in hell. Then, I bolster my courage and carry on. Kevin will keep mum. He's an O'Byrne. We are not cowards."

"I hope you're correct," she said.

Then she told me that Robert's body had been thrown into a commoner's grave at Bully Acre.

"He must be moved," I said. "He's no commoner, but a gentleman. And he needs to be buried near his fellow rebels."

Mrs. Nugent agreed, and we quickly hatched a plan for Robert to be disinterred and moved to St. Michan's churchyard. She said that she would take part in the plan; that she would help disinter and re-bury Robert. He couldn't be laid to rest near the Sheares Brothers, for they were in the crypt beneath the church, but they would move him to the churchyard and place an unmarked stone on his grave.

"Will you return and tell me when this has been undertaken? I need to know that his body is properly respected. I know that he would have done the same for me."

She nodded and rose to leave.

"If I could get out of here, I would move him myself," I said. "I've done the likes of it before. I'm not afeared of the dead, only the living."

25 March 1812

Harriet found her way to Mount Saint Joseph and entered the monastery grounds, which were silent as a tomb. She knocked on an interior door.

"What can I do for you, miss?" A monk stood in the doorway holding a candle in his hand.

"I wish to see one of the brothers, Brother Cullen, an old friend of mine."

The monk gave Harriet a skeptical look. "Please come in and I will see if Brother Cullen is free."

Harriet entered the foyer. The air was saturated with the scent of incense and Harriet heard male voices chanting. Several monks were transcribing books in an adjoining room. One monk held a paintbrush as he illuminated a manuscript. She thought, Just as in days of old, these men were saving God's word and civilization.

The monk returned. "I'm sorry, young lady. He's praying right now. This is his week of silence."

"I have an important message from Anne Devlin for him," Harriet said. "Would you please interrupt him and allow him to speak with me?"

The monk raised his eyebrows. "Wait here." In a few minutes, he returned with a petite, frail, bald man.

"Is Anne ill? Does she need my help? Is she in trouble with the Castle?" he asked.

"No, she's well and is in no trouble. She's asked me to fetch the story that you wrote about her. She wants to read it and correct any errors. Here is a note that she sent that gives me permission to take the book."

He took and read the note. "But I haven't written it yet. I only have notes."

"If you tell me the story, I'll write it."

"Who are you?"

"I'm Harriet Shelley, Anne's friend. My husband and I are members of the Society." Lying grew easier the more Harriet did it.

"Have you proof that you belong to the Society?"

"Isn't Anne's note sufficient?" Harriet hoped that he had never seen anything in Anne's handwriting. Harriet wrote the note in the Irish that Mrs. Nugent had taught her.

He glanced at the note. "Come into my cell. I'll tell you what I know but keep the deadly knowledge close to your heart."

Harriet's heart fluttered in fear and anticipation. She would finally learn the truth. Was she prepared to receive such knowledge of the evil perpetrated against Anne Devlin?

Anne Devlin

Aoife told me that she was unable to speak with Brother Cullen, for he was observing a week of silence.

"Did you tell the abbot that you needed to speak to him on my behalf?"

"No, I figured that he knew I was bringing a message on your behalf, because I told the monk my name. And I thought that, if they wouldn't allow Brother Cullen to speak with me, he likely wouldn't permit him to speak with Mrs. Shelley."

"Perhaps you're correct, but to be sure I need you to return to the monastery and insist that you be allowed to speak with him. Tell the abbot that I need Brother Cullen's help."

She assured me that she would return.

My time in Kilmainham continued to be hellish. Each day I asked when I would be tried and each day, I received no answer. Then I asked to see Dr. Trevor, and I was taken to his office and escorted through the West Wing, which other prisoners said was haunted by the spirit of a young rebel girl, who had first been starved but then supposedly immured within its walls. The area did feel eerie to me, but I saw no spirit begging for bread. I did feel for this spirit though, for the mode of punishment for me was to be deprived of food and drink. I knew what it was like to be starving and thirsty. I resembled the spirit and had compassion for her. Luckily, I had not yet been immured, although I had often felt extremely confined and sometimes dreamt I was buried alive within my cell's walls.

When I entered Trevor's office, I was not allowed to sit, but was forced to stand, even though I felt weak in the knees.

"What do you want? Why are you here? Are you ready for your hanging?" Trevor asked.

"I shall not be hanged, Dr. Trevor, and you know it. Women are not hanged in Ireland."

"You're wrong of course. A few years ago, Lady Betty of Roscommon was scheduled to be hanged but she was willing to become the executioner in order for her life to be spared. Perhaps you'll do the same. Or maybe for your hanging, we should dress you in the clothes that you wore when you arrived. You like dressing above your station as a man, don't you? Then we could rightfully hang you and no one would know the difference."

I ignored him. "I need to see a judge. I've been here for months and have never appeared before the court to plead my case."

"So, you're eager to appear before a judge and then to be hanged? I can arrange that."

"I have the right to a fair trial, just like anyone else."

"What makes you think that will happen?" he asked. "Did any of the other traitors receive a trial? No, none except your rich pet. The rest of you are nothing, mean nothing; you are expendable rubbish."

"I wish to see a lawyer; I have the right to a solicitor."

"You have no rights. Take her back to her cell. And no supper for you tonight, Devlin."

I heard the latch of the spy hole lifted, and something being shoved through it. I reached for a match, struck it, and read the piece of paper, which announced a reward of £500 for anyone who revealed the whereabouts of Michael Dwyer. I knew all along that Trevor had lied about my cousin who was still loose in the mountains. I wondered who had placed the notice in my cell. Was it someone who wished to inform me that they were still searching for Michael or someone who thought that I would betray him? How would anyone surmise that I would take £500 to betray my cousin? Besides, in truth, I had no knowledge of his whereabouts.

Once more Mrs. Nugent came to my cell in the guise of a good nun. Once more we whispered in the corner of my cell. She told me that all had gone well in digging up our leader and placing him in hallowed ground. A monk by the name of Luke Cullen had helped her and our comrades. She told me that in death Robert's face looked serene. Even so, the thought of his severed head was gruesome to imagine. Then she told me some wretched news. My cousin Michael had surrendered to the British, because they had arrested his sisters and had begun to torture them in the same way that they had persecuted me.

"What will become of him? Are they about to hang him? Will he get a trial?" I asked.

"No one knows," Mrs. Nugent said. "But he is here in Kilmainham. He has asked to see you but has been denied."

My confinement began to take a toll on my body. It was becoming increasingly difficult for me to move about. My legs were heavy, and my entire body ached whenever I moved. Sometimes my limbs felt like they were on fire. My spirit ached too, especially in knowing that my family members were still prisoners in this vile place. It was Christmas 1803 and twenty-one of my friends and family members, including Michael Dwyer, were in Kilmainham Gaol. We celebrated alone in each of our cells. I began to feel I was more dead than alive.

One evening I defied my deadly feelings and stirred my spirit. I softly sang.

> Come all ye brave United Men, I pray you lend an ear
> And listen to the verses I now will let you hear
> Concerning noble Billy Byrne, a man of great renown
> Who was tried and hanged at Wicklow as a traitor to the crown.

Soon I heard a voice join me, as I continued.

> It was in the year of ninety-nine, we had reason to complain
> We lost our brave commander, Billy Byrne was his name
> In Dublin he was taken and brought to Wicklow Gaol
> And though we wished to free him, for they'd take no bail.

Then another voice joined us:

> And when they had him taken, those traitors they came in
> There was Dixon, Doyle and Davis, and likewise Bid Doolin
> They had but little scruple, his precious blood to spill
> And Wicklow lost through perjury the pride of Pleasant Hill.

And then more voices, as the guards shouted for us to cease our rebel song. But we continued. As we sang, I saw Kevin O'Byrne walk by. He bowed and with his baritone voice sang the loudest of us all.

> When they came forward for the Crown, they against him swore
> That he among the Rebels, a Captain's title bore
> They swore he worked the cannons, and the Rebels did review
> And that with that piece of cannon, he marched on Carrigue.

A great swell of voices joined in the darkness as the men banged cups against their prison bars.

> God rest to Billy Byrne, may his name forever shine
> We'll not forget his noble death in the year of ninety-nine
> May the Lord have mercy on him and all such men as he
> Who stood upright for Ireland's right, and died for liberty.

As we completed our song, a guard came into my cell and dragged me out. He said, "You're going to the hole, Devlin. Let's see how you like singing alone in the dark."

Everything became shadow after they placed me in the hole. It was as if I had truly descended into Dante's hell with no guide, no Beatrice. I had to feel my way around the cave-like cell into which they had shoved me. I stretched out my hand and felt the wet, slimy wall. I wondered whose hands had touched these walls before me. Perhaps the heroic Sheares Brothers, perhaps Robert Emmet himself. I kept reaching until I had walked the pit's circumference. So, this was it, I thought. This was like being buried alive. I was still on my feet. I was still standing.

Mr. Emmet told me about the French *oubliette*, far worse than a mere dungeon. The *oubliette* is a hole in the ground that the French authorities force people to descend into and then they cover the hole with a grate. They make it a place where you are forgotten and then starved to death. Was this Kilmainham Gaol's version of the *oubliette*? Would I be forgotten? Would they feed me here? I was used to no food by now, but, maybe instead of hanging me, they intended to starve me to death or break me by depriving me of light.

I gathered my wits and once more sang, but this time no voices joined me, for I was truly alone. Even so, I sang my song of Billy Byrne, and it echoed against the walls of the dark hole, where it reverberated with the songs and chants of others who had also been cast into this hole. I thought about Kevin O'Byrne and wondered about his fate. Would he be true to the cause? Where were they taking him when he passed by my cell?

I only kept time by noting the occasion of my curse—another month had transpired. After this, I was returned to my cell and learned that Kevin had been on his way to his execution when he passed my cell. They tried to shut him up, but he sang the Billy Byrne song as the noose was slipped over his head. And a kind guard informed me later that Kevin had told Trevor that he would take my place on the gallows. Kevin wished for me to be spared. My heart ached to know that my cousin gave his life for me, even though Trevor continued to taunt me with hanging even after my cousin was executed.

My heart suffered for Kevin and Kathleen, yet I was proud of Kevin for proving that his blood ran green not red. That he didn't turn traitor to the cause. I like to think that he and Billy are singing together now as we on earth continue our struggle.

I was periodically returned to the hole for rebellious behaviour and for leading more tributes to Billy Byrne. I thought of Kevin as I did so. During that time in the hole, Robert began to fade in my memory. He seemed but a shadow rather than a human being. When I returned to my cell, I had to conjure his memory, and the outlines of his physiognomy took shape once again.

For the longest time, to keep myself from going mad, I imagined the possibility of escape. The matron's underling, Miss Flanagan, was new and therefore not hardened to the realities of prison life. She lamented every time I was thrown into the hole. She whispered to me each time she escorted me there or fetched me from the darkness, "I'll help you.

What would you have me do? Do you need my prayers? I'll say a novena for your soul."

I told her that I didn't need someone to pray for my soul. Instead, I needed her to provide a viable escape plan, which included a way to get me out of the country, for I knew that if I escaped and remained in Ireland, I would never be completely safe. I told her to contact Russell, who would help me.

I needed her to bring me matron's garb. I needed her to leave the doors unlocked down the long corridor leading to the exercise yard. I needed her to unlock the gate to that yard. If she did the compassionate thing, I could walk free. I could begin again, start over. I felt terrible, for I began to wish that I could forget about Robert and the United Irishmen and women. I could recover my health. I could stretch my limbs and look up at the healing sun. I could feel the rain fall on my limbs and cleanse me. I could breathe fresh not fetid air. I could see fields of sunflowers and purple heather. I could gaze at the field of shimmering stars. Everything depended on Miss Flanagan's kind and noble heart.

I was in such a dream state, when I heard Dr. Trevor's raspy voice that reminded me of Satan himself. "Anne Devlin, wake up. Are you dead, girl? Get up, you wretched wench. It's time that we talked again. Your cousin, Kevin O'Byrne, is ready to talk and he says that you will too." Trevor didn't know that I knew that Kevin's head rested on a spike outside of Kilmainham. His mouth was open as if in song or so the kindhearted Miss Flanagan told me.

Harriet listened to the story that Anne had told Luke Cullen. It was an obscene story of torture, deprivation, starvation, and mental trauma. Perhaps Anne didn't want to relive that story by telling Harriet all or parts of it. Perhaps she never even told Brother Cullen the entire truth, for even though he spoke of her as if she were a perfect saint, he told what happened on the surface. He did not speak of the likely horrific emotional state Anne must have been in when she saw Emmet hanged and decapitated. And he did not speak of the emotional state of what it must be like to be deprived not just of liberty but of light. Or what it must be like to be treated worse than an animal. Harriet wished to know the entire truth so she could write it for Anne and for history. The world should know what happened to an ordinary woman, not a saint, who loved her homeland so much that she defied the government in order to seek Erin's freedom.

26 March 1812

My dear Godwin,

I continue to consider your advice to quit Ireland and return to London, where I could continue my political work but from abroad and perhaps through other means of persuasion. I shall think more about it; I do have other plans in mind, but for now, I do not fear that I, any of my loved ones, or any innocents will suffer while we remain on this island. So far, we have not been accused, even though Lawless informed me that the Crown is aware of me. And I have not learned any further facts about the 1803 rebellion or any of its participants, so there is no knowledge that I could share regarding who aided Emmet in his poorly planned Quixotic quest.

I suppose that if, like you, I had witnessed the French Revolution, it is likely that my caution while here would be greater. But I have not beheld a Reign of Terror; no priests hang from the churches. No one is being guillotined in the streets. The streets are not awash in blood. No heads rest on spikes around town. Contrarily, no peasants rise up demanding bread, although they ought to, for they perish daily from the way that the rich and the Crown demean and starve them. In fact, the disheveled poor frequently congregate around the carriages of people who keep them in a starving state. They do not do this to harass the rich, but rather they gather to admire the fine silk gowns, fashionable hats, and gaudy jewels of the wealthy, to gawk at their blatant notion of superiority, as well as beg for bread or coin, which they are often denied. And, as I've previously noted, the idle rich ignore the suffering of the poor Irish and do not condemn the fact that the starving poor are hanged for stealing a penny loaf or for stealing thirteen shillings and four pence from the till at the greengrocer as I read about in the Dublin newspaper.

For now, I shall continue my work here, for it partially satisfies my hunger and thirst for action. I have begun to write a long poem that will focus on the downfall of tyrants. I dream of a just world and hope it will engender a worldwide revolution.

Your humble disciple,
P.B. Shelley

27 March 1812
Anne Devlin

The lass has not been here for several days. I do hope she's not come to a bad end.

In the evening after my babe is fast asleep, I spend time thinking about Trevor's attempt to get me to betray my comrades.

I was the only one of the rebels left and I intended to remain alive, but I would be sure to never speak of any of my colleagues no matter what the devils did to me.

In the winter of 1804, Trevor launched a new tactic on me. He told me that I was being transferred to live in Old Kilmainham among the female felons: the murderesses, thieves, prostitutes, and attempted suicides.

They moved me in shackles to the part of the gaol that housed those felons. Instead of being housed in individual cells, the prisoners were gathered in a large holding cell where they could walk about. No one abided by the rule of silence; they were often loud and boisterous. Some of them were drunk, because their visitors brought them whiskey to quench their thirst and the guards looked the other way, for the visitors always brought an additional bottle of whiskey for the guards. The whiskey made the prisoners and the guards louder and more ferocious.

One woman who drank excessively was a corpulent giantess named Katty the Goose. She stood six feet tall and weighed at least fourteen stone. Dominating the other women, she cursed like a sailor and bullied and threatened those she disliked. She stole others' rations. Trevor had told her that I was a traitor and that she could do whatever she wanted with me. At first, she kept her distance, and I managed to avoid her, but before long she began to harass me, calling me the same foul and degrading names that Trevor called me. She enticed other women to ridicule and mock me also. Everyone did, except those who had committed sexual "crimes," for they had often been forced against their will and disliked accusing women of actions that they had not initiated. Of course, I was not what Trevor and others had called me, and I continued to hold my head high to show them that I had nothing to be ashamed of.

One day, Katty stood before me. This woman knew that I had been tortured and that I had not spoken out about my comrades. Instead of seeing that as a virtue, she aimed to belittle me. She claimed she would do Trevor's dirty work.

"I'll hang you meself," she said.

She managed to procure a rope and walked around with it, pretending to lasso me as if I were a cow.

The guards laughed at her antics and her threats. They paid no attention to her insults but continued to drink their whiskey and play cards outside the holding cell. By threatening me, she thought that should break me and perhaps get me to confess. I was proving that I was not breakable though. I was and am no fragile colleen. I do not possess a coward's soul.

28 March 1812

Dear Godwin,

This evening, I attended a rally at Trinity College where I was invited to speak. Lawless had organized it on my behalf, for I wished to carry through on your recent suggestion that I must seek those whom I wish to join my philanthropic association. Lawless had reached out to many of the undergraduates, even though they are Protestants (many are sympathizers), and those who had attended the Catholic Committee meeting. He also informed some of their mentors. A fair number of listeners and sympathizers had arrived to hear my speech.

I stood on a platform at the campanile in the middle of the college and, even before I began, I noted that a plethora of townspeople had gathered as well; many men appeared to be inebriated.

As usual, I called for peaceful agitation and lawful protest but then I heard someone in the crowd shout, "Why should we listen to you? You're a damned bloody Englishman, probably a spy. We don't need you telling us what we should do."

I tried to mollify the crowd. I assured them that I was on their side in this struggle. That I empathized with their plight. That I was an Irishman at heart, to which some of them laughed. Even so, I persisted and said that I would stand by them as they strove to break the chains that bound them to England.

Just then, Yeomen rode through the front gate on horseback and threatened the crowd, telling them to disperse or they would be arrested. We all stood firm, but after a short standoff, they charged through the crowd and several people were trampled and were lying on the ground screaming for help. Lawless pulled me off the stage and hastily escorted me toward a side gate. I wished to return to help the injured, but Lawless insisted that if I did, I would likely be arrested for inciting a riot.

"But I've done no such thing. The gathering was intended to be peaceful."

"Dublin Castle cares not what your intention was. They would somehow concoct evidence against you, and you would be jailed. If you end up in the Castle or Kilmainham, you will have no influence. Or worse. You might be executed. We must preserve your life and well-being."

I insisted that my intentions were noble. I shall continue with my work but will perhaps need to be more clandestine so as not to arouse further suspicion. I vowed that no blood would be shed in my quest but clearly, I cannot control all aspects of my quiet revolution. I sometimes fear that you are correct, and Cadmus's teeth are rising up. We may need to depart Ireland for Wales as soon as we can.

Your faithful disciple,
P.B.

29 March 1812

Harriet was most concerned about Percy's emotional state and mental health. Following Dublin Castle's attack on a peaceful assembly, Percy swore that someone was breaking into their flat, and Harriet had to subdue his agitation, for no one was there. He insisted on calling for the constable, and they investigated the alley behind the flat and found no one.

"Percy, you must have had a bad dream," Harriet said. "Lie down again, darling."

He continued to pace. "I saw the man crawling through the window. He held a knife in his teeth. He looked like a bloody pirate."

"But the constable found no one."

"That doesn't mean it didn't happen."

"Percy, darling. We are safe. Please calm yourself."

Eventually, he settled and agreed to lie down. She stroked his back and whispered softly to him. After that she stayed awake all night; she kept hearing noises, and Percy repeatedly jumped up and raced to the window with a hammer in his hand. No one was there. The alley was quiet.

Harriet was at a loss about what they should do next. She still wished to stay in Ireland, for she remained committed to helping the Irish achieve freedom. But she was also worried about Percy's mental state. Perhaps he needed to return to England or make his way to Wales where he could rest and recuperate. He was severely agitated and seemed delusional. Perhaps, if he left to heal, she would remain in Ireland and become a genuine Irish woman.

Anne Devlin

Still no word from the lass. I do hope she returns unharmed. I should have told her that she was a risk with the Castle authorities for speaking with me.

Today, I cannot forget Katty who was merciless towards me. Even though the guards eventually confiscated the rope, fearing she might harm herself, for she was a bit mad, she continued with her antics and threats using other methods of harassment. One day when I was standing at the washtub washing the matron's and guards' clothes as we were forced to do, Katty came up behind me and said, "Maybe you need a good dunking; I heard that you're a witch. Let's see if you can float and then whether you can save yourself when I give you a little christening."

Before I knew it, she pushed my head into the tank, and she held me there. I blubbered and gulped water; I flailed my arms around. My feet were off the ground, and I kicked them. I thought this was an ignominious end and wouldn't have it, so I gathered all my strength, said a quick prayer, and used my arms to push against the bottom of the tub to raise my head. I caught Katty off guard. I turned around as quick as I could, landed on my feet, and gave Katty a great push. I had no idea where my strength came from; my guardian angel must have helped me. Katty landed on her back in the water that had splashed on the ground. She hollered for someone to help her, but no one came to her aid. Instead, the women who had abused me came forward and asked if I was all right.

One woman, Maeve was her name, took me in her arms and said, "Katty deserved what she got. She's pestered all of us for the longest time, Anne, but you especially. I'm genuinely sorry that we helped her in her evil acts."

After that, just like that devilish Dunn, Katty the Goose avoided me. In her case, she believed that I had help from supernatural forces. I do believe that, like Dunne, she thought I was a witch and that my familiars aided me, but, in fact, the angels themselves must have interceded for me, for God thought that I hadn't yet earned my death. Soon after that I was returned to the state prisoner wing. Trevor hadn't succeeded in having Katty do me in as he had planned.

I was returned to New Kilmainham and was fast becoming a hunger artist, like those who deliberately decline food to prove their stamina, but also to be a sort of sideshow. I had no audience of course and I had not chosen this for myself, but as time went on, it became easier not to feel the pangs of hunger. When I was shackled periodically for insubordination, I could see that the manacles were loose; with further emaciation, maybe I'd be able to slip them off so, in a way, a starved state helped me possibly escape.

While the guards slept, the new men on my row talked to one another. One of them was a solicitor named John Mason, who was Emmet's cousin. The prisoner, who had the task of dumping my slop bucket, told me that this Mr. Mason was writing a petition to have Dr. Trevor removed. He was gathering accounts of mistreatment from prisoners.

"How has Trevor treated you?" he asked.

"See for yourself." I showed him my arm, which was nearly bare bone.

"He starves you? When did you last eat?"

My mind felt foggy. How was one to know how the days passed? There was no way to count the days, for I had no writing utensil, and now that I was in a starved state, I no longer bled. "I can't say. It may be a week or more; I don't rightly know."

"The next time I come, I shall bring you some bread," he said.

Bless you was all that I could say, for I was extremely tired and wished to be left alone to sleep and dream of Wicklow, my mam and da, and my dear brothers and sisters. Sometimes of Robert, even though my memory of him had faded.

The good man, whose name was Colum, did as he promised; I received a modicum of bread each time he visited. Even though I remained famished, some of my strength returned.

30 March 1812
Anne Devlin

When Colum came to empty my slop bucket and to bring me some bread, he told me more about Mr. Mason's petition to have Dr. Trevor removed from Kilmainham. He recounted the various abuses that Trevor perpetrated. They included hanging a five stone weight off one prisoner, depriving state prisoners, like me, of food and water, stripping state prisoners of their clothing in front of all others in the yard, locking a state prisoner in with two felons and depriving them of water (one man drank his own urine in order to survive). Colum said that they continue to compile a record and that I must report any new forms of deprivation or torture. I told him of Trevor's repeated threats to personally hang me and his attempt to get Katty to kill me. He was already aware that most of my days were spent in the hole that was beginning to feel like my grave.

The abuse I suffered by being continually thrown into the hole was starting to affect my ability to see, and I told Colum about this. Being in prolonged darkness makes everything seem hazy, outlines of faces aren't as sharp, items you hold in your hand seem amorphous, I think that's the word. I hated being tossed into the hole, but I weathered it sufficiently each time, trying to fight the feeling that I was already dead. While in the hole, I closed my eyes and continued to imagine myself high on a mountain with the sun shining on my face and the wind blowing through my hair, even though in real life, they kept my head shorn to shame me for supposedly rising above my station and acting as if I were a man.

In addition to my eyesight failing, my limbs swelled. For what reason, no one knew at the time. The clothing that I wore became painful to wear, for my arms stretched the woven fabric and bit into my skin. My legs still felt heavy and were even more difficult to move, all because of my lack of exercise and from living in cramped and narrow quarters. It became so hard to walk that I required a cane. I felt and looked like an old woman, even though I was only twenty-three years old. Trevor performed an act of sorcery by making me age decades in a few short years. I wondered if my own kin would even recognize me or if I would recognize myself if I ever saw my reflection again. It didn't matter, for I knew that I remained myself on the inside, in my heart, where the true measure of a person is.

Time passed and eventually another winter rolled around. One evening, as I walked the perimeter of my cell to try to stop the aching in my legs, my cell door opened, and a small child stood in the doorway. The figure was hazy, and I couldn't discern what was happening, but the child cried out, "Anne, is that you? It's me, Jimmy."

"Jimmy, you're alive!" Somehow the blessed child had recovered from smallpox. His face was scarred but he was still a beautiful boy.

He ran over and grabbed my legs. We both collapsed on the floor and wept. For a moment, I felt peace descend on me, for one of my beloved family members was with me, and I was grateful. I thanked God for his mercy.

We held onto each other, but then the guard returned and said, "Get up, you two."

"Why? What's happening?" I asked.

"You're to be taken to Old Kilmainham, get up now and be quick about it."

"But my brother just arrived. Why must we go?"

"Dr. Trevor says that you'll be better off there."

"But it's even colder there than here," I replied. "Is he trying to kill me and my wee brother? We'll likely perish there."

"Quit arguing, Devlin," the guard said, as she pulled me to stand.

Jimmy started to whimper, but I told him, "Hush now, child, we'll be right as rain." I refused to allow Jimmy to share my fear of what was to come.

They led us out of the gaol, and all I could think was that I wished I had wings, for I would fly with Jimmy in my arms. Because my limbs ached so much, they didn't even need to manacle me, for they knew that I was crippled and had no way to escape.

It was late December and bitter cold and raining. I held Jimmy's hand and tried to keep him right next to me as I struggled to walk with my cane. Jimmy and I were completely soaked through and the guards who accompanied us never offered any form of protection, a cloak or hat.

When we arrived at Old Kilmainham, we were ordered into a crowded cell full of debtors and drunkards. By that time, Jimmy was feverish, and I asked the guard to please give us a blanket. He tossed us a threadbare blanket that smelled of urine and was crawling with lice. Instead of covering Jimmy with that, I covered Jimmy with my own body and prayed all night.

31 March 1812

When Harriet knocked on Anne's door, Aoife seemed shocked that she had return, and Anne beckoned Harriet to come over to her chair.

She touched Harriet's face. "I was worried about you, lass. Have you been well?"

Harriet didn't know what to say and was quite touched that Anne cared about her well-being.

"Yes, of course, I've just been busy helping Mrs. Nugent distribute alms and helping my husband with his project."

"So, he continues to rabble rouse?" she asked.

"He writes pamphlets with the hopes that people will join him and then peacefully agitate to end British rule."

Anne picked up her child and handed her to Harriet. "Do you wish to hear more of my story?"

Harriet thought for a moment and nearly blurted out, But what you've told me is what you think I want to hear. I want to hear the real story in your own words. I know what you told Luke Cullen. I've been writing it. But then she thought better and realized that perhaps Anne wasn't ready to tell her complete story and that no matter how much Harriet professed Irishness, she would have to prove to her that she was worthy of her story. She would need to earn the right to hear it. So, she told Anne to proceed, and Anne told Harriet tales of Queen Mab, the queen of the fairies, who descended from Queen Maeve. Anne's story was different from what Shakespeare told in *Romeo and Juliet.* Mab was not the midwife of unattainable dreams and the source of nightmares. Harriet rocked the baby next to her heart as she listened to Anne's tale, even though it was irrelevant to Anne's own rebel life.

After Anne finished, Harriet was disappointed but didn't let on that she hadn't wished to hear about Queen Mab. She bid Anne, Aoife, and Catrìne a good evening and walked home to find Percy scribbling away. Percy told her that, although he had thought they should depart for Wales, he felt re-invigorated after speaking further with Lawless, who promised that their work would bear fruit. Harriet wasn't sure what to do but she decided she would not leave until she'd recorded all of Anne Devlin's dreadful tale, so she sat near Percy and scribbled in her journal as she continued to record Anne's true tale.

Ten

Far From a Loving God

31 March 1812

Dear Godwin,

I am currently making plans to move on to Wales where I intend to continue to compose a long poem. It will be concerned with the future when all kings, bishops, aristocrats and the idle rich no longer exist, a future when all people are free to believe their own creed, and no tyrants hold power. It will be a bold and controversial poem that expresses genuine revolutionary ideas. I will rail against the existing establishment. My young character, Ianthe, modeled after my dear wife, will be shown this new, fairer world by the fairy queen, Queen Mab, which, according to my wife, is a favorite of the Irish. I have jotted down many ideas about this vision and have begun to write it. In it, Harriet is renamed Ianthe, and she is dead, but the Queen of the Fairies will awaken her. The Fairy says:

Soul of Ianthe! Thou
Judged alone worthy of the envied boon,
That waits the good and the sincere; that waits
Those who have struggled, and with resolute will
Vanquished earth's pride and meanness, burst the chains.
The icy chains of custom, and have shone
The day stars of their age. Soul of Ianthe!
Awake! arise!

Sudden arose
Ianthe's Soul; it stood
All beautiful in naked purity,
The perfect semblance of its bodily frame,
Instinct with inexpressible beauty and grace;
Each stain of earthliness

Had passed away, it reassumed
Its native dignity, and stood
Immortal amid ruin.

Perhaps my true political work will be to inspire through the creation of ideal literary worlds and through the founding of a utopian community of like-minded intellectuals and activists, rather than through leading reluctant men and women into freedom.

You'll perhaps be pleased to know that my Harriet believes she is carrying our child. She says that the fairies are delivering a baby to us, which is a delightful notion but clearly not in the least rational.

I shall write more later when our plans have been firmed up. Until then, I remain,
    Your faithful disciple,
    Percy

Anne Devlin

The lass didn't seem to care for my tale of Queen Mab. She said she preferred the British Bard's version. I shall have to think of another tale to keep her interest.

I've thought a lot about my time with Jimmy while he was ill. I did my best to tell Jimmy tales to soothe his spirit. We spent Christmas 1805 in Old Kilmainham. Jimmy suffered greatly during this time. Even though he survived smallpox, he had another ailment that would ebb and flow. He would suddenly grow well and then his fever and chills would return. I nursed him as best I could, based on what our mam had taught me, but had little that I could give him to better his illness. I wished that I knew more about healing and longed for a way that I could actually consult with my mam or Margaret King, but I had no way to contact them and, even if I did, I had no tonics or herbs to give him. I still didn't know whether my mam and da were in jail or if they had finally been set free. I learned that my sisters Mary and Julie had been released, and I supposed they were living on our farm, trying to maintain our dairy. If someday I could get out of this hell, I planned to return to the farm and then convince my sisters and the rest of my family to go with me to America, where we might start over and see the sky's canopy of stars.

Around the beginning of Lent, Jimmy rallied, and once he was no longer feverish, we were told that he would be moved.

"Where are you taking him? Why must he go? I take good care of him," I asked the guard, as Jimmy grabbed my legs and wrapped his arms around them. I didn't tell them that he was my solace, for that would have encouraged them to remove him from my care.

"Dr. Trevor thinks he belongs with his father."

"So, my da is still here in Kilmainham? Is that true? What's the charge against him?" I found it hard to believe that they kept him for two years, but they used his incarceration to torment me.

"Same as you, Devlin."

"Are you certain Jimmy will go to our da? You're not deceiving me, are you?" I could feel my ire rise, but once again I tried to hide my anger and fear for Jimmy's sake. The poor child had enough illness and sorrow to bear; he didn't need my fear seeping into his heart.

"That's what I've been told to tell you. Come on, boy, let go and get your things."

I wasn't sure what things Jimmy possessed, for all we had was the rags on our backs.

"No, I want to stay with my sister. I don't want to go," Jimmy said.

The guard tried to drag him away. Jimmy was screaming and I was crying; I could no longer control my emotions.

"Jimmy, don't be afeared. Be as brave as Cúchulainn the warrior. They say you're going to Da. He'll take care of you."

"What if they're lying, Anne? Please make them stop," he whimpered.

"I can't, Jimmy. You must have faith. Trust that you'll be safe." I took his hands and told him to let go. I kissed him on the forehead, as I bade him goodbye.

I watched as he was pulled from my cell. My heart felt as if was being torn from my body, for my Jimmy had been my salvation as I was his.

1 April 1812
Anne Devlin

To appease her thirst for a story, I told Mrs. Shelley about Maeve and her adversary Cúchulainn, who stole Maeve's cattle, tales that are bound to every Irish life, for, if she indeed wants to try to be Irish, she must know these tales. She said that she had heard some of these tales from her Irish friend. I had been thinking about how I told Jimmy these stories to help him have a brave heart, so it seemed natural to tell them to the lass too.

When she left and seemed satisfied, I reflected more on Jimmy and how he had been taken from me. I spent many months without my Jimmy. I experienced great emotional and physical pain. I thought about Dr. Trevor's treatment of me in terms of how he had given me my brother, someone to love and care for, and then cruelly snatched him away. This was part of Trevor's attempt to wear me down, to break my spirit. The more Trevor tried these tactics, the more I resisted. He could not use my family to destroy me. He didn't understand that I could be patient and remain loyal to the cause to which I had sworn my life.

I had once again been returned to Kilmainham, to my solitary cell. One evening, in the middle of the night, my cell door opened, and a guard stood in the opening holding Jimmy in his arms. Jimmy's body appeared limp; his head was hanging, and his legs dangled. My heart was in my throat as I screamed, for I feared that Jimmy was dead. The guard laid Jimmy next to me. I felt heat rising from his body and I felt his forehead, which seemed on fire. He wasn't gone yet, so I cradled him next to me.

"Oh, Jimmy, what have they done to you?" I cried.

He didn't respond. He couldn't. He was unconscious, but he was still breathing. I rocked him in my arms and cried out to God, blaspheming by saying, "How could you allow this innocent child to suffer? Could you do nothing to stop their war on us, their attempt to kill all of us Devlins?" I was in the worst state that I had ever been; I was in hell, the state of being far from a loving God.

I cried out to God all night, even when the guards told me to shut my mouth. I couldn't help myself.

At last, I fell asleep with Jimmy lying beside me.

In the morning, I awoke, but Jimmy was cold and stiff. When they tried to pry him from my arms, I fought the devils off. I told them that if they took Jimmy from me, I'd kill them for sure. After I scratched and clawed at them, they let me keep him and after I finally fell asleep, they stole him away. I had no way of knowing where they buried him and if they told Mam and Da that their youngest son had died in my arms.

2 April 1812

The fairies delivered on their promise. Harriet's dress had grown tight, and her breasts ached, which she understood were signs of pregnancy.

Eliza chastised her for her sexual congress with Percy that created new life. "What were you thinking in bringing a child into our lives?"

"I didn't bring the child into our lives. The fairies did. They brought me a baby."

Eliza scowled. "That's absurd. You and your foolish husband are losing your faculties. I fault Ireland and its whimsical tales for loosening the sinews of your minds."

"No, sister. Ireland has bestowed clarity, at least on my mind. Now, leave me be. I have writing to do." Harriet pulled out her journal and wrote what she knew of Anne's true story.

Harriet worried slightly about her pregnancy. She fretted that she should be gaining more weight, but their victuals were sparse, for they lacked funds to eat a proper diet. Percy deprived himself of food and gave his to Harriet so that their child would flourish. Whenever Eliza belittled Percy, Harriet defended him. He was still her savior, and she was his muse, his genuine love, his best friend.

One evening as he sat at his desk writing, he placed his quill in its inkstand and told Harriet that she was the subject of his new poem but in it he called her Ianthe. "Ianthe is dead, and Queen Mab awakens her."

"I'm grateful to be the subject of your poem but why am I called Ianthe and why am I dead?" Harriet thought of what Anne told her of Queen Mab. No Ianthe appeared in her story.

"I like the name and in making her dead she can be reborn as pure soul," he said.

Harriet wondered, Is that the way he thinks of me, as soul only? I'm a flesh and blood woman, not a soul walking around in a body. Also, does he wish me dead? She thought about asking, but instead asked, "Oh, then what does the name Ianthe mean?"

"The name means she who delights. In Greek myth, she was one of Persephone's companions. She went with Persephone to hell."

"The name is lovely, but I have no wish to die or visit hell even if it's temporary," Harriet replied. "And I'd prefer to be called by my true name."

Anne Devlin

I told Mrs. Shelley about the mummy in St. Michan's that reaches out and grabs you when you walk by their sarcophagus. Perhaps she will visit there and get a good scare that will keep her from learning too much about our rebellion or, God forbid, getting too involved in Irish politics. No matter how hard she tries, or no matter how many Irish tales she hears, she is not and never will be one of us, for she needs to have lived the experience of being an Irish woman in order to truly be counted as Irish.

After Jimmy died, I was racked with suffering. Perhaps God heard my blasphemy and despair and sent help. I don't know, but Mr. Dunn's angelic wife came to my aid. Mr. Dunn kept his distance from me, but through God's good grace, his wife did not.

When she learned that Dr. Trevor continued his war against me by trying to starve me to death and by taking the wee bit of love from me, when he took my brother Jimmy away and then brought him back where he died in my arms, she came to my aid.

When her husband was out of their flat, she brought me into their accommodation. She treated me like a human being. She wrapped me in a warm counterpane; she fed me beef broth and warm potatoes. She served me beer and tea. This blessed soul brought me to her apartment whenever it was feasible and safe to do so. I almost felt that I was being resurrected from the dead.

"Why do you do this for me?" I asked. "Won't your husband find out and punish you?"

"You've been treated cruelly, Anne," Mrs. Dunn said. "I know how they starve you, for my husband tells me that this is their aim. I can't be a part of their evil."

"But I don't wish for you to be penalized or reprimanded."

"What can they do to me? Throttle me? Starve me? Shame me? I frankly don't care. I know that others at Kilmainham are treated badly, but you receive the worst treatment because they despise your persistent courage, your continued rebellion. You know that most of the men cannot do what you do. Why do you think that is? How is it that you possess more valor than some of the men who became informers?"

"I can't say. I only know that, when I took my oath, I meant it and I did so for my sisters and brothers, all of them, all of Ireland. I would never betray them or us. Sometimes I am fearful though, but I am expert at hiding my emotions."

Mrs. Dunn regularly continued her charity toward me. I grew stronger; my limbs were less swollen; I was more mobile and sometimes didn't need to walk with a cane.

Then one day when I was convalescing in their apartment, Mr. Dunn walked through the door. He saw me sitting wrapped in a counterpane at their table. Before me, sat a half-eaten scone on a fancy china plate and a cup of tea with cream. Mrs. Dunn had lit the fire mid-day so that the room was cozy.

He became enraged and grabbed his wife by the arm. "So, you've been harboring and feeding this slutty rebel, have you? She's a traitor who ought to be hanged. Instead, you're treating her like a queen. You've undermined all that we've been trying to do." He twisted her arm behind her back and then shoved her against the bedroom door, where she fell on the floor.

"Stop it," I cried. I tried to stand, but suddenly my legs felt weak. "Leave her be!"

"And you, you've taken advantage of my stupid wife," he shouted. I'll fix you for that."

As he charged towards me, I gathered all my strength and stood up. "Don't come near me, Dunn. I curse you a second time. You know what could happen to you if I so choose." I was afeared of him, but my countenance did not show it. Somehow God had granted me the noble defiance to threaten Dunn. I was ready to curse him seventeen more times and he knew it.

By that time, his wife had stood and grabbed a knife from the sideboard. "If you touch her, so help me God, I'll not hesitate to do what I should have done long ago."

He looked startled and backed off, for his wife was slightly larger than him and her ire had been raised. He shouted for a guard. One of them came in and rescued me from Dunn's wrath and returned me to my cell, where I thanked Providence for my friend Mrs. Dunn and for God letting me live another day. Perhaps one day my luck would change, and I'd be free again. That night I dreamt of Emmet, not my usual nightmare of his execution, but of a moment when he and I sat in the warden's garden watching the stars glimmer overhead, and later we walked freely through the gates of Dublin Castle.

In the morning, I heard from Colum that Dunn had wrestled the knife from his wife, and then knocked her unconscious. She was taken to hospital. Poor woman. I felt awful that she was injured because she helped me. And I was also sad to realize that I would no longer benefit from her kindness.

3 April 1812

Dear Godwin,

I haven't followed your advice about departing Ireland, because I am beginning to make some headway here in terms of gathering men to join my philanthropy, so I am delaying our move to Wales. Lawless tells me that several men have approached him after reading my pamphlets and they are willing to unite with us in our effort to free Ireland through peaceful means, through petitioning Westminster and bringing MPs into our orbit. I have taken heart now that I know that all is not in vain. Contrary to your prediction that blood will be shed and that I will end

*up mimicking Emmet's fate, I have no qualms or fears about my work
here.*

*With that said, I have one request, and I must make it as if you were
my own father. For you see, my father continues to refuse to support us
financially because of my work in Ireland and because of my marriage.
He belittles the Irish and believes them unworthy of intervention. He
despises my thirst for justice. He thinks me irrational and impulsive.*

*I have reached out to him several times, but all I receive from him is
dreadful silence. Because I follow your political philosophy, I see you as
my guide in this world, more like a father than my own. In that vein,
I must beseech you to provide me with funds so that I can complete my
work here, which is inspired by your political writing. Have you £75
that I might borrow? I await publication of my "Songs of Liberty." Once
the poem collection is made available in England, I feel certain that an
income awaits me. I will quickly repay your compassionate generosity.
Know that the funds will be used to help purchase food for my wife, who
is with child.*

Your faithful adopted son,
Percy

4 April 1812
Anne Devlin

Mrs. Shelley listened to my tale of the dead nun and didn't say a word.
I expected some kind of reaction, but perhaps she grows used to my
stories that often contain death and grief. Again, much like my own
life.

After my encounter with Mr. Dunn and my threats against him, I was
confined in the dark once more. When Trevor learned of Mrs. Dunn's
kindness, he decided once more to starve me into submission.

In the dark hole, my legs swelled, and sometimes I wept because of
the pain. Once again, I wished to die, just to be done with this life of
suffering. But whenever I thought those evil, self-defeating thoughts, I
thought of my comrades and how my persistence in living demonstrated
to the English jailers that I was a fierce adversary. They could not break
me, at least not yet, and eventually we would be victorious, no matter
how many decades or centuries transpired; Ireland would be free, and
women and men would be equal.

One evening Dr. Trevor came to my cell; he visited me because the
guards told him that my arms and legs were swollen so large that my

clothing was tearing. "Anne Devlin, what are we to do with you? You remain a troublesome c-nt," he said. "I wonder what your pet would think of you if he saw how grotesque you've become."

"I care not what he would think of me. He would only think that you are a devil for treating me in such a heartless manner. Go away and leave me be."

"You shan't tell me what to do. I'm here to help you."

"And why would you do that?"

"I'm a merciful jailer."

I laughed, for he had never once shown mercy toward me or any of the other prisoners.

He started to lift my clothing, and I pushed his hands away, "What are you doing? Stop it right now."

"It's not what you think, you loathsome creature. You think that I want a piece of your filthy body? No, I want to relieve you of your suffering," he said, as he pulled a knife from his jacket.

"Do you plan to kill me?"

"Why would I do that? I'm waiting for the time when I can personally hang you," he said, as he aimed the knife at one of my swollen legs. I attempted to pull my leg away but, before I could move it, he cut a long gash in it, and I watched as fluid oozed out onto the floor.

I bit my tongue so hard that I was sure I cut it as well. I did not make a sound. Then Trevor butchered my other leg, and once again fluid flowed from it.

He put his knife back in his waistcoat. "What? No thanks? Surely, I deserve your gratitude."

"I'll only be grateful when you burn in hell for your evil actions."

He laughed as he walked out of my cell and slammed the door shut.

After that, I passed out. When I awoke, my legs ached as if that devil had burned them.

Not long after this, when Colum came to empty my slop bucket, he took one look at me and cringed. I knew that I had grown hideous, for I felt more like a cow than a human being.

He looked more closely. "There's a pestilence all over your face."

"What do you mean?"

"Your face is scaly with red patches. Let me see your arms."

I raised my right arm, and he pulled the fabric back. "It's on your arm too. Dear God, what has happened to you? Do you feel ill otherwise?"

"I always feel ill. This is nothing new. I have noticed more headaches though and chills."

"Let me see your leg."

I lifted my gown above my ankles, and he looked at the skin around where Trevor had cut my legs. "It's all over your leg too. I need to tell the guard. Perhaps it's contagious and you shouldn't be around anyone. I'm sorry, Anne, I fear that you will be alone once again."

Soon after, a guard brought a real doctor, not Dr. Trevor, into my cell. He examined my skin and said that yes, I was full of contagion, probably from Trevor's lancing of my flesh, and that I needed complete isolation. This meant, when they did feed me, they just shoved the food through the door, and no one came to empty my slop bucket, which ended up overflowing. This deprivation, this inhumane treatment, made me feel that I was no longer human, for I was not treated like a fellow human in any way.

When a guard walked by, I begged to see a priest, but I was ignored. I had become the invisible woman, a ghost woman, for no one came to my aid. I wanted to see a priest, for I wished to have the sacrament of last rites, but because I was a papist, the Protestant authorities ignored my request. So much for Trevor's mercy.

Eleven

Seeking Salvation

5 April 1812

Dear Godwin,

I am sorry to hear that you have no funds with which you can part. I did not know that your book publishing enterprise is not faring well and that your wife, her son, your stepdaughter Jane, and your own daughter Mary also require considerable funds. I had not realized that you had re-married after the death of your renowned wife.

Forgive me for my untimely request. I do hope that we can continue correspondence, and that when I return to England, I may meet you and your family to further solidify our friendship.

I remain your faithful disciple,
Percy Bysshe Shelley

5 April 1812

My dear Sir Charles,

You will be pleased to know that, because of your tutelage concerning the desperate condition of the Irish people, I continue to live in Ireland working on Catholic Emancipation and a Repeal of the Act of Union. I have addressed the Catholic Committee headed by Daniel O'Connell and have written a proposal for a philanthropy that will work peacefully toward these goals. I know that these aims are dear to your own heart since you were forced to convert to the Anglican Church to enter Parliament.

I feel certain that you will also be pleased to learn that I have written poems about liberty that are soon to be published. As I await their publication, I have started to experience deprivation, for my father, Sir Timothy, continues to withhold my allowance and forbids me to borrow against my inheritance from my grandfather.

As an uncle of sorts, would you be so kind as to dispatch funds to me? I need money to purchase victuals for my wife (who is with child) and her sister. I need little in the way of material sustenance; I live on spiritual food, the kind that comes from writing poetry and broadsheets about freedom. I also need funds, because my work here may soon be over, and I will need to secure passage to Wales. The three of us can't stowaway as I would if it were just me fleeing the country.

I await your reply.
      Yours in gratitude,
      Your "nephew," Percy

6 April 1812

Whenever Harriet left the flat, Eliza continued to follow her but kept considerable distance. Harriet noticed that someone followed her when she walked to Anne's. She tried a different path but saw the same person behind her, walking and stopping whenever she stopped. The person was heavily wrapped in several shawls and Harriet decided to stop and gaze in a store window. She turned around and the person was gone so she walked on.

But then she felt uneasy, believing that she was still being followed, so she turned around and saw what she assumed was the person who had been following her, but it was someone else dressed like a soldier.

"Why are you following me? Are you from Dublin Castle?" she asked in a trembling voice.

She noticed that the person looked to be a female, even though she was dressed in male garb.

"No, Mrs., I'm not. I know U."

Harriet was astonished. She recalled from what Brother Cullen told her that these were code words used by the United Irishmen and Women. Was this a United Irishwoman bringing her a message? "I don't know what you mean."

The woman repeated, "I know U."

Harriet hesitated. "I know N."

"Good," she said. "I thought you were one of us, for you visit Mrs. Campbell."

"How do you know that?"

"I watch her door to make sure no one harms her. I've seen you regularly visit her."

"Yes, she and I are friends," Harriet remarked.

"Then, if you're friends with her, you'll wish to come to a meeting in St. Michan's crypt. It's on Friday evening. Bring no one with you."

Harriet thought of the mummy in the crypt as well as of the ghost of a Viking warrior that supposedly haunted the place and wondered if she dared enter into its deadly world. Even though she felt great trepidation, she swallowed her fear and asked, "What's the meeting concerning?"

"We know that you wish to join our Sisterhood, and we have news concerning a child you claim is your charge," she said, as she handed Harriet a note that inscribed the place, date, and time of the meeting.

Harriet wondered how this woman knew that she wished to join the Sisterhood. She told no one but Catherine, but would Catherine tell others without informing her? She was curious but thought that she'd have to assume that Catherine had changed her mind about her joining the Sisterhood.

"Which child?" Harriet's hope rose. Perhaps Mrs. O'Byrne realized that she did not have the capacity to take care of her child and would now allow her and Percy to adopt Sinead.

"The one that you and your husband befriended."

"Do you mean Sinead?"

"I know nothing about a Sinead, but I do know of a Devin."

"Devin? A judge convicted him of theft and made him join the military." Harriet hoped that Devin was not hurt or in trouble.

"He's escaped. He's free and is asking for you."

"I must tell my husband," Harriet replied as she began to walk away.

"No, stop, you must tell no one and bring no one with you when you meet with us. Keep the note in a private place." The woman turned away from Harriet and walked down an alley. She didn't look back.

Harriet felt most peculiar. Even though she longed to join the Sisterhood, she wondered if she should trust this stranger, who, by all accounts, appeared to be a member of the United Irishwomen. Should she speak to Catherine or Anne about this, or should she trust her own judgment? How did this woman know of their informal guardianship of Devin and of his escape from the military? She felt as though she must tell Percy, but worried that, if she did, she might jeopardize Devin. She would have to determine for herself whether or not to attend this meeting and face her fears.

She tucked this knowledge away as she entered Anne's home and listened to more of Anne's tales.

Anne Devlin

Whenever the lass leaves to return to her atheistic "rebel" husband, I spend more time thinking about my trials. I can't say how long I lived in such a wretched state from what the devil Trevor did to me. It must have been months. Eventually, my infection subsided through God's mercy but, even so, my resolve was eroding, until one night I heard a voice whisper through the slit in my cell's door. The voice said, "Take heart, Anne Devlin. Your father Bryan is free as is your mother Winnie. Perhaps you'll be set free too." Knowing that my dear parents were free gladdened my heart and engendered some hope.

I arose as quickly as I could, but by the time I reached the door whomever had spoken to me had moved along. I thought at that moment that God was at least merciful to my family, and I said a prayer of thanksgiving. Perhaps Mam and Da would locate Nellie and return to my sisters on the farm. I closed my eyes and also said a silent Thanks to whomever was brave enough to relay this good news to me. Clearly, there were Devlin allies in the gaol.

Even so, my legs ached so that I could hardly sleep. I tossed and turned on the straw bed and waited until one of the jailers brought me my bread. Colum was now allowed to empty my slop bucket, and he told me that news of my condition had reached Dublin Castle, and he had heard that I would soon have a visitor.

"Who might that be?" I asked. "Why would they send a visitor? I remain an enemy of the state by their accounts."

"I don't know. But perhaps Dr. Trevor's cruelty towards you is being acknowledged. Don't lose heart at this point, Anne."

Sometime later, a gentleman from Dublin Castle examined me. He said his name was Dr. Howard. I said little to him, for all he had to do was look at my skin and limbs, which were both in a frightful condition.

"You poor creature. I shall pass your suffering on to his Excellency," he said. "Perhaps he will grant you mercy."

About a week later, I was placed among the women prisoners. Katty the Goose kept her distance, which I was grateful for, for I hadn't the strength to confront her and protect myself again.

I was still in great pain, so the authorities decided that I would benefit from visiting Lucan Spa to drink its waters. Michael Dwyer's wife remained a prisoner as well, and she offered to attend to me, but Dr. Trevor would not have it. Instead, my sister Julie traveled from the farm and accompanied me. I did not have complete freedom however, for two dragoons and a turnkey oversaw my visits. They carried pistols to prevent me from escaping. How they ever thought that I had the mobility to run is far beyond my imagination. I could barely walk, and I still needed to use the cane as support.

Even though we were not allowed to speak freely, I felt better merely by being in the company of my sister. The medicinal waters had little effect, but the companionship and proximity to someone who cared about my well-being made me feel human once more.

Not long after, we learned that Mr. Pitt, the Prime Minister, was not long for this world. It was believed that once he passed, the new PM, Mr. Charles Fox, would have mercy on us state prisoners and that I would be released. I could hardly contain my joy, for I had spent three years in captivity. When I closed my eyes, I tried to imagine what it would feel like to feel the sun shining on my face and to see the evening sky dotted with distant stars, to gaze at and try to discern the features of my loved ones. I practiced this feeling frequently to keep my senses and sensibilities as sharp as I could, despite my growing disability. I believed that I would be reunited with my family soon.

I was lost in this reverie when my door was thrown open.

"Get up, Devlin," the guard ordered.

"Am I to go free?" I asked as my heart beat wildly.

"I'm not at liberty to say," she replied. "You're to come with me."

I struggled to arise using my cane. Even though the jailer had been curt, she took pity on me and assisted me to stand.

When I entered the hallway, I saw a line of state prisoners, my comrades being escorted down the hall and down the winding steps. I followed in suit, growing stronger by the minute, for I believed that when I reached outdoors, I would be a free woman.

As I walked out of Kilmainham, I turned around and looked up at the five dragons and silently mocked them, for they had not conquered me. I was to walk free! I looked up at the sky and even though it was raining, I was thankful, for I felt that the rain was cleansing me and perhaps resurrecting me, giving me new life.

A carriage stood in front of the gaol. The guard told me that it was for me.

"Are you taking me home?" I asked.

No reply. The guard got in after me. I wondered why someone from Kilmainham would accompany me but didn't ask, for I was nearly in a state of delirium. I felt that soon I would be on the road back to Rathfarnum and would be in the arms of my loving family.

Soon the rain stopped, and the sun came out; I could tell that we were headed east from the position of the sun. Suddenly the carriage halted, and then the driver turned into the gates of Dublin Castle.

"Wait! Where are you taking me? I thought that I was being released through the beneficence of Charles Fox."

The jailer laughed. "Did you now? Dr. Trevor has other plans for you."

I felt my head swim; I felt like I might drown. I had been tricked.

My new accommodation was a little closet, one that resembled the place where they had kept me three years ago, a fearful symmetry. It was only slightly larger than the straw pallet they'd placed on the stone floor as my bed. They gave me no light or fire. I was sure that this would now become my narrow grave.

7 April 1812

My dear Sir Charles,

I cannot tell you how grateful I am that you have once again rescued us. Your generous allowance of £200 allows us to stay here in Ireland a bit longer. I cannot convey the ways in which the receipt of these funds makes me glad and saves us from destitution. Harriet (and our unborn child) and Eliza can now eat heartily. I have a few pounds sterling to contribute to the success of my philanthropy, some to pay my publisher so that my poems will be printed, and a fair amount will remain that we can use to travel to Wales and set up our communal life. I have decided that my colleague Lawless will continue our work here, and I will establish my utopia in Wales where my friend from Oxford, Thomas Jefferson Hogg, will join us, the first of the gifted and intelligent humans who will help us grow our community of like-minded seekers of truth and justice. In my artistic commune, I will write my poetry and create a following. My poetry will inspire others to seek freedom from tyranny. Art will be our salvation, as more people become better able to exercise reason and imagination.

You, sir, are my great benefactor. Please accept my most sincere thanks. I shall in time endeavour to repay your kindness to me and my loved ones who also hope to transform the world.

Your favorite "nephew,"
P.B.

8 April 1812

Percy had once again changed his mind. They would now depart for Wales, even though Harriet wished to stay in Ireland. She decided to attend the meeting and learn of Devin's whereabouts and how she could be of service to him, and then would join the Sisterhood. Perhaps if Percy waited to depart, Devin could travel with them to Wales if they hid and disguised him. Harriet didn't tell anyone about her plan but told Percy that they must wait to depart because of her pregnancy.

"Percy, you recall how ill I was when we sailed. I fear that, if we experience a storm again, I will miscarry. Please, may we delay our departure?" She also fretted about the sea voyage and the possibility that this next voyage would fulfill her nightmares.

He looked at her with concern. "Of course, darling girl. We'll wait to travel as long as you need to feel comfortable." He agreed that they must safeguard the pregnancy so he said that they could delay their move for a few weeks.

Anne Devlin

I expected a visit from the lass, but she did not arrive and then I was too busy with the washing to think more about her. I do hope that she is well. The last time we saw her, Aoife remarked that on her way to the market she noticed that someone appeared to follow Mrs. Shelley as she walked down the street but then turned down a side street. I should warn the lass that she may be followed because of her visits.

Later in the evening, I sat in my chair after Aoife and Mr. Campbell had taken to their beds, and I thought more about how Trevor had dangled freedom before me and then swept it away like a great tidal wave. Now I was back where I started, in Dublin Castle, essentially in a closet, not quite the *oubliette*, but close to it, for I felt as though Dr. Trevor wished to hide and forget me. He had not succeeded in hanging me, as he had hoped, but if he locked me away and told no one I was there, I would surely starve to death or die from loneliness. All the hope that I once possessed, the dreams of freedom, of sitting with my family in the Wicklow Mountains, of walking on the road in the sunshine with the sapphire sky overhead, of escaping to America, of walking to freedom with Robert beside me, had vanished. Now, my mind was troubled and the sinews that had held madness at bay started to loosen.

My dream world became horrifying, and I couldn't tell what was real and what wasn't. Even though I was alone, Trevor seemed to taunt me with a hanging rope, as he called me all the vile names that he could muster. He'd say, "Here, Anne Devlin, you rebelly wench, you tart, you filthy whore, come here and I'll end your misery; I'll send you to hell to meet with your pet. You two will then be joined as you were on earth. You'll entwine your flesh and never part. Now, wouldn't you like that?"

Part of my mind knew that Trevor was not really there in the cell harassing me, but when you are alone for long periods and have no hope of rising from the grave they've placed you in, you imagine all sort of things: men in the form of devils, just like Dr. Trevor, evil men, like the turnkey Dunn with his knife pressed to my throat, and Major Sirr with his hanging rope ready to hoist me into the air, appeared before me.

I tried my best to keep these terrifying visions at bay and to think of my mam and da and my brothers and sisters, but those beneficent visions were impossible to conjure. I was even beginning to forget what my loved ones looked like.

Along with the evil hallucinations, I saw the starving ghost, the girl who had supposedly been buried in the walls of Dublin Castle. She begged me for food, and I told her repeatedly that I had nothing to give her. I was indeed sorry for her but also sorry for myself, for I was famished like her.

"But you still have flesh," she said. "You're still alive, unlike me. You must have some victuals stowed away. I know you do! Now, give them over or I'll do something that you'll regret."

"You can't hurt me or, if you do, I would be most grateful. I'm nearly dead anyway," I replied.

"Starving to death is the worst fate, for your hunger is never satiated. If you die now, you will hunger for eternity."

"So be it; I don't care," I replied.

I really didn't wish to die of starvation, for I feared what the starving lass told me was true. I did not wish to hunger for eternity. I banged on my cell door. I cried out for my mam and da, for a guardian angel, for Jesus himself to appear with bread and wine, loaves, and fishes, but no one came to my aid.

In the end, I prayed for death. I felt that I could no longer continue without breaking and telling everything that I knew about my co-conspirators and the dozens in and around Dublin that supported our work. I was tired, broken as if I had been stretched on the rack or pushed into one of those medieval torture machines that I saw in the gaol, the iron maiden that pierced your flesh in a thousand places, just like you were Jesus himself. I could no longer pray to God to strengthen my weakened resolve, so I asked him to send one of His angels to lift me from this life that was no life but rather a living death.

Twelve

Betrayal

9 April 1812

Harriet descended the stairs into St. Michan's Crypt and felt a chill.

"Is anyone here?" she called out.

Her words reverberated in the cavernous crypt. Weak light from the staircase barely illuminated the place, and, in the shadows, she saw row after row of tombs, which made her tremble. The first tombs were those of the Sheares Brothers, members of the Society who met the same fate as Emmet but were further dishonored by being drawn and quartered. Perhaps meeting here was contrived to test her courage, but, even so, she wished to get away from the place as quickly as possible.

"It's Harriet Shelley. I'm here to meet those who wish to free Ireland."

Someone groaned and laughed.

Harriet panicked, for she had been told that the ghost of a Viking warrior haunted the place, and she had no wish to meet him.

Then, she looked in the corner and saw the mummified nun who beseeched heaven to help her. Her heart beat wildly, and she was ready to run up the stairs but then she heard someone step forward from behind one of the tombs.

"Devin, is that you?"

The person's face was covered with a scarf. "Are you alone as you were instructed?"

"Yes, of course."

"Are you willing to swear allegiance to the Society?"

"That's why I'm here. And to learn of my ward."

"You will learn of your ward after you prove yourself. You're not afeared of the dead, are you?" Harriet thought that an odd question and wondered how this stranger knew one of her greatest fears.

"No," she said, even though she felt great trepidation. She recalled how she could not help retrieve the dead woman from the river. When they found the baby, it was as if touching the dead would somehow infect her and lead her to her own death and that of her child's. She still feared that she would perish while young. In her dreams, she'd seen herself drown. But then she thought of Anne's courage when she unearthed and reburied Sam. She silently swore that she would draw on Anne's courage and pluck up her own.

"Turn around," the woman said.

As Harriet did so, the woman wrapped a scarf around Harriet's eyes and led her up the stairs.

"Why do I need a blindfold? Where are you taking me?"

"Of course, I can't reveal that," she replied.

She held Harriet's arm tightly, and Harriet felt even more fearful. Her heart beat frantically, but she took several deep breaths to try to calm herself. At that point, she heard other voices, and then feet shuffling up the stairs to the courtyard, as the stranger escorted her up the steps. Once in the courtyard, Harriet felt herself being helped onto a wagon, and she felt warm bodies surrounding her.

After what seemed like a long ride, she was helped down from the wagon and her blindfold was removed. The moon was a quarter crescent, partly covered by clouds that stretched across the sky, hiding the starlight. The leader lit a torch and handed it to another woman.

"Here's your shovel," the leader said as she directed Harriet to a small heap on the ground.

"What am I to do?"

"Dig, of course."

She and the other women quickly unearthed a shallow grave. One woman held a torch over the grave, and Harriet saw a girl who looked to be around her own age. Her long hair was nut-brown with little golden tendrils surrounding her sweet face. The girl's eyes were wide open as if in death she had witnessed terror.

"What's her name?" Harriet asked.

"Ianthe," the leader replied.

Did these women know of Percy's poem? Was the girl's name really Ianthe? Had she, like her Greek namesake, been to hell?

"What happened to her? How did she die?"

"Does it matter?"

"Yes, of course," Harriet replied as she swayed.

"She died giving aid to fellow rebels, if you must know; she drowned while helping rebels cross the river," one woman said.

Harriet's knees buckled.

"Are you alright?" the leader asked as she reached for Harriet.

Harriet felt woozy but stayed upright. "Yes, I was just surprised by the girl's unusual name and her mode of death."

The leader shrugged and then told Harriet to lift the girl's shoulders while she grabbed her feet. Harriet's hands trembled as she touched the flesh of the dead girl whose skin felt like rock.

"Where are we to put her?" she asked.

"We've opened a tomb back at St. Michan's; she needs to be placed in sacred ground," the leader said.

Harriet was once again blindfolded and wondered why. She had little knowledge of Dublin's geography, but why were her soon-to-be sisters intent on keeping her in the dark? In the wagon, she felt the dead girl's cold body next to hers and she shook with fear. She kept trying to keep her head and remember that she was being tested. That she would soon be able to help Devin. She thought of Anne and all that she encountered in Kilmainham and told herself that this short test was nothing like what Anne experienced.

The wagon stopped, and her blindfold was removed. The leader directed her to pick up the dead girl and help carry her into the graveyard. As Harriet carried the child, she felt as though she carried herself to her own grave. They faltered a few times and Harriet nearly stumbled. The leader led the way to an opened grave.

"Have a look, Mrs. Shelley," the leader said. Harriet was horrified when she peered into the open grave and saw a pile of bodies in a mass grave. Why would the Society place their members in a mass grave?

"Are we at St. Michan's? This doesn't look right. Who are all of these others?" she asked.

"Our comrades, our sisters," one of them said.

"Have they no names? Why are they buried together?"

"You ask too many questions, Mrs. Shelley," the leader said. "But, of course, you need to know what you risk if you become one of us. You risk death. We need to finish our task and get you sworn in. We need you to begin to act on the Society's behalf."

Harriet felt that she was being rushed, and she still wanted to know why these girls and women were placed in a mass grave. It made no sense, for it did not honor those who died in service to free Ireland. She began to doubt the authenticity of this enterprise, but speculated that she was just being overly anxious, too fearful, and that she should continue to risk joining the Society. Surely, confronting her fears was necessary for her to actually become a true Irishwoman and the test they had given her forced her to embrace what she feared most, death.

As she thought about all of this, she wondered if this mass grave would indeed be her fate if she took the vow. She shook with fear, even though she was trying her best to channel Anne's courage. Then she remembered that

Anne told Luke Cullen that she had often been afraid in Kilmainham, but she never let her face show it, so Harriet attempted to put on a blank face as she stood as tall as she could to denote confidence and courage. Even so, her knees shook uncontrollably.

The women surrounded her.

"Now, Mrs. Shelley, you'll take our oath," the leader said. "You have proven yourself and I would wager that, if necessary, you would do anything we ask of you. Is that correct?"

"If necessary, yes, but . . . what about Devin? Is he here? May I see him?"

"Not until you take your vow."

As soon as she completed the oath, Harriet expected to receive the green scarf that Luke Cullen mentioned was the mark of the rebel. She expected that Devin would appear and run into her arms. Instead, she was struck from behind. As she blacked out, all she heard was, "Take her to Kilmainham and charge her with treason."

Now she sat in a damp cell, just like Anne Devlin did, and waited to hear what would become of her. She felt duped by those who used her love of children to get her to believe that she would become a true Irish woman and a true rebel. She should have consulted Percy, Anne, or Catherine. And why was the girl Ianthe relegated to a mass grave? And who were the others piled high in that common grave? Were they all rebels who had been murdered by Dublin Castle authorities? Once more, she feared that these women spies, these traitors to the Irish cause, had been showing her her potential fate.

10 April 1812

My dear Godwin,

The most terrible thing has happened. My darling wife has disappeared. She's been missing for a day. I fear the worst. I have contacted the authorities, but no one knows where she is. She's vanished.

I was out late with my friend Lawless and then when I came home, I slept on the sofa so I wouldn't disturb my wife. In the morning, I saw that our bed was empty. I asked her sister where Harriet was and she said, "What? She's not here? I thought she went to bed when I did. Where could she have gone? Perhaps she's with that Anne Devlin character."

"That's impossible. She never met Devlin."

"You're wrong. She told me that she regularly visits that woman. And out of concern for her safety, I've been following her. Last evening,

I must have dozed off and she went out. I thought I heard her come in later so was unconcerned, but now it seems she never came home." Eliza anxiously wrung her hands. "This is your fault, Percy. You asked her to visit that Devlin woman, and she did. Then she seems to have befriended her. I knew that something terrible would happen to her. I tried to protect her." Eliza glared at me and grew red in the face.

"Why didn't you tell me that Harriet was visiting with Devlin?"

"If your wife was not willing to confide her activities to you, why should I? You never should have brought us to this God-forsaken place. I should have insisted, as the eldest, that we return to England, where we belong."

"I haven't time for your drivel, Eliza. I must search for my wife," I replied.

I raced to Anne Devlin's abode and knocked furiously on her door, but no one answered. I thought that odd, since Anne told me that she does not leave her flat. Perhaps she and Harriet left Dublin City. But why would they do so? Were they in cahoots regarding an uprising? That seemed absurd to me, since Harriet is a pacifist like me.

I thought that perhaps someone on John Street saw them walking out of town. I knocked on several doors and showed them a sketch of my wife, a fair likeness.

An old man opened his door. "What can I do for you, sir?"

"Have you seen this woman?"

The man squinted at the sketch and studied it for a minute. "No, sir. Why would such a lovely girl walk about on these streets?"

"She may have been with a friend, Anne Devlin. Do you know her?"

"Anne Devlin? She's a cripple. She never leaves her home."

"So, I've heard. But I have reason to believe that she and my wife may have walked down this street and fled Dublin City."

"That I doubt. I haven't seen Anne Devlin in years."

I felt perturbed, for I had seen Anne in the cemetery and didn't believe that she never left her home. I decided it was futile to speak further with this doddering man, so I said, "If you see my wife, please come find me." I handed the man my card.

"Of course, sir," he said as he pocketed the card.

I knocked on another door.

"What do you want?" a woman peeked through a crack in the door.

"I'm sorry to disturb you but I'm looking for my wife. Here's a sketch of her."

The woman opened the door. Surrounded by a bevy of unwashed children, she peered at the drawing and said, "She came here looking for me sister, Kathleen O'Byrne, but I haven't seen her since."

"And why would she want to find your sister? You say her name is O'Byrne?" Then I recalled that that was the name of children Harriet felt responsible for, one of whom had died in the Foundling Hospital.

"I haven't the slightest idea."

"Do you know where my wife is?"

"No, sir, I don't. If you can spare me some money, I will keep an eye out for her."

The woman looked dubious to me, but I offered her a few pounds.

As I continued to search, I thought, If Harriet deliberately left, why would she leave me? I adore her; I'm committed to her and our child. I have made her the heroine of my epic poem. This question plagues my heart and mind.

In the meantime, our friends Lawless, Mrs. Nugent, Harriet's sister Eliza, and I endlessly search the streets. I walk along the River Liffey worrying that some ill fortune occurred, and that my dear Harriet is injured along the banks or, worse yet, drowned in that filthy water, like a dead woman we found under the Ha'penney Bridge. Today, we saw constables pull a woman from the river and I rushed to see if it was my girl, but, Thank Goodness, the drowned girl did not in the least resemble my beautiful wife. Even so, I worried that the river's next victim could be her, for Harriet believes she will die by drowning.

I'm sure you're aware how much I love my darling girl. She is a young creature and rather delicate. She is becoming learned through my tutelage. She has a compassionate heart and is my partner, my love, my best friend. She inspired me to come to Ireland and free the wretches. Together we bring justice to this broken world. I must find her and secure her well-being, lest I go mad.

Your worried friend,

P.B.

10 April 1812

Harriet had been confined, as Anne Devlin was, to a narrow, dark cell. Like her, she slept on sodden straw. Like her, she felt rats nibbling her toes. She tried not to cry out, but she didn't have the fortitude to stay as silent as a sphinx or a cloistered nun. All of this seemed like a nightmare in that she was being treated as if she were Anne Devlin.

When Harriet was brought into the prison, her hair was shorn just as Anne's was. She noticed that other prisoners still possessed their locks and wondered why she had been degraded in this way. She held her head high though, as she remembered what Anne had told Luke Cullen about how she maintained her dignity. She was innocent of any wrongdoing, aside from believing that she was joining a secret society, and surely loving Irish children was not a crime.

Harriet asked the guard who brought her stirabout whether she would receive a trial. She said that she didn't know. Guards were never informed about plans for the prisoners. Harriet told the guard that she would like to know how she could be charged with treason, for she had done nothing treasonous.

"Perhaps, Mrs., you was seen in the company of undesirables, those that work against the state."

Harriet didn't reply, for indeed she had been in the company of a woman that Dublin Castle loathed and feared. She decided at that point to keep mum, for no good could be had by revealing her actions, even though she was growing to trust this somewhat helpful guard. Perhaps she should rethink trusting strangers though; look where such trust delivered her.

Harriet asked herself, what have I done? And will I actually be brave enough to withstand what will happen to me? Will knowledge of Anne's courage sustain me further? Have I, like Sarah Curran, who led to Emmet's downfall, ruined our lives by trying to become an Irish rebel?

12 April 1812

My dear Mr. Curran,

I write in the hope that you will come to my aid, for my wife is missing. Today, as I was once perusing Harriet's things, I found a note among her keepsakes. All it said was "Half nine, Friday evening, St. Michan's crypt."

I dashed to St. Michan's only to find the crypt locked. I felt crestfallen, as I sat in the church and thought about Dean Swift's ironic proposal that the Irish eat their young. Is that metaphorically what happened here? A young woman who thought herself kin to the Irish and wished to help them has been sacrificed for some unknown reason. I know I sound as though I've gone mad, but I nearly feel this is so.

I know you think that we foolishly followed in Robert Emmet's steps. I may have but to my knowledge my wife did not. She's an innocent

*young woman. And she is carrying our child. I must find the two of them
and ensure their safety.*

*Please, I am desperate. If you have a heart for my plight, I beseech
your help.*

> *Your servant,*
> *Percy Shelley*

12 April 1812

Harriet was taken in chains to see Dr. Trevor, the devil who had tortured
Anne Devlin.

He looked her up and down. "Mrs. Shelley, we are quite aware of your
excursions around Dublin and your frequent visits to John Street. Tell me
what you were doing there."

"I don't know what you're talking about. I don't know where John Lane
is. I am a visitor here," she replied as she kept her head lowered, not wishing
to look the devil in the eye. "I wish to know what I'm charged with and why."

"Well, like your friend Anne Devlin, that slutty bitch, you've been charged
with treason for joining a forbidden society."

"I don't know what you're talking about."

"Why were you in the crypt at St. Michan's then?"

"I was fascinated by the tales I heard of a Viking ghost, and I wished to
see if he would appear to me. I'm collecting sightings of the supernatural for
my husband who is writing a book about Irish history and folklore."

"Ah, yes, your husband the writer and interloper, the interfering British
subject who arouses the Irish to violently rebel."

"He's done no such thing. He advocates non-violence," Harriet said.

"No, Mrs. Shelley, if that were so, then why did a riot start at Trinity
College when he spoke?"

"I don't know, sir," she replied. "I was not there, but I was told that it
wasn't a riot, but rather a Yeomanry action that deliberately injured innocent
people."

"Is that so? Which innocent people were they? The ones who wish to
overthrow the British government, just like you and your interfering
husband? Are you, your husband, and that bitch Devlin planning another
rebellion?"

Harriet remained silent and stared directly at Trevor.

"Take her back to her cell and remove her slop bucket." He crossed his
arms. "I believe you'll wise up, Mrs. Shelley, after you are deprived in the way
that Anne Devlin was. As Anne Devlin's comrade this is what you deserve."

Harriet resolved at that moment to try to imitate Anne Devlin. She would do her best to not speak about Anne or her friends, to not reveal all that she knew about her and Robert Emmet. Even with her resolution, she found it difficult to sleep, for she worried about Percy and whether he would soon join her. She wondered if he would be brave enough to remain silent. She now wished she had told him what she learned from Brother Cullen, for she felt certain that, if he had, it would bolster Percy's courage and calm his agitated mind.

13 April 1812

Dear Godwin,

There is still no word about my dear Harriet. I continue to walk the streets with Lawless searching for her. I've shown my sketch to people in pubs, but no one recognizes her. I continue to search the riverbank.

This evening as Eliza and I further searched Harriet's belongings for clues, I found her journal. I knew that she had been writing each evening, but I was deeply involved in my own work and paid little attention to Harriet's scribblings. As I opened the journal, I felt as though I was invading her privacy, but thought what is privacy at this point? Harriet is missing and perhaps, if I read her journal, I would discern if she had been unhappy with me and left on her own accord. So, I read it and found that all this time, while she had been visiting the rebel Anne Devlin, she obtained Anne's tale from a Carmelite brother and that she was writing Anne's tale of her imprisonment for her. The tale Harriet has written is truly a dreadful one of prolonged suffering and endless torture. Some of Emmet's story is recorded too and it too is horrific, but it pales in comparison to the incessant years of anguish that Anne Devlin endured. I am grateful to have read this tale, but now fear that because Harriet regularly spent hours with Anne Devlin, Harriet may have been taken prisoner because of her relationship with Anne. I fear the worst, even though Harriet has done nothing wrong other than befriend a broken woman while continuing to possess an "Irish" heart that longs, like mine does, for justice.

In addition, I learned that she wanted to be sworn into a secret society. I repeatedly told her that such societies work against our cause and only engender trouble. She should have heeded my warning and ended her mad romantic notions of becoming an Irish rebel.

Your disciple,

P.B.

17 April 1812

Dr. Trevor visited Harriet and informed her that she would no longer be fed. He told her that she deserved to starve for interfering in Irish politics.

"You're no Irishwoman, you know, Mrs. Shelley. You're a fake, an imitation, a desperately foolish Englishwoman with delusional ideas about freedom," he said with ire.

She said nothing, which made him even angrier.

"You have nothing to say after all the time you spent becoming Anne Devlin's confidant? I shall treat you as I treated her. No food, no water, no slop bucket, total darkness. We'll see how you like those living arrangements, my good lady."

He left her cell. Harriet thought, How he must loathe himself for his evil ways. Like Castlereagh, he eats the hearts of the Irish and the would-be Irish.

21 April 1812

Percy walked through the graveyard and placed Deora Dé on Emmet's grave, hoping that Emmet's spirit might help him find Harriet. Perhaps she left a clue in the crypt. When he descended the steps, he thought that he should have brought a torch, because there was no illumination and without it, he would find nothing. As he started to ascend the stairs, he heard footsteps.

"Who's there?" he inquired. He thought perhaps the fabled Viking warrior was in his midst, and Percy was excited to encounter him.

But instead, he saw a group of men. The man at the top of the stairs held a torch and those below him each brandished a weapon.

Percy raised his arms. "Gentlemen, I'm unarmed. Please lower your weapons."

"No, Mr. Shelley, we've been ordered to deliver you to Kilmainham Gaol," the man at the top of the stairs said.

"How do you know me?"

"Everyone who respects the proper relationship between England and Ireland knows you. You've gained quite a reputation."

Percy's heart beat wildly. "And why must I go to Kilmainham?"

"Major Sirr and Dr. Trevor wish to entertain you."

Percy quaked, for he recalled the names of both these figures from what Anne Devlin told the brother. The first had half-hanged Anne Devlin and the other starved and tortured Anne for three years.

"And why do they wish to entertain me?"

"They wish to discuss your writing with you," one of them replied as he chuckled.

"Am I being arrested? If so, what's the charge?"

"Sedition," the head man said. "Come along now."

"But I did nothing of the kind," he replied as one of the men grabbed his arm.

"You wrote incendiary work that promotes Catholic freedom and the abolishment of the penal laws. Take it up with your solicitor and the judge," the head man replied.

"But you can't arrest me. My father is a Member of the British Parliament."

All of them laughed.

"That means nothing to us," the head man said. "Come with us now or would you rather that we take you deeper into the crypt to convince you?"

They looked at Percy fiercely, so he went with them, reckoning that nothing ill would happen.

When he arrived at Kilmainham, he noted that five stone dragons looked as if they knew he was charged with treason, and that he would be found guilty as Robert Emmet had been. He looked back in defiance, for he was certain that the authorities dared not prosecute him. I am a future Baronet, he thought, if I choose to be.

Then his captors escorted him deep into the confines of the jail and told him to peer through a slit in a cell door. He saw Harriet lying on the stone floor. Her beautiful hair had been shorn and she looked weak and pale.

"Harriet!" he shouted. She did not move or look up. "What have you done to her? Did you drug her, torture her? You must let me stay with her. She needs tending."

Again, they laughed.

"No, no conjugal visits are allowed," the lead man said. "Besides, we have other plans for you."

At that point, they dragged him up a flight of stairs and stood him in front of a cell that contained a fireplace, a bed, and writing desk. A man stood inside the cell.

"Welcome to your new accommodation, Mr. Shelley," the man said. "You are so fond of that traitor Emmet; we've decided that his accommodation will be yours. Like him, you can write your last letters here at the desk where he confessed all."

"But I've not led a rebellion as he did. I have nothing to confess. What last letters are you suggesting?"

"The ones to your kin where you confess your treason. You've dabbled in Irish affairs. You fomented rebellion."

"I've done nothing of the kind. Who are you, sir?" Percy asked.

"Why I'm the superintendent here. I'm Dr. Edward Trevor."

Percy shivered, for he had read how Anne called him the Devil's Partner. Percy endeavoured once more to hide his fear as Anne Devlin did, but he could feel his his heart race.

"Mr. Percy Shelley, rest this evening. For we shall interrogate you tomorrow. In the meantime, here's some paper, a quill, and ink. You may write to whomever you wish."

Percy could not sleep. All night he thought of Harriet and what he had done that had led her to this place. If they had never come to Ireland, they would be safe in England. He realized that his plan to free Ireland had been folly, a type of madness, and all he wanted to do now was obtain his wife's freedom and to leave this wretched, loathsome country.

22 April 1812

As promised, Harriet was kept in the dark. Her guard, whose name was Fiona, had brought her news that Percy was now incarcerated as well. He was being kept in Robert Emmet's cell and Trevor interrogated him for hours. Harriet asked if she could see her husband and Fiona said that she would try to sneak Harriet in to see him in a few days.

"Must I wait that long? Please, I must be assured that he is well. He's a poet and extremely sensitive."

"I take great risk in removing you from your cell, Mrs."

"I know. Perhaps you can, in the meantime, take him a message. Tell him I'm well and that I love him. I trust him. Tell him to remain silent as the grave. I feel certain that we can withstand our sufferings, for we have Irish hearts."

She gave Harriet a skeptical look. "That I will do, Mrs. Now, here's some bread."

Harriet grabbed the bread. "You are truly my guardian angel. God bless you."

She rested easier then, knowing that Percy would learn that she was strong and courageous. That, like Anne, she did not possess a coward's soul.

23 April 1812

Harriet cried out for Fiona. A different guard appeared in her cell.

"Where's Fiona?"

"She's been dismissed."

"Why?"

"She was found carrying messages for you," she said. "You can bet that none of us will repeat her actions. Sure, we have families to feed."

Harriet's heart sank. "I need help. I'm pregnant but something isn't right. I'm cramping, and I feel ill. Please help me." She felt a gush of blood and an intense pressure below. She put her hand between her legs and held it in front of her face as the guard moved her torch close to Harriet's body.

"I'm bleeding. Oh, please, do something. I'm losing my baby." Harriet thought about how Anne said that fairies steal babies. That couldn't be what was happening but why was she losing her baby? Was it because of the deprivation that Trevor ordered?

"Ain't nothing I can do, Mrs," she said. "We ain't got no midwife. Besides, it's likely God's will for the trouble you caused."

"Surely, you don't believe that. Have you no heart?"

"Course I have, but I know nothing about such things. I'm a good, God-fearing woman."

"As I am," Harriet said as she continued to feel blood trickle from her womb.

"Well, if you are, God will let you keep your child. If not, that's the price you pay for sticking your nose into Irish business."

"I beg you to help me."

The woman thought for a moment and pulled a bottle out of her apron. "Here, maybe this will help."

Harriet saw that it was a bottle of gin. "Will this stop the bleeding?"

"Dunno, but it will ease the pain."

And with that she shut the cell door and walked away.

Harriet slept fitfully throughout the night. The gin took the edge off the pain, but she continued to bleed. When she finally slept, she dreamt that devils cast her into their dark, sweltering lair where they brandished her with pitchforks while their pet ravens pecked out her eyes.

When she awoke, she felt the bottom of her prison garb. It was soaked with blood. Her cramping had stopped. She laid her head on the straw and tried to return to sleep as she thought about her child and wondered whether it was a girl or a boy. Had it been born on Irish soil, she or he would truly have been Irish.

Even though Percy said that no blood would be shed in their quest for justice, Harriet shed blood. They had lost their Irish child.

When Harriet awakened, she thought she saw Anne sitting near her pallet. Perhaps she was stupefied from the gin, but she felt a warm hand on hers and returned to sleep. As she fell asleep, she recalled that Anne said that her ghost haunted Kilmainham. At least Anne's ghost was friendly and comforting.

23 April 1812

In the morning, Dr. Trevor appeared in Percy's cell, and he began to question him.

"I demand representation," Percy said.

"That's not possible. Don't you know, Mr. Shelley, that habeas corpus has been suspended? You've gotten yourself into a fine mess. Now, what can you tell us about Anne Devlin and her friends? Have you and your wife been plotting with Anne and the other traitors to threaten the Crown? Based on your writing and your association with Misters Lawless and Curran, we believe that you have."

"How do you know that?"

"Are you dense, man? We've followed you ever since you pasted your *Address* on the old parliament building."

"But, if you read my writing, you would understand that I have merely sought peaceful agitation and Catholic freedom."

"You should know that the Crown does not advocate Catholic freedom. You truly are naïve. Why should a young man such as yourself care about we Irish? You should keep to your own affairs."

Percy ignored him. "I wish to know what you have done to my wife. Why did she not respond to me last evening? Have you tortured her? You had no right to arrest her. She's an innocent victim."

"On the contrary, Mr. Shelley, she's an avowed member of an illegal society; she spoke the oath of the United Irishwomen. She has thus been confined lest she persuade others to join their diabolical society."

"But Harriet doesn't believe in violent upheaval."

"You, sir, don't know your wife well at all. I shall leave you now to brood on your transgressions against the king. In the meantime, you may write a final letter. You best make it a good one."

Percy sat at the table and felt despondent. What had he done to Harriet? How would he be able to free her? Trevor had suggested that she is in grave danger, as he was. They were both being charged with sedition. Perhaps the mocking dragons were right in their estimation.

Percy wrote to his father:

Dear Father,

If you still care about me, please, I beseech you, come to my aid and rescue me for I am in Kilmainham Gaol in Dublin along with my wife Harriet. Against my will and without my knowledge, Harriet joined a secret society, the Society of United Irishwomen, and we both have been accused of fomenting rebellion and are to be tried. Dr. Philpot Curran, a defender of the United Irishmen, has attempted to help us, but to no avail. The superintendent of this realm, Dr. Trevor, believes that I am the next Robert Emmet. I have argued with him, telling him that, unlike Emmet, my work intended to promote peaceful agitation. He says that I have been surveilled, that Harriet has been watched, and that because she befriended the Irish rebel Anne Devlin, Robert Emmet's colleague, and she took the oath of the United Irishwomen, she's also considered a traitor to the Crown. Harriet is being kept from me, and I fear that she will greatly suffer and will likely succumb to illness, for this place is full of pestilence and vermin. I can withstand whatever befalls me, but Harriet is far too delicate. And, then there's the fact that she is carrying our child, your first grandchild.

They have even placed me in Emmet's cell, and I write at the writing desk he used the night before he was executed. I wished to be his kin, but I do not wish to attain his ill fate.

Father, you must help me, Harriet, and your grandson or granddaughter. I beg your forgiveness and assistance.

Faithfully yours,
Percy

30 April 1812

Days passed and no word came from Percy's father. Percy feared that Dr. Trevor had intercepted his letter to prevent him from receiving aid. Or that perhaps his father had decided to leave them in prison so that he could further punish Percy for what he perceived to be Percy's folly.

Percy slept on the bed that Emmet occupied during his last days and thought about his fate, wondering whether there were actual plans to treat him as if I were Emmet's twin. How could this be happening? All he had wanted was to free the Irish from tyranny and now he was being persecuted. He felt his mind unravelling, for he thought for a moment that Emmet sat with him, telling him that he had been a fool. That his quest was absurd and Quixotic. That he should have remained in England where he belonged.

"But I wanted to continue your struggle. I have an Irish heart; I have become an Irishman."

"That's ludicrous. One cannot become Irish, even if you long to do so," Emmet said.

Percy shook his head. He wondered if he was dreaming. No, I'm awake. I finally met my idol, and he thinks me a fool.

He began to think that he would do anything to save his darling wife, including giving information about Lawless and others, including what he knew about Emmet. He knew in his heart that betrayal was wrong but, if he could turn evidence, he might be able to save Harriet. He tried to push such thoughts from his mind and hoped that there was another way to free Harriet and himself.

1 May 1812

Dr. Trevor visited Percy each day, trying to get him to confess, but Percy repeated that he was not a traitor and that they had no right to try him as one. He was not Robert Emmet. Trevor threatened Percy each day by taking him out to look up at the gallows, asking him to imagine hanging from a rope.

"I hear you're a poet, Mr. Shelley. You have a good imagination. I bet you can see yourself dangling here. That will soon happen, you know, for you are a traitor."

Percy told him that he dared not hang him, because parliament would exact justice against him if he decided to hang the son of an MP.

He smirked. "We shall see, Mr. Shelley."

2 May 1812

As Percy stood once more in front of the gallows, Trevor held a rope and taunted him in the usual manner.

"Why don't you hang yourself? You seem to think that you're a brave one, like Tone or Emmet," Trevor said. "If you won't do it, I'll gladly do it for you.

And I'll hang that pretty wife of yours. I meant to hang Anne Devlin, but your wife will do nicely as a substitute."

Percy lunged at him, called him the devil that he was and swore that if he touched Harriet, he would kill him himself. He was so enraged that his avowed pacifism was completely abandoned. He pommeled Trevor and knocked him to the ground, but then a guard stepped forward, grabbed his arm, and twisted it behind his back.

Percy was returned to his cell and left in the dark. He listened to the sound of weeping that came from below his cell and his heart ached, for he knew that Harriet was the captive who cried in the cell below him. He needed to rescue her once more.

3 May 1812

The next morning a guard appeared at Percy's cell door and said that Trevor wished to see him. Percy briefly remembered the pact he made with Hogg to commit suicide, if necessary, but he realized that he did not have the courage that Tone possessed, and he needed to stay alive to save his dear wife.

As he entered Trevor's lair, Trevor stood with rope in hand and escorted Percy to the front gate. They were accompanied by a guard who sported a large bayonet. The dragons leered down, and Trevor dangled the rope once more, as the guard held onto his arm.

"Shall we go to the upper chamber so you can hang yourself?" Trevor asked.

A guard pushed Percy. Even though he felt quite ashamed, he blurted out, "I'll give you names. I'll tell you what you want to know. I'll tell you about Anne Devlin and her plan to foment another rebellion. I'll tell you all I know about Emmet. Just release me and my wife."

"Well, now, you are becoming wise. I knew that the rebelly bitch was up to something nefarious. Let's return to your cell and you can write a confession."

"Will you free Harriet and me?" Percy asked.

"Not until we have your confession. And then we will need to take it to the Board of Governors of the Gaol. They will decide what's to become of you. Come along, Mr. Shelley," Trevor said as escorted Percy back to his cell.

Percy felt like a traitor to Ireland, to all Irish patriots, including his idol. Harriet was right. When pressed, he had abandoned his ideals. His activism and political ambitions had been folly and now he needed to save his own neck and that of his wife's. And in his betrayal of the patriots, he had not been assured that they would not be prosecuted. Emmet was correct. He was a fool.

In his cell, Percy examined his motivations. Why had he believed that he could free the Irish? The whole idea was absurd. He sat before the blank sheet of paper. Did he dare write a confession? What would he confess to? Being a poet, an idealist? A seeker of justice for all? A man ahead of his time who wished to topple all tyrants? That was the truth. The rest was a lie that he would have to fabricate to save them from execution.

He picked up the quill and dipped it in ink and began to write.

His cell door opened, and Percy looked up, thinking that Trevor was there to prod him to write. But instead of Trevor, Percy saw a man in a dark cloak.

The man threw back his hood and said, "Percy, what's to be done with you. You cause no end to trouble."

Percy wondered if he was once again imagining things. That he had gone mad. But then the man touched his arm.

"Father, oh, father, I'm so very sorry," he said as he fell into his father's open arms. "Are you really here?"

"I am. Now let's get you out of these less than desirable accommodations and get you home."

Trevor blocked the doorway. "Your papa saved your skin, Mr. Shelley. You'd better hope that he remains loyal to you, for I fear that you will cause further trouble for yourself and your family."

"Be silent, sir, and move aside," Sir Timothy said. "At least my son has lofty ideals and convictions. You, sir, seem to have none. Now have your guard take us to Mrs. Shelley."

Trevor smirked. "As you wish, my lord." He bowed deeply in deference, but Percy felt the bow disingenuous. Sir Timothy didn't seem to notice Trevor's mockery.

The guard escorted the two of them to Harriet's cell. Percy cried out when he saw once more the interior of the dark filthy cell that she had been kept in. The air was putrid with urine and excrement; he saw a rat race out the open door.

They found Harriet dressed in filthy rags and cowering in a corner. She didn't seem to know who Percy was.

"It's me love, Percy." He pulled the shawl off her head and saw that there were marks on her scalp where scissors had cut her. He covered her head once more, for he could not bear to look at the way they had disfigured her. At first, she struggled, as if she didn't know him, but then she looked into his eyes and realized it was him. She started to weep.

"Oh, Percy, I'm so sorry. I fear that our child is gone. The fairies took her."

She shook in his arms, and he tried his best to hold her close, gently caressing her, and telling her they were saved. "Please, do not cry, my darling; all will be well. And we will have other children far away from this place of pestilence and injustice. They will be safe."

She cried. "I wanted to save Devin, Percy. They told me I could save him."

"Now, my darling, you're delirious. I have it on good authority that Devin has been sent to India. Don't fret. There was nothing we could do for him." He dried her tears with the handkerchief that his father handed him.

Then, he held her tightly, nearly carrying her down the dark hallway, for several times she stumbled. His father walked behind them and the three of them walked out of Kilmainham. Percy felt overwhelming guilt, but also some relief that his father had rescued them. They did not speak as they climbed into the carriage; Eliza sat inside. Percy had no idea how his father had found her and didn't ask. He looked at Eliza who glared at him; she seemed to accuse him of having gravely injured her sister.

Sir Timothy ordered the carriage to make haste to Kingston.

"Stop," Harriet said. "We must go to Anne Devlin's. I need to bid her adieu."

"It's your extended relationship with her that caused us such trouble. We can't go there. That would be foolish," Percy said. "You must never speak of her again, for it causes me too much pain. Your acquaintance with her nearly cost us our lives. And it did cost our child's life."

Harriet cringed, but she blamed Trevor, not Anne. And she felt ashamed of Percy and realized that, unlike her, he did not truly possess an Irish heart. Didn't he still think that the Irish should be free of British tyranny? Had a short jail sentence broken his idealism and his thirst for justice? She wanted to scold him but thought that it would be best to ask these questions when they were not in the presence of his father and Eliza, who would likely feel gratified at her renunciation of Percy's actions, so she said, "Well, then we must return to Sackville Street, for there's something I must fetch."

"We haven't time, Harriet," Percy said.

"If it's important to your wife, then we will make time," Sir Timothy said.

Percy grew pale and didn't respond.

"I know what you want to fetch," Eliza said. "Here it is." She handed Harriet her journal.

Harriet felt great gratitude for her sister, who despite her criticism of her visits with Anne, now seemed to understand the importance of Anne's story and that ordinary women's stories were surely a part of history.

Harriet silently pledged to keep Anne's story safe until Erin was free. And then all would know of her valor, heroism, and suffering. People would learn how to be courageous from her example. Harriet thought that perhaps she would write and tell her that her story, which she learned from Brother Cullen, sustained her when she took her place in Kilmainham Gaol, or tell her that she felt her presence after she lost her child, or maybe she would just write to let her know that she remained her friend, for her own suffering in no way compared with hers. She would try her best to emulate Anne Devlin as she lived what she hoped would be a long life.

On the remainder of their journey, no one spoke. Under a steel-gray sky, they passed Dublin Castle, Trinity College, and the shuttered parliament, where countless desperate people had convened outside and were listening to Lawless urge them to emancipate themselves. Percy turned his head when he heard the crowd cheer. He shut his eyes and drifted to sleep, while Harriet slept and dreamt of her lost fairy child.

At the last minute, Sir Timothy tried to persuade Percy to return to England, but Percy said they would press on to Wales as planned. He asked his father to reinstate his allowance and Sir Timothy didn't respond.

Percy had failed in his Quixotic quest. Neither of he nor Harriet had become Irish; neither of them had saved the Irish from British tyranny. The morning star did not shine on them and no fairies twinkled in the gloaming.

1 June 1812
Anne Devlin

The lass never returned. Perhaps she lost interest in my tales because I'm not a genuine storyteller like my mam. I hope that the girl has not reached a bad end, for she seemed a kind young woman, perhaps too naïve and delicate for this land where we perennially suffer. She claims an Irish soul, but how can that be? She once told me that she and her atheist believe the pagan notion that when we die, we are born into another body. That seems like heathenism, but I know little about the afterlife. I only know that we can experience hell right here on earth. So, if this heathen belief is true, maybe she once had been Irish in another life.

I now wish that I had told the lass some of my own story. Even so, I would never have told the entire truth to her. I know that it is a sin to tell a lie, but omission allows us to keep secrets in our hearts about ourselves and those we love.

Towards the end of my time in Dublin Castle, I prayed for death in that solitary cell where no one tended me; I received no food or water. And I was kept in complete darkness once again. I despaired, believing, and hoping that I would die. Then, out of nowhere, an angel appeared.

A woman appeared in my cell and said to me kindly, "Anne Devlin, I'm here to help you."

"Who are you?"

"My name is Martha Hanlon. The jailer told me about you and what Dr. Trevor did to you. Please may I examine you?"

I could barely lift my head and look at her. So, she bent down and helped me sit up.

"Please," I said. "Please get me out of here. I'll do what they want. I'll tell them everything if they'll only let me go."

"That's the fever talking, Anne. I'll minister to you and get you examined by a doctor and then I shall write to Secretary Long and demand that he visit you to see for himself how cruelly you've been treated."

"You would do this for me? Why?"

"Your reputation as a fearless woman is growing. Everyone at Dublin Castle and Kilmainham know how you've been treated. It's time that the world knew."

As she said this, I fell into her arms and wept for the longest time. I couldn't stop weeping, for it was as if a dam held back a great flood of tears that had been filling my heart and were now being released.

She did as she said. She tended to me, and my fever dissipated. Secretary Long visited me and after he looked at my shrunken frame, my withered limbs, my filthy, swollen body, he wept.

He ordered that I be given a bath, new clothes, and a new cane. And when that was done, he personally opened the door and said, "You're free, Anne Devlin. God go with you."

I was fearful as I picked up my cane, left my cell, and found my way to an exit. No one stopped me, but even so as I passed people in the hallway, I worried that someone would start laughing and tell me that once more I had been tricked. That they would grab me and throw me into another cell where I would surely rot. Or that they would bury me in a wall, and I would be like the eternally hungry girl. But no one did and my heart raced with the thought that I would truly be free.

When I got outside, I looked up at the sky, which was an azure blue. I felt the sun shine on my face and had to close my eyes, for the bright sun nearly blinded me and everything appeared hazy, as if a halo surrounded all things and people, as it still did to this day. I heard robins twitter and the bells at St. Patrick's Cathedral chime. Even though I could barely walk, I held my head high as I passed through those gates that Robert Emmet had tried to storm to free Erin three years ago. And as I passed, Robert walked by my side as I headed home toward Rathfarnum, and then arm in arm we both ventured on to Wicklow, the garden of Ireland, my mam's, and Mother Ireland's birthplace. Together, we sat atop Lugnaquilla, the highest mountain. We lifted our faces to the stars above, breathed in their light, and looked down at the four green fields that we knew would one day be ours again.

Afterward

As far as I know, Percy and Harriet Shelley never met Anne Devlin, but they sojourned in Dublin in 1812 working for Irish independence. It is true that Shelley eventually met Margaret King, who befriended him and his second wife, Mary Godwin Shelley, when they lived in Italy. And it's also true that Mary Wollstonecraft was Margaret King's governess, and that King claimed that Wollstonecraft freed her from superstition and had emboldened her to become an Irish rebel. And, much later in Percy's life, when he was married to Mary Godwin, when they resided in Italy, he became acquainted with Sarah Curran's sister Amelia, the artist who drew a portrait of Percy's and Mary's three-year-old son Will just prior to his death.

Sadly, in an act of desperation, similar to the drowned woman in my novel, at the age of twenty-one, Harriet Shelley drowned herself and her unborn child in 1816 in the Serpentine Pond in London's Hyde Park (the child was thought perhaps to be Percy's), two years after Percy abandoned her and their daughter Eliza Ianthe and their son Charles when he eloped with Mary Godwin. He eloped with Mary while he was still married to Harriet, who was pregnant at the time with Charles Bysshe Shelley.

After Harriet's suicide, even though Percy Shelley and Mary Godwin married in order to be granted the right to raise his children, Percy Shelley was denied guardianship of his children because of the history of his illicit relationship with Mary Godwin and his espoused atheism. The children were adopted by a vicar and his wife, and Ianthe and Charles never saw their biological father again.

And tragically, even though Percy was an accomplished sailor, he drowned at the age of twenty-nine in Italy in a treacherous storm off the Italian coast.

While researching my debut novel, *Vindicated: A Novel of Mary Shelley,* winner of the 2021 May Sarton Award in Historical Fiction (Cuidono Press, Brooklyn, 2020), I discovered that young Percy Shelley, an admirer of Robert Emmet, traveled to Dublin in 1812 to attempt to complete Emmet's failed 1803 rebellion to free Ireland from British rule. Having taught at Trinity College in Dublin and at Oriel College, Oxford

University, I was absolutely intrigued by Percy Shelley's rather naïve and idealistic notion that he could free Ireland. And through my teaching of Irish literature and history, I knew that by 1812 Anne Devlin, Emmet's colleague, and housekeeper, was living in Dublin after having been incarcerated and tortured in Kilmainham Gaol. Based on this knowledge, I began to imagine Percy meeting Devlin so that he could learn more about Emmet, in order to complete Emmet's rebellion. The result is a novel that imagines that meeting, while juxtaposed with Shelley's misguided efforts to save the Irish. My hope is that readers will learn of Anne's bravery, that she will be further inscribed into history, and that Percy Shelley's audacious political idealism, although misguided, will be as well-known as his poetry. I also wished to redeem Harriet Shelley, who had been falsely accused of betraying Percy. The more I learned about her generous heart and her interest in and love of Ireland the more I wished to instill her character with agency. Both Anne and Harriet have stood outside of history, but now I've inscribed them as heroines—not saints or queens—just ordinary women working toward human liberation and political justice. And both demonstrated, in my novel, that they possessed courageous souls.

I consulted many sources while conducting research, including but not limited to Paul O'Brien's *Shelley and Revolutionary Ireland* (London and Dublin: Redwords, 2002), Robin McKown's *The Ordeal of Anne Devlin*, Niamh O'Sullivan's *Every Dark Hour: A History of Kilmainham Jail* (Dublin: Liberties Press, 2007), Percy Bysshe Shelley's *Shelley's Poetry and Prose.* ed and selected by Donald H. Reiman and Neil Fraistat, Janet Todd's *Rebel Daughters: Ireland in Conflict 1798*, and Patrick M. Geoghegan's *Robert Emmet* (Dublin: Gill Books, 2002).

The title of my novel is taken from the title of a poem by Emily Brontë. Since the Brontë sisters' father Patrick was originally named Patrick Brunty, an Irishman, whose brother fought with Wolfe Tone, it seems fitting to connect Emily with the story of Anne Devlin and Percy and Harriet Shelley.

Finally, I thank my writing group, members of the Creative Girls in Iowa City, IA: Mary Helen Stefaniak, Mary Vermillion, Ann Zerkel, Marianne Jones, Kris Vervaecke, Eileen Bartos, and Marjorie Carlson Davis, who read countless drafts of this novel. I also wish to extend thanks to David Duer for his writerly advice. And I owe Julene Bair, my graduate school colleague, and my Irish historian friend Professor Gillian O'Brien many thanks as well for reading and commenting on drafts of this novel. In addition, I thank the wonderful writers Carol Roh-Spaulding and

Tea Marrocco for writing endorsements. I also owe a debt of gratitude to Jeff Chown, my colleague at Northern Illinois University, with whom I taught in Dublin where I first learned Anne Devlin's tale while visiting Kilmainham Gaol with my students. I must also thank W.W. Norton Publishing and Carcanet Press (in the U.K.) for their kind permission to use Eavan Boland's poem "Outside History" in her collection of the same name. I extend thanks to Bedazzled Ink Publishing, particularly Elizabeth Gibson and C.A. Casey, who support my work and the work of women writers who write about women. Perhaps this novel will help more women and men gain courage as they learn of the extraordinary lives of ordinary women neglected by the writers of history.

Kathleen Williams Renk taught British and Women's literature for nearly three decades in the U.S. and abroad. Her scholarly books include *Caribbean Shadows and Victorian Ghosts: Women's Writing and Decolonization* (Univ. Press of Virginia,1999), *Magic, Science, and Empire in Postcolonial Literature: The Alchemical Literary Imagination* (Routledge, 2012), and *Women Writing the Neo-Victorian Novel: Erotic "Victorians"* (Palgrave Macmillan, 2020). While earning her Ph.D. in English at the University of Iowa, Williams Renk studied fiction writing with James Alan MacPherson. Her short fiction, creative nonfiction, and poetry have appeared in *Iowa City Magazine, Literary Yard, Page and Spine, CC & D Magazine*, and *the Scarlet Review*. In November 2020, Cuidono Press (Brooklyn) published her debut novel, *Vindicated: A Life of Mary Shelley. Vindicated* won Story Circle Network's 2021 May Sarton Award in Historical Fiction; it was also a finalist for the CIBA Goethe Award and was longlisted for the Chautauqua Literary Prize. *The Rossetti Diaries* was also longlisted for the Chautauqua Prize

In her spare time, Williams Renk plays violin and guitar. She also loves to hike on the Front Range in Colorado where she lives.

Visit Kathleen's website: http://www.kathleenrenk.com

* 9 7 8 1 9 6 0 3 7 3 5 9 5 *